Deeper Than Lies

Deeper Than Love, Book 2

...

EMMA ASHE

This is a work of fiction. Similarities to real people, places,
or events are entirely coincidental.

...

DEEPER THAN LIES
First edition. January 11, 2019.

Written by Emma Ashe
www.emmaashe.com/books[1]

ALSO BY EMMA ASHE

Deeper Than Love

Deeper Than Desire, Prequel[1]
Deeper Than Destiny, Book 1[2]
Deeper Than Lies, Book 2[3]
Deeper Than Secrets, Book 3[4]
Deeper Than Temptation, Book 4[5]

An Indecent Apposal

Something Real, Prequel[6]
Show Me Your Secrets, Book 1[7]
Claiming The Secretary, Book 2[8]
Second Chance Romance, Book 3[9]
All For Her, Book 4[10]
Better With You, Book 5[11]
Anyone But You, Book 6[12]

...

1. http://www.emmaashe.com/books/deeper

2. http://www.emmaashe.com/books/deeper

3. http://www.emmaashe.com/books/deeper

4. http://www.emmaashe.com/books/deeper

5. http://www.emmaashe.com/books/deeper

6. http://www.emmaashe.com/books/apposal

7. http://www.emmaashe.com/books/apposal

8. http://www.emmaashe.com/books/apposal

9. http://www.emmaashe.com/books/apposal

10. http://www.emmaashe.com/books/apposal

11. http://www.emmaashe.com/books/apposal

12. http://www.emmaashe.com/books/apposal

<u>An Indecent Apposal Volume 1, Books 1-3</u>[13]
<u>An Indecent Apposal Volume 2, Books 4-6</u>[14]

...

<u>An Indecent Apposal Collection 1, Books 1-6</u>[15]

Get notified of new releases & free reads:
<u>www.emmaashe.com/signup</u>[16]

---

13. http://www.emmaashe.com/books/apposal-set

14. http://www.emmaashe.com/books/apposal-set

15. http://www.emmaashe.com/books/apposal-set

16. http://www.emmaashe.com/signup

ACKNOWLEDGMENTS

This book wouldn't even be here without the encouragement of some of the finest writers I know. Thank you for cheering me on Skylar Hill, Cici Coughlin, and Natalie Richards.

DEDICATION

For Tony

CHAPTER 1 | Ellie

So that's *Hot Stuff?!* I crane my head, trying—and failing—to see across the crowded dance floor. It's too dark to see much. I mean, I can tell he's big. The guy is at least a head taller than anyone else in here, but *hot?* Gag me. He's my sister's fiancé, which means I don't need to know if he's hot.

I need to know if he's a cheater.

"You know your glare can't actually set him on fire, right?" The club is so noisy Holly has to lean close. Her breath is hot in my ear.

I scowl. "Maybe I can. Maybe I've been secretly developing laser eyes."

My best friend laughs. "When it comes to Wren, I would believe it." She hooks her arm through mine, sipping on a neon-colored drink as we watch my beloved older sister touch Hot Stuff's arm. They laugh.

"She looks really happy, Ellie."

"Wren's always happy," I say, sipping my own neon-colored drink. It's too sweet and turns my mouth sticky. "And then they cheat on her and she's devastated. I love my sister, but we have crappy taste in men. We can't help it. It's genetic."

Holly faces me. The disco lights have turned her pale hair green and red. Her blue eyes look electric. "Please don't do this."

"I have to."

"No, you don't. If it works, you're the woman who kissed her sister's fiancé. If it doesn't work, you're the woman who *tried* to kiss her sister's fiancé."

"Gross!" The idea of kissing my sister's fiancé is worse than my overly sweet drink. I nearly gag. "I'm not going to kiss him! That's horrible!"

"Then what—"

"I'm just going to get chatty. Flirt a little. Make sure he tells me he has a fiancée and she's beautiful and brilliant, like a good guy would. If I have to, I'll invite him to leave with me, and if he gives me his number, we'll know he's an ass."

"Or." Holly holds up one finger. "You could wait and get to know him."

I glare at Holly because she's right and also because we've been over this. Technically, the guy's name isn't Hot Stuff. It's Tate Matthews. But ever since I read this text where Wren called him Hot Stuff, I can't get it out of my mind. I mean *really*. Hot. Stuff. Ugh.

Anyway, Wren met him while visiting her mom's family in Paris. She does this every summer and she always tells me everything. Except this time, she dated the guy for two months before even mentioning him. Then they spent all last month living together, and *now* they're saying "I love you," giving out nicknames, and getting *married*. I've never even met him.

Hot Stuff flew in this afternoon to visit and Wren picked him up from the airport. They decided to celebrate his arrival with dinner and dancing and I was supposed to come, but I got stuck at the farm—which turned out to be a huge blessing because *now* he doesn't know what I look like. I mean, sure, he could've Facebook stalked me or whatever, but thanks to my crazy work hours I can't remember the last time someone took a picture of me that didn't involve sweaty ponytails and riding breeches. Cleaned up, I look way different. *Now*, I can ambush him and find out if he's horn dog cheater.

"It's like the universe planned this," I mutter.

"What?"

"Nothing." It's a great idea—it *is*—and yet my stomach is in knots. I take a deep breath. "Sometimes you have to do something terrible to do something right."

"That doesn't even make sense."

"Yes, it does. Look, Holls, you know how hard Wren took her last break up. She's getting *married* to this guy. I've never seen her so in love. If he turns out to be a troll, she'll be devastated. Remember Brian the Super Jerk?"

Holly nods grimly. "And Craig from her freshman bio class."

"And James the gigantic tool."

"James was *your* gigantic tool, not Wren's."

I blink, flashing back to a six feet plus of dark hair, darker eyes, and a pair of fast hands. Not coincidentally, the last fast hands that have touched me in almost a year. "You're right," I say at last. "But I think my point is still made. Wren and I cannot be trusted to pick out boyfriends, let alone husbands, and—"

"And I want to know where my uptight friend has gone. Even if you're not going to touch him, you're still inviting him to leave with you."

"If he leaves with some girl who offers him a go in the parking lot, he doesn't deserve my sister."

Holly goes quiet, and I know she agrees. "This isn't like you," she says at last. She's right too. Outside the club, I'm a respected professional rider. I have clients, sale horses, a *business*. I might only be twenty-three, but I have goals, and I'm usually not prone to dramatics.

But I'm also not prone to discovering my sister is about to get married to a guy I've never met, and run off to New York, and leave everyone we love behind, and—

Get it together, I tell myself. I grab Holly's hand and squeeze. "You love Wren as much as I do. Help me make sure she's going to be happy with that idiot."

"That 'idiot' could be your brother in law. Do you really want to mess this up?"

"No, but I would rather Hot Stuff be mad at me for the rest of our lives than see Wren heartbroken. Please, Holly?" After a ridiculously long moment, she sighs, and I know I have her. I grin. "You're the best, you know that?"

Holly rolls her eyes, and we watch Wren and Hot Stuff share another laugh over something he said. The DJ fires up another remix of some Top 40 Hit, and the crowd cheers. More people rush to the dance floor, someone jostling me as she passes.

I barely notice. Wren is patting Hot Stuff's forearm, telling him something. She moves away, purse in hand. I push up on my tip-toes trying to see better. Is she going to the bathroom? For another drink? It doesn't matter, I guess. Hot Stuff is alone now and my opportunity is here.

I adjust my already low cut dress until my breasts are on the verge of exploding. "Okay." I turn to Holly. "How do I look?"

"Like a crazy woman with weird tan lines."

I scowl again and peer at my shoulders. She's right. Thanks to spending most of yesterday afternoon working on the pasture fencing, pale lines from my tank top crisscross my skin. "Ugh, I'd hoped you wouldn't be able to see them."

"You can't. Not really." Holly rubs her forehead like I've given her a headache. I probably have. "You're still crazy though."

Sadly, she's absolutely right. "Sometimes you have to do crazy stuff to protect the people you love," I tell her. "Wren will forgive me...eventually." The thought makes my stomach squeeze again. "Hold my drink?"

Holly eyes the half-finished peach martini. "How many of these have you had?"

"Three?"

"And when did you get your brilliant idea?"

"Sometime around the second. I'm not drunk though. I know what I'm doing. I *do*. I'm going to flirt with him, maybe invite him outside, and if he says 'yes' I'll out him for the ass he is. It's a good plan. It'll work."

Holly opens her mouth and then shuts it. "Good luck," she says at last.

I nod and totter across the dance floor, needing four or five strides before I get my balance. I love heels, but I spend most of my time in boots, and it shows. I probably look like a five-year-old wearing her mommy's shoes.

To compensate, I stick my chest out. *You can do this. You can do this.*

Four feet away though I'm suddenly not so sure. Hot Stuff turns and the strobe lights catch his face: full lips, high cheekbones, and a hard edged jaw. He's wearing dark jeans, and a black dress shirt, the tails untucked and the top buttons undone. Hot Stuff is indeed hot. So hot, in fact, I forget I'm staring—with my mouth open—until he smiles.

"Hey, there."

Oh, God and he has a southern accent. Wren really does have amazing taste in jerks.

So do you, I remind myself, snapping my mouth shut and matching Hot Stuff's smile. "Hey, yourself. Are you having a good time?"

"Better now."

Jerk Alert bells go off in my head and any doubt I had about my plan vanishes. He's having a better time now that my sister isn't here? He's an ass.

I'm so going to take you down, I think, widening my smile and shimmying closer. His gaze briefly dips, taking in my cleavage and the form fitting dress, and now I hate him even more.

"Do you live around here?" I ask.

He shrugs. "Just moved back."

"Lucky me."

A smile tugs at one corner of Hot Stuff's mouth and, again, I see what Wren sees in him. He's pretty. I know you're not supposed to call guys that, but he is.

I ease a little closer. "So where'd you move from?"

"Ireland."

"Wow!" For a second, my sexy girl coming onto him thing slips and the real me shows through. I can't help it. I've always wanted to go to Ireland. Some of the best show jumping riders in the world have trained there.

Focus, Ellie! "Wow," I repeat, sounding a little more like the drunken party girl I'm supposed to be. "That's really far away."

"Not nearly far enough."

Oh. Well, okay then. Hot Stuff has gone from flirty to broody. He glares out at the dancers like they have personally offended him. I slide another step closer though and his attention snaps back to me. It's probably a trick of the light, but his expression seems to soften.

Not. Good. "So what brings you to Atlanta?" I ask. *You better say my sister*, I think.

Hot Stuff frowns. "Work. I'm applying for a manager position."

Hmm, he didn't mention Wren, but he isn't exactly flirting anymore either. For several seconds, we stare at each other.

"Are *you* local?" Hot Stuff asks. "What do you do for fun?"

Fun? What's that? I train horses and when I'm not training horses I'm thinking about training horses. Until tonight, I couldn't have even told you where this club was, but I could tell you the location of four tack shops, six breeding farms, and about a dozen stables. I like to think it's because I know my market. Wren says it's because I'm not well rounded.

"Oh, I don't know," I say at last, making a show of playing with my hair. It needs a cut and the overlong ends brush past my elbows. "I guess it depends on the person you're with."

The half-smile turns into a full-fledged grin, and my stomach sinks. My poor sister. He's a cheater.

"Yeah?" Hot Stuff asks.

"Yeah." I take a deep—*deep*—breath and force my hand to cup his arm. The muscles beneath my palm tighten. "I mean, we could stay here and have fun...or we could go somewhere else..." I trail off, hoping innuendo will be enough. I don't have a ton of experience with sexy stuff. Okay, I have almost no experience with sexy stuff. Work doesn't leave me a lot of free time, and it seems like every guy I date turns into a huge jerk.

Hot Stuff's left eyebrow raises. "Somewhere else?"

Ugh. Think. I shift from foot to foot and wobble, hip bumping into the glossy-topped table.

Hot Stuff puts one hand on my arm, gently squeezing. "Are you okay?"

I don't think so. I blink, blink again. The floor feels like it's tilting under my feet, and that wobble definitely wasn't from the heels. Maybe I am drunk?

Maybe this *is* a bad idea.

"Do you need me to get you a cab?" he asks.

I lift my face to tell him I'm fine, and realize we're inches apart. I'm close enough to smell the bourbon on his breath, close enough...to kiss.

Run! Except I can't because Hot Stuff's hand has suddenly found my wrist. I can feel the heat of him. He comes closer...closer...

"Ellie?"

My stomach lurches. Wren. I spin around and see my big sister standing only a few feet away. She has a drink in each hand and looks like she's biting down a laugh.

I launch myself away from Hot Stuff. "He's a cheater, Wren! He was going to kiss me!"

"Cheater?" Wren puts the drinks on a hip high table and trots to my side. She presses a cool hand to my head like she did when I was little and sick with the flu. "Honey, Caleb's single. Are you feeling okay?"

"No, I'm fine—wait. *What?* I thought you said his name was Tate."

Wren cocks her head, her smooth brown ponytail slipping down one shoulder. "No. *That's* Caleb." She motions to the guy beside me before turning in the direction of another. One who could also be called hot.

Oh, crap.

"*That's* Tate," she says, hands going to her hips. "Caleb was about to kiss you."

CHAPTER 2 | Caleb

What the hell? The pretty brunette takes another wobbly step away from me and squares her shoulders. She looks from Tate to me and back to Tate.

"Nice to meet you," she says at last and offers him a hand. "I'm Ellie, Wren's sister."

Tate and Ellie shake like this is completely normal and she wasn't just flirting with *me* because she thought I was *him*.

I don't even know where to begin with this shit and it looks like Wren agrees. Eyes narrowed, she glares at her sister. "What's going on?"

Ellie chews her lower lip for a long moment, no doubt searching for something to say that won't sound crazy.

Newsflash, sweetheart, you are *crazy.* I lean one arm against the tabletop, and give Tate a sympathetic look. *See what you're marrying into, buddy.*

Tate won't meet my eyes, but he scratches his temple with his middle finger in response.

Fine. Your funeral. He may not have had his fill of party girls and their games, but I have. I barely escaped Mandy. I may be home again, but I'm not going back for another round of crazy. In fact, I can't believe I almost fell for it again. Or maybe I can. When it comes to women, I have terrible taste. If she's a beautiful party girl prone to bad decisions, she's the girl for me.

Or she was, like I said I've had my fill of crazy.

"OhmygodWren!" Another girl shoulders her way out of the dance floor and into our group. She's curvy and pale-haired and moves like she could run a mile in those four-inch heels. "It's not what you think!"

"Holly?" Wren glances from her sister to the Holly girl, corners of her mouth turned down. "What are you doing here?"

"Uh," Holly manages. Her eyes are huge and guilty. "I came with Ellie."

Ah, the partner in crime. Crazy always travels in packs. I'm going to need more booze to handle this. I start looking for our waitress. Unfortunately for me, there's no sign of her. The club is way crowded, and someone is breaking out glow sticks, the universal promise of bad decisions to come.

"Why are you here? You guys said you couldn't come—are you *spying* on me?" Wren's voice skews higher and I wince. Wren's a nice girl. When Tate introduced us, I never expected to like her as much as I do. She doesn't deserve whatever stupidity her sister and friend have cooked up.

"Of course I'm not spying on you!" Ellie starts toward Wren and then pauses, thinking hard. She's definitely drunk. I wasn't entirely sure earlier, but there's no mistaking the glassy, overbright eyes and the sway to her step now. "Okay, it's a little like spying, but not like you think. I was never going to kiss him. I was just going to flirt with him so we'd know if he was an ass."

Oh, there's some logic for you. Our waitress squeezes a group of guys blocking the tables, and I catch her eye, signaling for another drink. If only there were a universal hand sign for keep-them-coming-until-I-pass-out. Normally, I would just leave, but Wren's my ride, and at this rate, we're not getting out of here any time soon. I predict tears with a side of screaming.

Actually...I eye Wren. She's drawing herself up to her full height—all barely five and a half feet of her—and both her hands are clenched. Actually, it may be screaming with a side of tears. If she starts throwing punches, I will be impressed.

And not really surprised because insanity runs in families and clearly the Ellie girl has issues.

"Look, Wren." Ellie reaches for her sister's arm and Wren pulls away. "I can explain."

"No," Holly says, wide-eyed. She steps between the sisters and wraps one arm around Wren's shoulders. "*You* stay put," she says to Ellie. "*I* will explain."

Holly pulls Wren and Tate away as the waitress returns with my bourbon. "Thank you," I say and pass her a ten.

Her face lights up. "Sure thing, honey."

"Keep them coming," I say, shaking the glass. She nods and disappears into the thickening crowd. The night is definitely heating up. People are flinging themselves around on the dance floor and pounding back drinks at the bar. Maybe a dozen feet away, a gorgeous girl with waist-length dark hair and a wicked pair of legs twines herself around a guy who holds her like she is his everything.

I used to look at Mandy like that, I think, and it feels like a kick to the gut.

"Well, this is awkward."

I glance down, bourbon almost to my lips. Ellie is now standing by my side. She chews the skin next to her thumb, watching Holly talk to Wren and Tate. Whatever Holly's saying, they don't seem to be impressed. Actually, Tate seems kind of horrified. He's standing even straighter than usual and staring down at Holly with that calculating expression he usually reserves for the courtroom.

I turn back to Ellie. "You thought I was Tate? What was that? Some sort of game?"

Wren's sister glares at me and crosses her arms. Moments ago, I would've said that was to better highlight her assets, but now I think it's just because she's pissed. I honestly don't think Ellie realizes how close she is to popping out of that dress—or how hard I'm struggling not to look at her almost popping out of that dress.

"It was...an experiment," she finally manages.

"An experiment?" That makes zero sense. I eye her. "How drunk are you?"

"Not nearly enough." Ellie looks up at me through a fringe of bangs and even though I know she's a drama queen and I can't stand drama queens, those big, brown eyes hit something low in my gut. "I owe you an apology," she continues. "I was being...stupid."

"No kidding." Okay, I could've been more gracious, but I'm still annoyed. Freaking party girls.

Ellie forces her shoulders back. "Okay, I deserved that. Can we try again? I'm Ellie."

She offers me her hand and I finish my bourbon in one quick swallow. Her palm is surprisingly cool against mine. "Caleb."

"How do you know Tate?"

"I'm his best friend."

At least she has the good grace to wince. We spend another uncomfortable moment watching Tate, Wren, and Holly talking. Holly points at Ellie and then twirls one finger around her temple in the universal symbol for crazy. Everyone nods and Ellie huffs something under her breath.

"I'm Wren's *sister*," she mutters. "I was worried about her."

"Funny way of showing it."

Ellie blows at her bangs again. "Yeah. I guess. It's just...Wren and I have really bad taste in guys. I'm worried Hot—I mean Tate—is going to hurt her."

"Tate's a great guy. She's lucky to have him."

"*She's* lucky?" Ellie wheels around on me, wobbling dangerously on her heels. The club music swings into deep bass line, and she leans forward so I can hear her. "Try *he's* lucky. My sister is amazing."

"So amazing you have to jump her fiancé?"

"There wasn't going to *be* any jumping. I was going to flirt with him to see if he was cheater." Ellie fidgets with her hair, tugging it this way and that. It's distracting as hell. "I had to make sure he's worthy of her. But *now* we'll just have to wait it out. It could take months for his true colors to show."

I pause. *Is it just me or did she make this sound like my fault?* "Your crazy is showing," I say, rolling my bourbon glass from palm to palm. It's no good though. I can still feel her skin against mine. "You might want to tuck that back in."

She rolls her eyes like *I'm* the ass. "You don't understand. She's been hurt too many times."

"Welcome to the real world. It happens."

Ellie looks at me for a long moment—too long actually because it gives me plenty of time to notice how she's exactly the right height to fit under my chin and how her curves look in that fitted dress. Damn. Why am I attracted to wild party girls?

When I left for Dublin, I gave up on two things. One, I swore off girls like Ellie and Mandy. Christ, *Mandy.* We'd been engaged when she slept with that polo player. Kept the ring on and everything. My friends said it was because she was wild. My father said it was because I wasn't enough to keep her still.

Which brings me to the second thing I gave up: my father. I promised myself I didn't need his approval—which was good because I was never going to get it anyway.

And now here I am, back to take over his breeding farm and unable to take my eyes away from Little Miss I Have a Plan.

I can't decide if that makes me pathetic, or incredibly stupid.

"They're getting married," Ellie says finally, glancing away from me. "I hadn't even met him until now."

Wow. Okay, I kinda sorta understand why she's upset. I met Wren weeks ago. I took a few days off from the breeding barn I managed, and flew to Paris for a weekend. We had dinner together and by the time I left, I knew all about Wren's art doctorate, her love for all things French, and the fact she only has one living relative: her sister, Ellie.

Which means I've spent more time with Wren and Tate than she has.

I rattle the ice in my glass. "They're good together."

Ellie shakes her head. "Well, clearly you're the expert."

"You would be too, if you hopped a plane." Although to be honest, the only reason Tate probably brought me in is because A. I'm his best friend and B. no *one* has better radar for crazy than I do.

Actually, B is a bit of a stretch. Tate's so in love with Wren he can't see straight. The girl could be green with scales and he'd be thrilled. Normally, this would be cause for major concern, but after meeting Wren, I couldn't be happier for him. She's straight up amazing. No crazy there.

It all went to her sister instead.

"I'm not an expert on them," I say at last, finishing the last of my bourbon. "I only met Wren last month."

And I suddenly remember how Wren described Ellie as her 'baby sister.' I take another long look at Ellie's curves. Baby sister is definitely not the way I would describe this girl.

I clear my throat. "You'll like Tate. He's great."

"So great she said they would probably move for his job," Ellie says quietly, so quietly I pretend I didn't hear her.

Too bad I can't push it from my mind. She's scared of being left behind. I get that. I don't want to, but I do. When I was growing up, my mom traveled extensively for our farm's breeding program. She was always looking for broodmares with certain bloodlines or stallions with international potential. It was amazing for her, and miserable for me. Left at home, I spent most of my time with my father—the Colonel—and it was horrible. I spent almost ten years plotting my escape.

And now you're back. I sigh, and look around for the waitress again, spotting her on the other side of the dance floor.

"Well?" Ellie asks.

I blink. I have no idea what she's talking about. "Well what?"

"You said you moved back from Ireland. Why?"

"I'm taking over the manager position at a local farm."

"Wait." Ellie turns her head to one side, long brown hair sweeping in a shining curtain across her shoulder. "Caleb...what's your last name?"

"Reese."

She's still staring at Wren, but her expression has hollowed. She looks like she's going to be sick. "Caleb. *Reese.*"

"Yeah."

Those big, brown eyes swing to me, and stick. "Like *Michael* Reese's son?"

I stiffen. "How do you know the Colonel?"

"He owns the place I work at." Her nose wrinkles as she looks me up and down. "You're here for the manager position? I'm your competition for it."

CHAPTER 3 | Caleb

It takes me five whole seconds before I can form words again. "You're my *what*?" I manage at last.

"I'm your competition for the Jacks or Better job." Ellie straightens her shoulders again, studying me with interest. My body tightens in response. "I know the Colonel told you about me."

"He told me someone else was applying. He didn't tell me she was—was—" I shake myself. "The job is mine, sweetheart. Not only am I his son, but I am very, very good at what I do."

"So am I. *Plus*, I'm the rider who's going to put his homegrown mare in the Grand Prix ring."

I frown. She's got me there. Beckon was the year before I left. The only thing I really remember about the filly was her size (smaller), her color (dark bay, no white), and her attitude (foul). Then, maybe two years ago, the mare started making a name for herself in the lower levels. She won two competitions in Wellington before returning to Jacks or Better for more training. The Colonel thinks she's our best homebred yet, and he very well might be right.

"Cute that you think that matters," I tell her. "Riders are a dime a dozen. Actual professionals? Way more rare."

"Is that what you call sleeping with your father's assistant trainer?"

I go still. It's been six years since I fell for Mandy and that's *still* the first thing everyone remembers? I nearly laugh. Who am I kidding? Of *course* it is. This is the horse industry. Everyone knows everyone and everyone gossips.

I step a little closer, crowding Ellie. "Jealous, sweetheart?"

She blinks. Good. I've caught her off guard. But she's caught me too. This close, I can smell her perfume—something soft and clean—and I can see that amazing cleavage again. Christ, it makes my mouth go hot.

There's a flurry of movement over Ellie's shoulder, and I glance up. Smirk. "I think you may have a problem."

Ellie whips around, spotting the 'problem' right away: her sister's leaving. Wren strides away from Holly like a woman on a mission, and Tate dashes after her, his expression panicked. He should be. If I had any drink left in my glass, I would lift it in solidarity.

Good luck, my man, I think. *You're going to need it.*

"Oh no!" Ellie gasps, and takes off after both of them.

I sigh and follow, Ellie's little friend falling into stride next to me. "Holly," she says in greeting.

I lift my chin. "Caleb."

"Nice to meet you."

I start to ask the curvy blonde if this all seems normal to her—because she's sure as hell acting like it is—and shut my mouth. I don't want to know. I just want to go home.

Outside the club, the air feels like a sauna, humid and overfull with the promise of thunderstorms. Welcome to the south. After so many years of rain and cold, I actually missed it. The sun's been down for hours now, but everything is still warm and close.

Ellie catches Wren underneath a parking lot light and they begin to argue. Tate—probably because he learns faster than I do—stays out of it, hovering at a distance in case his girl needs help.

"Wren, please." Ellie's holding onto her sister's elbow for dear life and Wren keeps trying to shake her off. "I just thought—"

"*No!* You didn't think! You *never* think!" Wren rips herself away, and power stomps to Tate's car. Ellie stares after her, eyes huge and round, and I have the sudden stupid urge to put my arm around her shoulders. Then, as if she feels me staring, Ellie's gaze flicks to me. The haunted look disappears, replaced instead with cool determination. She nods in my direction as if we are about to start a game, which I guess in a way we are.

But not at all like she thinks. Competition for the manager position? Please.

"That actually went better than I expected," Holly announces, but whether she's talking to me or to herself, I can't tell. She turns to me, blonde hair falling around her shoulders. "I guess I'll see you around then, yeah?"

"Not if I see you first."

She laughs, and pats my arm. "You're funny."

Crazy. Both of them. I watch Holly rush to Ellie's side. She leads the other girl toward the line of taxis waiting by the entrance. They don't look back and I can't seem to stop staring.

Why am I still so annoyed?

"Caleb!" Tate waves me toward him, and I gotta say, the guy looks a bit wild-eyed. Poor bastard. I follow him to his car. Wren is already inside, chewing her thumbnail to death. Tate nods his head toward Ellie and Holly. "Think it'll be better by the wedding?" he asks, dropping his voice.

"No."

He pulls a face. "Yeah. Well at least, you don't have to see her before then."

"Ellie? Oh, I'll be seeing her."

Tate throws me a sideways W-T-F look.

"Remember the Colonel saying I had competition for the job?" I ask.

"Yeah."

I glare at Ellie's back as she climbs into her taxi. "Behold my competition."

***

Tate drops Wren off at the bed-and-breakfast they're staying at, and drives me out to Jacks or Better. The farm is maybe thirty minutes outside of town, and for once, I'm grateful for the drive. Between the bourbon and the jet lag, I feel like I'm moving underwater. I need time to think, to plan, but every time I close my eyes I see Ellie shimmying closer, and every time I open them, I remember I'm back home.

Tate runs the windows down, and hot, humid air hurls through the BMW. "Tonight was different."

I pause. "You aren't pissed?"

He grunts, and shifts into a lower gear as we take the last bend before the farm's main drive. "Not as much as Wren. I think Ellie just made a bad decision."

"Having the chicken instead of the steak is a bad decision. That was..." I have no words to adequately express that level of bullshit so I wave my hand in a circle. Tate seems to get the idea anyway. He shrugs, making a right into Jacks or Better.

"Seriously," I continue as the smell of fresh cut grass fills the car. "That was a whole new level of crazy. Do you really want to marry into it?"

"Absolutely."

I twist around in my seat, studying Tate's face for signs of lying, but no matter how hard I search, I can't find any. I fling myself back around. He means it. I actually envy that. I've never been that sure about a person—even when Mandy and I were doing well, I was never that sure about her, never that sure about anything.

Actually, no, that's not true. I'm sure I want a future in showjumping. I've shaped my whole life around it: all the work for Jacks or Better, another six years working for two farms outside of Dublin. It's everything I am.

And the deeper we drive into Jacks or Better, the more that realization begins to feel like a death sentence. Coming home wasn't supposed to be like this. I wasn't supposed to be this pissy. I wasn't supposed to fight another employee for the manager job.

I wasn't supposed to play my father's games anymore.

What am I doing here? I wonder, scrubbing both hands over my face. "Did you really not know who Wren's sister was?"

Tate raises his right hand. "Swear to God. I mean, I think Wren mentioned she rode horses, but I pretty much forgot. We got onto other...things."

Part of me wants to be seriously annoyed, but I can't really bring myself to be. Tate and I have been best friends since college. A lot of people in the horse industry don't bother with university, but I wanted a business degree to better understand how to make a farm work. I knew the day to day stuff, but I wanted—needed—more. If I was going to do better than the Colonel, I figured university was the best way to start. Tate was the same way. Like me, he knew what he wanted: fancy job, big house, traveling the world. Unlike me, he isn't walking into an established business. His parents are teachers. They'd give him the world if they could.

Tate drums his fingers along the steering wheel. "I mean, I know we've moved pretty fast, but damn. Didn't realize I'd missed that. The only stuff I remember is Wren's real dad and stepmom died in a car accident so she's all the family Ellie has."

I wince. She's all Ellie's got? And she's leaving? Ouch. "Does she get along with Wren's mom?"

"I don't think they spend a lot of time together. Lynn stays in Paris, and Ellie is supposed to be a workaholic. Wren says she doesn't get out enough."

"Look what happens when she does."

"No shit." Somewhere in the dark, a horse whinnies, and Tate glances at me. "Anyway, who hasn't made bad decisions while drinking peach martinis?"

I eye him. "You think this is funny?"

"Yeah, a bit." He grins, face green from the dashboard lights. "More than a bit. Usually, you would too."

I sit back against the seat, tapping my fingers against my thigh. "No, I wouldn't."

Tate fiddles with the radio, and for a few minutes, there's nothing but the sound of air rushing through the open windows. "Are you okay?"

"You look different today, Dr. Phil."

"And you still look like an asshole. I'm not trying to play therapist. You want to talk? Talk."

Fair enough. I glance out the window. In the dark, the trees are a curtain of shadows rushing by, and as we slow down for the last turn, I can hear the high-pitched whine of crickets. "It's this place, this *town*. It was a mistake."

"You mean coming back?"

"I mean everything. The Colonel calls me, and asks me to come home, and against my better judgment, I agree. I quit my job. I asked Aiden to come on. Then I find out he doesn't want me to take over the farm, he wants me to *interview* to take over the farm. That's bullshit."

"No doubt. But you knew that before you flew over. Why'd you still come?"

"Because it wasn't just me anymore. I had Aiden quit his job at the farm to follow me. He's supposed to ride for Jacks or Better now and he's depending on this as much as I am—more so. He takes care of his sister's kids."

Aiden's also one of the most talented show jumping riders I've ever seen. His feel, his sense of timing, hell his ability to get the most from his horses, blows most riders out of the water. If life were fair, the guy would have sponsors lining up. Since life isn't, he's been coming up through the ranks on his own, getting rides and horses as he can. He was living in his car before coming to my farm last year. This was—*is*—a huge opportunity for him. For both of us.

"That all?" Tate asks.

For two whole seconds, I'm beyond pissed because really does there need to be more? Then I realize what Tate's getting at. "And I want the damn job."

"So get it."

I raise one brow. "At Ellie's expense? Is that what brother-in-laws are supposed to say?"

Tate frowns. "Probably not, but you've wanted this for as long as I've known you. You want it? Go get it."

He pulls to a stop next to the Colonel's Range Rover, and we both take a long look at the house. The antebellum mansion is dark, but one window burns bright. My father's still awake. Waiting for me? God, I hope not. I don't have the energy for one of our arguments.

"Seriously," Tate adds. "There's no way she'd be better at this than you would be. Don't fall for the Colonel's head games."

I crack my knuckles. "It's not just the head games. I'm walking back into that shit I left behind with Mandy."

Tate winces. We've been friends since college and he knows the story. "You know how I felt about Mandy," I say. "But to everyone else, I slept with an employee. They think I used her, and it's *still* following me. Even Ellie threw it in my face."

Tate laughs.

"It's not funny."

"It's totally funny." He turns to me, expression all lawyer-y and composed. "Look, you're not the first guy to break some rules, and get burned. Was Mandy underage?"

"God, no."

"Was she willing?"

"Hell, yes."

"Then what's the deal?"

I grind my teeth. "It made me look like I can't keep my hands off the staff. You should've heard the Colonel's freak out—and when Mandy went public with our drama? It burned my professional standing to the ground."

"So build it back up."

"By standing on your future sister-in-law?" I really can't believe he would suggest it. Tate's a nice guy, an honorable guy, which sounds cheesy as all hell, but it's a big deal to me. He doesn't screw people over.

"Yeah, I know," he says, picking at the leather on his steering wheel. "But Caleb, you're a good boss. You're driven, but you don't ask anyone to do something you wouldn't. Your guys bend over backward for you. I know you'll treat her well."

The compliment makes my skin crawl. Some of that is because I'm no good with niceties. The rest of it is because if—*when*—I make farm manager, I won't treat Ellie nicely at all. I don't need her propensity for drama. I'll fire her.

CHAPTER 4 | Ellie

A door slams and I open my eyes, blink. There are footsteps on the stairs and for two seconds I'm confused because Wren isn't supposed to be home. She was going to stay at that bed and breakfast with Tate. I must be hearing things. I must be—car keys jingle as they're slung across the kitchen counter and I snap upright.

It *is* Wren! I launch out of bed and run—head throbbing—down the hallway just in time to see my sister stomp into our bathroom and slam the door behind her.

I jiggle the handle and, in answer, Wren turns on the shower. "Please, Wren? Can we talk? I want to apologize."

Nothing.

"Please?"

Still nothing. I lean my forehead against the door and tell myself I have no business getting teary. It's my fault Wren isn't speaking to me, but I can't help all the panicked feelings squirming through me. Wren's the only family I have left and she's getting married.

And moving to New York.

And...leaving me.

More tears burn my eyes and I wipe them away. "Okay," I shout. "Good talk. I'll see you later."

Still no answer, but I didn't really expect one. Briefly, I consider stealing Wren's car keys so she can't get away from me, but I figure I'm on thin enough ice. I don't need to add to it—and just like that, the memory of Caleb Reese hits me all over again.

I stuff down a groan. I flirted with my competition for the manager job. Thin ice doesn't even cover it. In fact, I don't think there is a word that covers it. Last night, I breezed out of the club fueled by peach martinis and a hazy grasp on what I'd done, but this morning it all came rushing back in painful detail.

I have to fix this, I think, retreating to my bedroom. Holly and Parker grin at me from various photos as I shuffle through my dresser. Eventually, I find an embroidered Jacks or Better polo and a pair of khaki shorts. I don't bother with makeup since I'll just sweat it off, but I take a minute to smooth down my ponytail and tuck in my shirt. There. Better.

Sort of.

Aside from the headache, I don't feel terribly hung over, but my face looks pale in the mirror and my eyes are shadowy from exhaustion. Not good considering I probably have ten hours' worth of work ahead me. Thank goodness I love my job.

I grab my sunglasses from the hook by the kitchen door and head down the spiral staircase that leads into the tack room. Wren and I have shared the second floor stable apartment for almost three years now and I still love it—the way your shoes clatter on the black iron steps, how all the polished wood glows in the sunlight, and the *smell*. I hit the bottom step and stretch, inhaling the amazing scent of conditioned saddles and bridles.

"Morning, Sleeping Beauty." Sam, our head groom, is sitting on a tack trunk and cleaning one of the jumping saddles. He dips a sponge into glycerin soap and begins another round of gentle circles against the cognac-colored leather. "Nice of you to join us."

I grin. "I'm not late. I'm on time."

"Which means you're late. If you want to be on time, you should be early." Sam doesn't look up, but I can hear the smile in his voice. He turns the saddle over to inspect the stitching. "Boss'll be here soon. You ready?"

"I was born ready."

Sam grunts.

"Are you nervous?" I ask him, and for the first time, Sam looks up. His eyes are wrinkled with worry.

"I'm...concerned."

It makes my heart hurt Sam is probably close to seventy with grey hair, grey whiskers, and an *impressive* swear word vocabulary. He's been in the horse industry his whole life. It's all he knows. I don't want him to be concerned about anything.

"You shouldn't be worried." I drop onto the tack trunk next to him and start to clean a set of stirrup leathers. "The Reeses are lucky to have you."

Sam grunts and goes back to cleaning, ears turning red. "I have a bad feeling about the whole thing. Pitting you against his son? Making the son work for what should be his inheritance? Something's off."

Sadly, I agree. When the Colonel told us he was retiring, I kinda panicked. He looked great. He seemed normal. Why retire? Then he asked me to think about taking the farm manager position. I'd already been doing most of the stuff already, but if I had the full title I'd get way more input. Not only would I be riding Jacks or Better horses, I would be directing the farm's breeding program. It would be an amazing opportunity.

Then the Colonel announced his son also wanted the job, and we would both have to interview for it. Under normal circumstances, I would worry. I mean, who can compete against family? No one, that's who. But the Reeses have never been normal. From what I've heard, Caleb is a stereotypical playboy, and after three years of working for the Colonel, I know he's, well, the *Colonel*. He appreciates hard work—something I'm sure Caleb wouldn't know a thing about.

"Besides," Sam adds, "the kid'll want his own staff, his own people."

I wipe off the stirrup leather in long strokes, and try to think of Caleb Reese as a "kid" and fail. He's too big, too male, too *arrogant* to be kid-like. Then again, I guess to Sam we're all kids. "Well, that's *if* he gets the job, and I don't think he will. I've worked for the Colonel for three years, Sam. Nights, weekends, every horse, every opportunity, I've done everything for him."

"That's true."

"He wouldn't screw me over."

Sam doesn't look up from the saddle he's cleaning and my stomach squeezes. I'm confident I'll get the job. I am. But after last night, well, I'm less confident about pretty much everything. "I met him," I add, watching as Sam's hand slows. "Caleb."

"Yeah?"

"Yeah, we didn't exactly hit it off."

Sam puts down his sponge and now I'm the one who won't look up. "What did you do?"

"Something stupid."

He sighs. "It had to do with Wren, didn't it?"

"We don't know anything about this Tate guy and she's *engaged* to him."

"Ellie, if your sister is old enough to get married, she's old enough to fight her own battles."

I concentrate on the stirrup leathers. Sam's right...and he's also wrong. Dead wrong. Wren and I are more complicated than that. We've been through too much together. "She's the only family I have left," I say. "I'm worried."

"You need to be worried about having done something 'stupid' in front of your possible new boss."

"He won't be my new boss." And stupid doesn't even begin to cover it. If it were possible to die of embarrassment, I would be six feet under. I pop to my feet and hang up the leathers. After I blurted out how I was Caleb's competition, his eyes almost bugged out of his head and he got that broody look again. I may be nuts (okay, yeah, after last night I probably *am* nuts), but that boy has serious mood swings.

"It'll be fine," I say.

Possibly a lie.

"I can always find another job," I add.

Definitely the truth.

"Damn right," Sam says. I stop dead. Sam's worked with my family for years. He was with my dad before the accident, and he's been working with me ever since I turned pro at eighteen, but that's one of the best compliments I've ever gotten. Actually, it's one of the only compliments I've ever gotten. "You're a good kid, Ellie."

"I'm twenty-three."

"You're a good kid," he repeats and hangs the saddle on a rack to dry. "And you're a damn talented rider. But the Reeses can take you places you can only dream of. This is not an inexpensive sport."

Nor is it something I need to be reminded of. At Jacks or Better, we specialize in showjumpers. Young foals can go for six figures. Trained horses can sell in the millions. My family doesn't have money. We work for families that do. If I want to ride in the Olympics, if I want to make my life about horses, I need people like them to believe in me.

"Are you telling me to make nice with the jerk?" I ask, smiling.

"I'm *begging* you to make nice with the jerk. If he gets the job, we need him on your side. I'm too old to move and train all your new grooms."

I laugh and it almost—*almost*—whisks away the dread in my stomach. "I'll think about it."

"Think about it while you make me coffee," Sam says, concentrating on buffing the saddle's flap to soft shine.

"Sure thing." Jacks or Better horses might run on the finest feed money can buy, but the rest of us run on Folgers. After pouring the water into the coffee maker, I turn for the door. "I'll be right back. I want to check on Beckon before the staff meeting."

"Damn mare." Sam grunts and pulls another saddle onto his lap for cleaning. "Watch she doesn't take your arm off."

Sam and I both laugh. It's funny because it's true. Beckon is not the kindest mare you will ever meet, but she can jump like nobody's business. I trained her entirely myself and we're due to compete in her first Grand Prix competition in a month.

I shut the tack room door and make my way down the brick aisle, nodding and smiling to the grooms. "There's coffee brewing in the tack room," I tell them.

"Thank God," someone mutters and I grin. I don't blame them. We have almost thirty horses here—a mix of show horses, client horses, and a couple broodmares—and it keeps everyone busy. It's not just the feeding and watering and stall cleaning. It's also the mowing and fence repairs and accounting and the list goes on. And on. In fact, it never ends.

I turn at the atrium and walk down the north aisle, making it four or five steps before Beckon's elegant dark head appears at her stall door.

"Hey, pretty girl," I say, and she pricks her ears, looking at me like I am everything she loves.

Until I'm within touching distance then she pins her ears and flashes her teeth.

"Nice to see you too." I coax Beckon back into her stall so I can check her hay and water. When those look good, I take a moment to run my hands over her smooth, black coat. No bumps. No scrapes. No swelling. It's probably something most people would take for granted. I mean to the untrained eye, the farm probably looks like a horse palace. Nothing bad could happen here, but that's the thing about horses: they're always getting hurt. For such enormous animals, they're frustratingly delicate. Sam says most of them were "born trying to kill themselves," and he's about right. Thankfully, Beckon has been super healthy.

I pat her shoulder. "I'll turn you out later."

Beckon clicks her teeth in response. I let myself out of her stall, but I linger for a few minutes, taking in the sun-drenched hallway, the beautiful horses, and the sweeping fields around us. Miles of black four-board fencing weave across the grass and I can spot two yearlings playing in their paddock. For horse people, Jacks or Better is heaven. For me, it's heaven and home.

Hope I haven't screwed that up, I think. After all, the farm might feel like home to me, but it *is* home to Caleb.

I'm just about to turn back when I spot a black SUV winding up the tree-lined drive. It's the Colonel. I squint, trying to see if he has anyone else with him. Crap. It looks like Caleb's riding shotgun.

I shake myself. No. Not crap. This is good. I need to patch things up with Wren (gulp), apologize to Caleb (ick), get three horses ridden, the invoices reviewed for payment, and finish the grooms' schedules for next week (easy).

Oddly, listing out all my responsibilities slows my heartrate and deeps my breathing. *You can do this*, I think. *You're* already *doing this*.

I square my shoulders and head for the tack room.

CHAPTER 5 | Caleb

It's been six years and Jacks or Better doesn't look like it's aged a day. It's still the same miles of black fencing, still the same pastures fertilized until they're electric green. The horses wandering through the pastures might be different, but the bloodlines are undoubtedly still the same: French, German, and the occasional American Thoroughbred.

Everything's the same so why does it feel different? No, not different. *Wrong*. Maybe it's the effects of last night, but I'd actually been contemplating packing my stuff when the Colonel banged on my bedroom door this morning and demanded I get up.

"The staff meeting starts in twenty," he barked through the door jamb's crack. "I want you there."

This is as close to 'good morning' as our family gets. It sounds cold, but I'm okay with it. I can't imagine the Colonel wanting to talk about anything beyond the farm. Actually, I can, but I don't want to. Horses are a safe topic. Everything else? No way. We haven't agreed on anything since my mom died.

"And you think *I* have problems," Mandy had always reminded me. In the beginning, she did it with a laugh we could share. Later, it was a laugh at my expense. "Your family is so..."

Mandy said a lot of things, but she never finished that sentence. Ever. I guess she was leaving me to fill in the blank for her. Like that was going to happen. I think even in those very first days I knew I couldn't trust her.

I flex both hands against my knees and roll my shoulders as the Colonel steers his Range Rover up the stable's winding drive. My eyes feel gritty and I can't shake the cottony taste in my mouth. Helluva a way to start an interview, but whatever.

We curve around the last bend and the stable's main tower rises above the trees, sunlight sparking off the copper weathervane. A heartbeat later, the trees part and all of Jacks or Better sprawls into view. Fifty stalls shaped around a wide courtyard, hundred year old pecan trees shading the paddocks, and a three different sand arenas set up for schooling. It's the most beautiful place in the world, and I have a growing pit in my stomach.

"You're hungover," my father says at last. His voice is even, but his knuckles stand up white beneath the skin.

"Yes."

"Is that really the way you want to start this?"

I pause. Of course, it isn't, but admitting it will only make the whole thing worse. The only thing the Colonel hates more than overindulgence is overindulging while *knowing* you shouldn't. Honestly, I'm the same way, which *also* makes the whole thing worse.

Two yearlings race the SUV up the drive, veering away from the fence line at the last possible second. I watch the larger one strike at a passing butterfly. "Is that one of Laughter's foals?"

The Colonel squints. Frowns. "Yes."

I try not to smirk, and fail. I may be hungover—fine, I *am* hungover—but no one knows his horses like I do and the subtle reminder makes the Colonel's jaw clench.

My father pulls into an empty parking space, shuts off the Rover, and turns to me. The morning light does him no favors. He looks older than ever: close-cropped grey hair gone thin, once muscular chest now verging on sunken. Deep grooves bracket his mouth, and with every word they grow deeper. "Do you really think you can do this? Jacks or Better is an established business, not a start-up."

"Is it? I hadn't noticed." The words shoot out before I think about them and I scowl. Great. Now I sound like a bitchy teenager.

The Colonel's whole face hardens. "This is a *serious* business," he begins, winding up for a lecture we both know by heart. "I've spent my whole life creating a reputation known throughout the world."

"I know."

"I'm not just handing over a flourishing business. I'm handing over my life's work. My—"

"Look," I say, grinding the word through clenched teeth. "You're the one who called me back. *You're* the one who asked *me* to come home."

There is the smallest twitch beneath the Colonel's left eye. "I did," he says at last, and pauses, then: "I might have made a mistake. I don't know if you're ready for this."

"Ready for it? Seriously? I brought two start up breeding farms into the black. I picked stallions, broodmares, and the young stock. I hired the riders. I planned the programs."

"But nothing at this level."

And there it is. I grind my teeth together until it hurts. He's right. I didn't. Few farms have the kind of capital Jacks or Better does, and that's why my accomplishments mean so much more. Those two operations needed every penny we scored, every diamond in the rough broodmare or yearling we found, but I can't say any of that to my dad because he won't understand a word of it, not really. He looks down on people who don't come from the same affluent background he does.

"I'm just not sure you're the right fit," the Colonel continues, "even if you are my son."

Now *my* eye is the one twitching. I hate how his tone of voice makes me feel ten years old again.

I hate even more how much I want to prove him wrong.

"And somehow Ellie Lenox is a better bet?" I ask.

He doesn't say anything, and I don't know what that means. Whatever it is, I don't like it. I grab the door handle, ready to jump out and stalk back to the house, but something makes me pause. "Then what is this? Why am I here?"

"Because I want you to be the right fit, and I'm not sure you won't walk away again."

Honestly, I should've seen it coming. That was a nice move. Very manipulative. Now, if I tell him to shove it, he can tell everyone I left because I always leave, and if I stay, I have to play his reindeer games—and make no mistake, they *are* games. Days before I was supposed to fly home, the Colonel called me and said I had competition for the job.

"What are you talking about?" I'd asked him. "You said the job was mine. I already quit my position here. We had an agreement."

He'd made some harrumphing noise. "Well, if you don't want the position anymore. I can give it to her."

Like *I* was the one being difficult.

"You and the other candidate will interview over the course of a week," he'd continued. "At the end, I'll make my decision."

At the time, I'd thought it was almost cute how he called it an interview. I'd called it "pitting people against each other."

Now, it just looks like a warning I should've heeded.

Inside the barn, a horse neighs. I take a deep breath and shrug, neck and shoulders popping. "Then let's call it quits. You don't think I can handle the farm? Fine, but we both know I can—and we both know no one else will do better."

The Colonel clenches his jaw and glares at me like I'm going to back down. I don't. I glare right back. It makes something nameless zip through his eyes. He's deciding something, and if I had any guts, I'd walk away before he does it, but the farm is all around me—sun dappled horses and ecstatic green pastures—and I can't.

"We'll discuss this later," the Colonel finally says, opening the driver door and stepping onto the gravel. The smell of fresh cut grass floods the SUV. "Will you come in with me?"

I blink. I can't remember the last time my father asked me to do anything, and the shock propels me out of the Rover and into the sunshine. Down the slope, someone is already weaving back and forth with a ride-on lawnmower while the horses look on with interest.

The Colonel walks into the stable, stiff-legged and back straight—the way he gets when he's hurting. After a fox hunting accident in his forties, he needs a cane, but he won't use it unless the pain in his hip and knee is excruciating.

Or when no one is around to see him, I think, following him. We head down the wide brick aisle toward the tack room. Even though the staff has probably been there since six, the farm looks like it's waking up. On either side of us, horses are being prepared for their day—two being groomed, another being saddled, a few more being lead out to the pastures.

A couple of grooms nod in greeting, but the Colonel doesn't acknowledge them or their plastered on smiles. It's like the whole place suddenly holds its breath.

Guess I'm not the only one who's been subjected to the tyrant, I think.

"Through here," the Colonel says, opening a dark stained door on our right and revealing the bright, wood-paneled tack room. Inside, Ellie and a much older man are sitting on a glossy wooden trunk, sipping coffee. I think they're trying for casual, but Ellie's bouncing one foot against the floor and the older man—Sam Ray—is twisting and re-twisting a rag in his hands.

Ellie stands in one smooth movement, eyes pinned to my father and last night's killer smile at the ready. To his credit, Sam doesn't bother standing. My father might be the boss, but everyone knows Sam Ray is a legend without compare.

"Morning," the Colonel says, and snaps the door shut behind me.

"Morning," Ellie echoes. She won't look at me.

And I can't stop looking at her: toned legs, dark eyes, and that sweep of hair. Last night, it was loose. Today, she's tied it up into a thick braid and I suddenly wonder what it would feel like wrapped around my hand.

The Colonel strides to the corner desk and picks up the file folders sitting on top. He takes a moment to flip through them and then levels his attention at Ellie. "What's our status?"

Status? I suppress a groan, but Ellie seems to brighten. "Good," she tells him. "Beckon is in fine form. Today's her day off, but I'll jump her tomorrow. The grooms are finishing up and I'll start riding once they're done. We need an order of hay, but Sam is already on it and the farrier is scheduled for tomorrow."

The Colonel nods. "And the vet check for Galloway?"

"Wednesday at noon."

"The client billing?"

"Done. I want to review it once more though for any discrepancies." Ellie's gaze never swerves from the Colonel. She doesn't fidget. She doesn't mumble. I can barely believe this is the same girl from last night. The Colonel keeps going, and Ellie has an answer for everything. She's good at this—way better than I expected—and I'd be lying if I said that didn't make me ever so slightly uneasy. Technically, she's already been doing the manager job, and from the sound of it, she's been doing it well.

"Good," the Colonel says once he's asked her about everything under the freaking sun. "Very good. Now onto other business: have you met my son, Caleb?"

Ellie opens her mouth and I cut her off. "Oh, we've met." I face my father, and savor the surprise in the old man's eyes. "Guess where?"

The Colonel's face goes blank and then annoyed. He knows whatever I want to say, he isn't going to like. "As we previously discussed," he says, frowning. "This week will determine your futures at Jacks or Better."

Ellie tenses, dark eyes going bright with interest. *Want.* I feel it too. Maybe it's being back or maybe it's looking at my competition, but everything in me has gone tight.

The Colonel places the file folders back on the desk and helps himself to coffee. "I've changed my mind. The interview won't be necessary." He takes the longest moment of my life to stir creamer into his cup. "Caleb, you will be running the breeding operations. Ellie, you will be in charge of training."

It's like a blow to the stomach. For a second, I can't breathe.

Ellie steps forward, face ashen. "But—but—I don't understand, sir. The last time we spoke—"

"I changed my mind," the Colonel repeats.

Ellie blinks like her world just spun around, which I guess it pretty much has. Briefly, I feel bad for her. I know how this feels. I would've thought three years of working for my father would prepare her for this stuff. Maybe she hasn't been paying attention.

She stands up straighter. "But I've been doing the work for months now. I'm ready for this."

"I disagree. From now on, your respective positions will be collaborative."

"Define collaborative," Ellie says, mutiny stamped into her voice.

The Colonel raises one brow. "When you want to make a management change to benefit one of the horses, you'll run it by Caleb. If Caleb wants to change how one of the horses is going, he'll come to you."

"If he wants to change how one of the horses is going," Ellie repeats softly, like she's about to faint.

Or freak out.

My money's on freak out. She's already grinding her teeth.

I smirk—I can't help it—and she catches me, dark eyes going even darker.

"You will both represent the farm and our horses," the Colonel continues. "You'll figure out a way to make it work. You'll have to."

Ellie crosses both arms and faces me, mouth tight. "Can you give me an example of your proposed management changes?"

I hesitate. Where do I begin? The new advances in pasture management? The breeding program's need for a new mare line? "Feed," I say finally. "We need to go clean. The preservatives, additives, it's all got to go. New research has found links between food and various health and performance problems."

Ellie goes super still. "My horses don't have health *or* performance problems."

"Really?" I give her a sarcastic smile. "There isn't one hard keeper here? One horse who gets a little colicky? One—"

"No, because they're *managed*. You don't fix something that isn't broken." Ellie rolls her eyes, and my temper spikes.

You want to play, sweetheart? Let's play. But before I can open my mouth the Colonel cuts in: "*Collaborative*," he says through gritted teeth. "Or I'll fire both of you."

CHAPTER 6 | Ellie

Collaborate with Caleb? I brace one hand against the desk so I don't fall down. It's a little embarrassing, but the Colonel doesn't notice. He's too busy staring daggers at his son.

Sam looks at me and shakes his head. I know what he's thinking: *You couldn't play along for a* minute? Or maybe: *You do nothing by halves, you know that? He hates you.*

It's a lot to say in a look, but somehow Sam manages it. I shrug. He's right. I shouldn't have flirted with Caleb last night, and I shouldn't have rolled my eyes at him right now. But honestly? I couldn't help it. His idea is ridiculous. He thinks he's going to revolutionize the farm with feed? It's so stupid it's almost enough to make me forget I need to play along with him to keep my job.

Almost.

The Colonel clears his throat. "Do you know who she *is*?"

"I know enough." Caleb shoots me a contemptuous look and all my insides wither. "I know what *matters* about her."

Ah, crap. Sam and I exchange another quick glance. His face has gone positively gray. He's probably picturing our future...or lack of one if I get us thrown out of here.

There's only one way to handle this, I think, squaring my shoulders. "He thinks he knows me because I flirted with him, sir."

The Colonel switches his attention to me and stares at me as if I have just spoken in tongues. Now isn't an appropriate time to notice how he shares the same strong jaw and high cheekbones with his son, but my stupid brain does anyway.

"What are you talking about" the Colonel asks.

"Last night, I flirted with Caleb," I repeat, re-crossing my arms to hide how my hands are now shaking. "But, in my defense, I thought he was someone else."

Sam makes a choking noise and tries to pretend he swallowed his coffee wrong. He whacks one hand against his chest.

"You thought Caleb was someone else," our boss says slowly.

I give him my brightest smile. "Exactly. I mean why else would I flirt with him?"

Behind me, Caleb makes a rude noise deep in his throat. The Colonel looks from his son to me and back again. He doesn't know what to say. We've worked together for a long time and I think that's a first.

"Look," I say, pushing up my chin and trying to sound like I'm not scared to death. "You can fire me. That's fine, but you're firing your head trainer, your head rider, and you have the fall classic in a month." I pause to let all that sink in, but all it does is lay out everything I have here, everything I've worked for. I force a shrug like none of it matters. "I mean, if you've found someone else to ride Beckon by all means, do it. Fire me."

My tone makes it sound like I'm daring the Colonel when really I'm bluffing. Sort of. Everything I've said is true, but it's omitting one of the biggest factors: I love Jacks or Better. It's the closest thing I've ever had to a home and I don't want to lose it.

"Your choice," I add and I'm so *so* grateful my voice doesn't crack.

The Colonel's lips twitch. He's trying not to smile and I can't decide if that's a good sign. He turns to Sam. "What do you think?"

Sam glowers at me. "I think you'd be a fool to fire her. She'd be your competition. Pardon the expression, sir, but you'd rather have Ellie in the tent pissing out than outside the tent pissing in."

I wrinkle my nose in disgust and Sam shrugs. "It's true," he grumbles.

"No, it's not," Caleb says, leaning back against the desk so his long legs stretch out in front of him. "Riders are a dime a dozen. You don't need her, but if you want to keep her? Fine. But there needs to be *one* manager. You can't collaborate on these things. There has to be one manager and one vision."

One vision? I nearly laugh. *Pretentious ass.*

"It's called being practical." Caleb shakes his head and takes a step toward me. Last night, he had been tall, but in my heels I had been tall (okay, sort of tall) too. Now, I'm in my regular boots and he towers over me. "Running a business means eliminating liabilities, and *you* are a liability. If you think your behavior from last night is remotely acceptable, I can't work with you."

Hot, embarrassing tears prick the corners of my eyes. "How dare you? I would never do anything like that when I'm riding for Jacks or Better!"

"Ha!" Caleb turns triumphant. "So you *do* admit it was unacceptable behavior!"

"It isn't even an appropriate comparison!"

"You're right. It's worse." He looks at his father. "She flirted with me because she thought I was her sister's fiancé. That's the kind of person you're dealing with. She has no integrity, no personal pride. Do you really want her representing your farm?"

"My private life has no bearing—"

"Are you kidding me?" Caleb's eyes drag up and down me and I can't stop a furious blush from climbing my cheeks. "How old are you anyway?"

"Twenty-three," I manage and Caleb rolls his eyes like this too is unacceptable on my part. He turns his back to me.

"Look, Colonel, I don't know what she's told you, but no one is irreplaceable. If you want Jacks or Better to be a premiere farm then hire the best, professional people you can afford."

The Colonel clears his throat. "She *is* one of the best, professional people I can afford." Caleb shifts like he's going to start arguing again and the Colonel cuts him off: "You two will make this work."

"The hell I will."

The Colonel straightens. "You owe me this. You owe your mother."

It's as if the air has been sucked from the room. Everything goes tense. The Colonel's wife had always been a bit sickly, but after Caleb left, she took a turn for the worse. It was a year before I arrived, but I was told he didn't even come home for the funeral.

I sneak a glance at Caleb. He's gone pale. The dig about his mother has hit something deep. Painful. I don't want to feel sorry for him, but somehow I do.

The Colonel glares at him. "If you want the job all to yourself, then prove you can do it better."

He can't, I think. Caleb doesn't compete or even *ride*. It should be a reassuring thought, but it's not. I've given years to the farm, and the Colonel makes it sound like he'd be fine replacing me. The revelation has a lingering sting. I had no idea. I thought my work had meant more to him.

"We're on the verge of selling Beckon," the Colonel continues, "and making the Jacks or Better name. It's everything I've worked for—everything your mother worked for—and you owe us your help." A tight nod from Caleb and the Colonel relaxes the tiniest bit. "The Classic is in a month, but you know what the run up will be like, and I expect you to be there. With. Her."

Caleb and I both flinch. "The run up" is an awfully casual way of describing a set of parties that's anything but casual. Usually, the Colonel and I go together, working the beautifully dressed crowd for contacts and buyers. It's stressful enough, but going with Caleb? Ugh.

"In one month," the Colonel continues, "I want to be holding the Classic trophy and a buyer's contract for Beckon and I want you two to make it happen, do you understand?"

"Of course." My agreement is immediate, and seconds later, I wonder how I can possibly deliver. I'd have a better chance of creating world peace. I smile at Caleb like I'd rather set my hair on fire than have him help me, and Caleb smiles back like he'd happily pass me a match. We both face the Colonel.

"It won't be a problem," I lie.

CHAPTER 7 | Caleb

And just like that, the Colonel treats me like I'm ten again. I watch him stalk from the tack room, his little hanger-on scurrying after him. When she reaches the door, Ellie casts a quick glance back, but I can't read her expression. It's probably fury or disgust.

I roll my shoulders, and my spine pops. Well, she doesn't need to bother. I'm disgusted enough with myself for both of us. Doesn't change my mind though. There needs to be one manager, one decision maker.

And I really, really want it to be me.

"Well," a roughened voice says behind me. "It's been a bit of a rocky start, but I'm looking forward to working with you."

Stomach sinking, I turn around and Sam Bishop sticks out a hand. For one whole minute, I wish he'd just punch me in the face. The man is practically a legend in the business. He didn't deserve to get caught up in this, but my temper got the better of me. It was the Colonel and Ellie and...I mentally kick myself. I have no excuse.

"Sorry about that." I shake Sam's hand and the old man squeezes my fingers way more than necessary. "I dragged you into our family issues. It wasn't right."

Sam's faded brown eyes briefly widen in surprise. "I didn't get along with my old man either."

I nod like that explains it, but honestly there's way more to the Colonel and me than that and I don't want to go into it. In fact, it's why I went all the way to Ireland to get away from it and now look at me, I'm acting like I never left.

At least you have the job, I remind myself. When I walked in here, I had no idea the Colonel was about to change his mind. Except did he, really? I have to keep employees I don't want. Who's really in charge?

Sam shifts from foot to foot. He must be seventy, and at the moment, looks every minute of it. His shoulders are sharp beneath his plaid shirt, and there are dark circles beneath his eyes. "If you like," Sam says at last, "I can go over the accounts with you later today."

"Thank you. I would also like to meet the staff."

The old man scratches his temple, tips of white hair curling from beneath his dark blue cap. "Everyone?"

"Everyone," I confirm. A lot of owners don't bother with grooms or stable hands. I'm not like that. Never have been. "I'm not an elitist."

Sam grunts and I don't bother defending myself. After that outburst, I totally look like an elitist. I try not to worry about it and fail.

"Coffee?" I ask him, taking a mug from the cabinet. There's a dull ache behind my eyes, payback from last night's indulgences.

"Sure," Sam says, settling onto a tack trunk and pulling a saddle into his lap. "I take it black."

I pull out another mug and help myself to the coffee pot, dumping for scoops of sugar and loads of cream into my cup. Stuff still tastes like death, but the jolt of caffeine helps me feel less blurry.

Unfortunately, it also makes me more observant and I spot Ellie grinning at me from a framed picture above the coffee maker. She's holding up an armful of first place ribbons and laughing at the camera.

"We have excellent staff," Sam says, jerking me back to reality. "You'll like the grooms. I've trained them myself."

I turn around and offer Sam his coffee. "And the girl?"

"The *girl*—" distaste at my term ghosts across the old man's face "—is one of the most promising young riders in the country. She's going to go on to do great things. If you want Jacks or Better to be taken as one of the best barns in the world, you would do well to keep her."

Ellie's brave, I'll give her that. Not many people can stand up to my father's rapid fire question sessions—and not only did Ellie stand up, she seemed to almost enjoy it. More of the crazy right there. She probably enjoys arguing too. "Maybe," I say at last.

Sam grunts, and takes the coffee I've poured for him.

"I have my own rider I'll be bringing in though," I tell Sam. "Name's Aiden Macken."

"Never heard of him."

A prickle of annoyance hits me. "He's good. With the right opportunity, he'll be great."

"So that's it?" There's an edge to the older man's voice now, like he's on the edge of an explosion. "You're not even going to try to work with her?"

"Of course not. You've needed a second rider for months now. Now you have one."

It's true. No matter what I think about Ellie personally, no one can keep up with this many horses for long. In addition to Beckon, there are three other up and coming young horses. They're already competing and we need to see what they can do. Then there's the young stock, two to four year olds who will need to be handled and eventually broken. She can't be everywhere and Sam and I both know it.

Or he should know it. Right now, the old man is deep in thought, leaving me to notice the tack room still hasn't changed since my mom designed it. The dark wood paneling and brass accents glow in the growing sunshine, and the brick floor is smooth underfoot. Everything is a testament to functional elegance except for the huge antique mirror by the rider lockers, and the matching crystal chandeliers overhead. They'd belonged to my grandparents and my mom had wanted to keep them somewhere she'd see them every day.

I finish the last of my coffee in one long pull and try not to make a face. Man, that stuff is horrible. "When does Ellie school Beckon?"

"Usually early morning. The heat's been bad. She tries to keep the mare out of it."

"Good. I'll come by to watch tomorrow."

Sam nods. "Do you want to meet the staff afterward?"

"That'll work. Can you fill me in on the buyers interested in Beckon? I understand it Adele Mar has come to the table."

Sam's eyes briefly widen as he nods. I understand the sentiment. The equine world is rife with money: the Firestones, the DuPonts, the Bloombergs, the Gates, I could go on and on. But Adele Mar has always been a special case even among the trust fund set. She loves her horses, and has kept some riders working for her for decades. In other words, she has money to burn, takes care of her animals, and she's loyal. Some people owe her their professional standing.

I wouldn't mind being one of those people.

"Prestigious potential client," I say, studying the rows of saddles and bridles that line the walls. "She's known to return shop too. Why not buy the mare now? If she wins the classic, she'll be worth twice what she is now."

Sam grimaces. "*If* she wins. You and I both know all that can happen between now and the day of the classic."

I watch him, something nagging at me. "Adele Mar knows that too. What aren't you telling me?"

"The mare's talented, no doubt, but she's difficult. It will be hard to find another rider who fits her as well as Ellie does. She brought Beckon up herself. They're good together."

"Other riders could be good with her too."

"True." Sam nods. "But rumor has it that Mrs. Mar is looking for a new Olympic prospect for her current rider, and that isn't Beckon. She needs time to develop, and everyone knows there are no guarantees."

He's right. In fact, it's about the only thing you can count on with horses. "We still need the mare sold."

Sam eyes me. "Do we? We have several sales horses available—Echo has potential buyers coming tomorrow. A few sales would easily float us."

"I'm thinking long term." I pause. "So what's the plan? How's Ellie going to handle convincing Mar this is what she wants?"

"There's no convincing Adele Mar of anything, but they'll both be at the Wesley party later this week. I'm sure Ellie will speak to her there."

Then I'll need to be there too, I think, frowning as I realize being at the party will not only mean working with Ellie, but also getting closer to Mandy and our old circle of friends. *I can do that.*

"Caleb..." Sam's voice brings me back, but the old man takes his time with his next question. He slides his rag over and over the saddle's flaps, filling the air with the smell of leather and glycerin. "I know what your father wants Jacks or Better to be, but what do you want?"

Everything. I want *everything*: legendary bloodlines, competition wins, and a world class reputation. Basically...I want everything my mom dreamed of. I want to make it happen because it meant the world to her, and now it means the world to me.

"I'm not sure where I want to begin yet," I say at last, and the honesty surprises me—surprises both of us because Sam looks up from the saddle with his fuzzy grey eyebrows halfway up his forehead. "I do know I want this place running like a business."

The grey eyebrows drew close together. "After what happened last night, I'll assume that's directed at Ellie. Look, Caleb...I know riders like Ellie. They always come through. They always make you proud. They are *not* easily replaceable."

"Maybe," I repeat, trying to stay neutral and knowing I'm probably failing. The old man must think of Ellie like she's some kind of granddaughter. "But Aiden is very, very good, and I have every confidence in him."

Unlike some people hangs unspoken between us. Sam has gone totally silent, and if I were the Colonel, I would ask him if he heard me. Since I'm not, I put my empty coffee cup in the sink, and say I'll see him around.

CHAPTER 8 | Ellie

It's nine o'clock by the time I drag myself up the spiral staircase and into our apartment. I stand at the fridge for a few minutes trying to decide what to cook for dinner and then decide I don't care. I'm too disappointed, too angry, and too tired.

Not so tired I can't send another text to Parker asking her to call me. Maybe this time she will. I hope so. I face my fridge again.

"Bowl of cereal it is," I mutter, but I don't even make it that far because I hear a bump in our living room and my stomach squeezes. Wren's still here.

I kick off my boots and pad down the tiny hallway to the equally tiny living room. Wren is obsessed with all things French. We have vintage wine posters and pocket-sized tables, chairs trimmed in gold paint and the prettiest Oriental carpets. It looks like we spent a ton, but Wren picks up everything from junk sales and antique shops. She has an amazing eye. If it were up to me, we'd probably be living on lawn chairs.

Which is why I get so scared when I see half the living room packed away. I huddle in the doorway and watch her roll up her Eiffel Tower posters and slide them into tubes.

"Wren...please?" For two heartbeats, I'm convinced she's going to keep ignoring me and then she spins around.

"Don't," Wren spits. "You don't get to be hurt that I'm mad at you."

"I'm sorry. I know. I just thought—"

"No, you didn't think. You never think, Ellie. That's part of the problem."

I wince and we stand there for a moment or so in silence.

Wren sighs. She rubs one hand across her eyes. "It's my fault you're like this. When Mom and Dad died, I thought I was doing the right

55

thing by keeping you in training, but you've never really had to grow up and be with other people."

"What?" There's more edge to my voice than I intend and Wren glares at me. I glare back. I can't help it. I hate it when she makes my career sound like something less than what other people do. "I have plenty of people in my life. I have Holly and Parker—"

"Who's in *Seattle*. If she'd been here, she would've stopped you."

"I made a mistake," I say.

"Yeah, a big one. Tate thinks you're insane. What were you thinking?"

"Apparently, I wasn't." I flop down on our couch and Wren's decorative pillows bounce to the floor. I pick one up and play with the tasseled edge.

My sister stands over me, hands on hips. "Talk to me about what's bothering you or I'm out, Ellie. I'll stay with Tate until the move. I'm serious."

She is too. I've done some epically stupid stuff over the years, but I've never seen Wren as angry as she is now. Her eyes are pink from crying and there are grooves bracketing her mouth.

"You're leaving," I say.

"So?"

"So you're *leaving*."

"I've been in Paris for months now. If anything, I've already left."

The words suck the air from my lungs and I stare at her. I hadn't thought about it like that, but she's right. I try to swallow and realize my throat has funneled shut. "You said...you said you would come home after visiting Lynn, get a job around here."

Wren's mouth presses thin. "Yeah, but...things changed."

"Tate."

"Not just Tate. If I want gallery work, I have to go to New York." She drops onto the couch next to me and touches my knee with her hand. Her left hand. I find myself staring down her enormous diamond engagement ring.

"You know how much I want this," Wren continues. "And you know how much you have to sacrifice to get what you want."

I look away. It's true, but it still feels like a low blow. I gave up a lot to pursue my riding: high school graduation, dance, dating, friends. Most people don't want to put up with someone who will have to cancel plans because a horse colicked or a fence fell down. Holly does because she grew up riding, but even she gets frustrated with me.

"I never gave up *you*," I say at last.

"I'm not giving you up either. I'm moving for work."

"And for Tate."

"And for Tate."

We go quiet and I study the new blank spots on our wall. Wren painted the whole apartment in this warm white. It was almost blinding until she put up pictures—old travel posters, photography. Even with my old photographs of my best friends, Holly and Parker, smiling down at me, the apartment feels cold.

I slide lower on the couch. "I really am sorry."

"I know. I knew you were sorry the minute I confronted you—didn't stop me from being angry though. I wanted you to make a good impression on Tate."

A good impression? Like I'm twelve? I stuff down my sigh as Wren curls up next to me. Her dark hair is coming loose from its topknot and it tickles my neck and jaw. "I can't believe you thought Caleb was Tate," she says.

"Please don't remind me."

Wren laughs. "Oh, I'm going to. Probably for..." She taps one finger to her chin, pretending to think. "Yeah, the rest of your life."

I groan. "You know what's even worse? I have to work with him. We're competing for the same job."

"*What?*"

"Yeah," I say, trying to keep the pinch of frustration out of my voice. "The Colonel says he's going to pick between us. In the meantime, we have to work together."

"Well, shit."

"Pretty much." We both fall silent, slumped boneless on the couch together. It would be nice if I weren't so gut wrenchingly disappointed. "There's no way this is going to work. Caleb's awful."

"Really?"

"What do you mean really?" I sit up. "Haven't you noticed?"

"No. He was actually pretty nice."

I study Wren, trying to decide if she's lying. We share the same coloring and features as our dad, but Wren has her mom's dark, expressive eyes. She watches me closely and I'm almost positive she isn't lying. I'm not sure if I'm glad about that. Caleb Reese is nice? Hmmm.

"Well," I say at last. "You were in Paris. I'm pretty sure everyone is nice when there are so many good things to eat."

"True, but he could've been rude and he never was. I talked about art all night and he was probably bored silly, but he never let on if he was. He didn't act like an ass at all—"

I roll my eyes so hard they hurt.

"He *didn't*," Wren insists. "I bet you two would get along great if you would relax. Think of all you've accomplished. I bet he'd love to talk shop."

"I thought I hadn't accomplished anything. You're always telling me to get out and be more rounded."

"It's true. You need to." Wren plays with the edge of her white button up. Even during packing, she's still pristine. If that were me, I'd be covered in stains. "You never get off the farm unless it's for a horse show. There's a huge world out there. Don't you want to see it?"

"You make me sound like a shut in."

"You practically are! All you talk about is horses!" Wren catches herself and sighs again. The worry lines around her mouth deepen. "I worry you'll hide here for the rest of your life. Dad wouldn't have wanted that."

I pick at my polo shirt, refusing to look at her. I know how this argument goes. We've had it enough times, I could probably recite it by memory now and the whole thing makes me tired.

Or maybe it's just the Reeses who have made me tired. They have that effect.

Wren squeezes my hand. "It doesn't mean I'm not excited for where you might end up."

I shrug. "If Caleb the Ass doesn't get my job first."

"Are you seriously worried about that?" Wren turns quiet and worried. "No fooling around, no exaggerating. You really think you won't get the manager job?"

"I don't know. He's the Colonel's son, right? How can you compete with that? Plus, he wants me gone. He told Sam he has his own rider coming in. It's only a matter of time before he gets me fired. We're supposed to collaborate, but there's no way that'll happen. Caleb has a plan and it doesn't include me—you know what's even worse?"

"It gets worse?"

"The Colonel acted like he'd let Caleb do it *if* he could prove he could do a better job. Six years of loyalty, six years of giving everything, and he'd be happy to let me go."

"I'm so sorry, Ellie." Wren cradles a pillow in her lap, crushing it death. "That's awful."

And it's so true, I feel even worse.

She sits up. "Something to think about though? You're seeing a side of the Colonel Caleb probably grew up with. Tate said he's had it pretty rough."

"Pretty rough?" I make a scoffing noise. "You're so right. It must be really hard to have money and opportunity and a farm like Jacks or Better. What was I thinking?"

Wren laughs. "Okay, yeah, fair point." She hesitates. "You really think he'll fire you?"

I nod, miserable. "If he gets the chance."

My sister's face goes tight. "I'll talk to Tate. Caleb can't do this. Tate will make him understand—"

"I thought we just had a conversation about not interfering in each other's lives?" I sound pretty assured for someone whose heart just swung into her throat. I'm so lucky to have Wren. "Telling Tate to defend me is just like me flirting with Caleb because I thought he was Tate."

"They're so not the same."

"Do you want your fiancé to think we're both crazy?"

"Ellie..." My sister's mouth screws up. She blows out a long sigh.

"When I'm right, I'm right."

The tiniest of smiles. "Okay, yeah, you're right. I don't know what to tell you. Just try to...be nice, I guess. His family life wasn't like ours. They weren't close and not everyone thinks Jacks or Better is heaven on earth."

"They don't?"

"Funny."

It's kind of not though. Wren isn't very horsey, which is fine. Loads of people aren't. But when you're born into a horse crazy family, well, it's been tough on her. Lynn was so far away, and my parents never really understood Wren's fascination with art the same way they understood my fascination with riding. Dinner table conversations never circled around what new technique my sister was learning, but there was plenty of talk about how the sale ponies were doing or who might win an upcoming horse show.

Wren and I talk about everything, but we've never talked about that. I mean, I've tried, but she won't go there. She always cuts me off and it's those memories that make me decide I have to be glad Wren's making her own life.

Even if it's away from me.

I stand up. "I'm beat. I need to go to bed. Are you staying here tonight?"

She nods. "I'll make you breakfast in the morning. Tate's coming by. You can apologize."

"Oh, goody."

Wren shoots me a dangerous look. "Please try to get along with him?"

"Does it matter?" I joke. "I mean he already thinks I'm nuts."

Wren's smile vanishes. She shifts from foot to foot. "Actually, I'm the one who might have said you were crazy. Tate just thinks you're acting out."

"'Acting out?'" Now I know why he's best friends with Caleb. They're both condescending, know-it-alls. "How old does Tate think I am?"

Wren's eyes narrow. "You really want me to answer that?"

I open my mouth to argue and stop. I don't want to do this. "Sure thing. I'll apologize."

Wren's shoulders sag with relief. She hugs me and pretends to gag. "You stink of horse."

"Some of us think it's nice."

She points to me. "One of us thinks it's nice. The rest of us know you need a shower."

"Fine." I turn to go and stop, spin back around to my sister. In the golden lamplight, she looks like the Madonna from her favorite painting. "You still haven't told me what Tate's like."

"Oh." Wren's dark eyes go faraway and the softest smile ghosts across her lips. "He's wonderful. He's really thoughtful and supportive and I had no idea relationships could be so easy. He doesn't want to play games. He just wants to be with me."

"Sounds amazing," I say—and it does. None of my relationships have ever been that good. My life is pretty great anyway, but having that? It would make it even better.

Wren's smile turns a little goofy. "He makes me happy, Ellie."

He does. The thought hits me low in the stomach. I don't think I've ever seen her so happy and even though I'm still pretty sure I'm going to dislike Hot Stuff, I'm glad for her. "Good," I say. "You deserve that."

Her cheeks go pink. "You're my favorite sister."

You're all I have left, I want to say, but I don't because it will only make her feel bad, and more than anything, I want her to be happy.

CHAPTER 9 | Caleb

Sam wasn't kidding when he said the girl—Ellie—practiced early. I'm at the stables by seven, but she's already in the riding arena, working back and forth in the pink morning sunlight. There's almost no noise except for the mare's soft snorting and the rhythmic beat of her hooves against the sand footing. I stand by the gate, sipping on terrible coffee again, and watch Ellie ride Beckon toward a set of brightly colored jumps.

Arranged at different lengths and heights, the obstacles are designed to make Beckon listen to her rider and pay attention to her body. Not that Beckon really seems to need it. The mare slips over the poles like a shadow, landing on the other side in a soft spray of sand.

To the untrained eye, Ellie looks damn near motionless in the saddle, moving and folding in perfect rhythm with the mare. She makes it look effortless. But even to the trained eye, she's good. When she corrects Beckon, the moves are fluid. Her voice stays soft. There's something almost familiar about her riding too. I can't put my finger on it.

Ellie turns Beckon toward the rail and the sunrise illuminates all their edges. Briefly, they're on fire, and it's all very picturesque until Ellie canters the mare past me and Beckon pins her ears and flashes her teeth.

"Good morning to you too," I mutter, leaning against the arena's top rail to watch them finish up. Moments later, Ellie murmurs something to Beckon and pats the mare's neck. They slow to a walk and head for the gate. I follow along the arena's edge, reaching the entrance just as Ellie swings down from the saddle. She takes off her helmet, shaking loose a thick braid.

"Morning," I say, and Beckon snakes her head around, clicking her teeth at me. I take a step back—not because I'm chicken, but because

I would prefer to keep my nose on my face. "I see she's still evil. How wonderful."

Ellie hooks a few strands of hair behind her ear, and gives me a bright smile. "They say animals can judge character better than we can. Do you think that's true? Because I think it's true and that's so interesting to me right now." Ellie drags her eyes up and down me and even though she's being sarcastic and I should be annoyed—okay, I *am* annoyed—heat still pools in my gut. I also can't get a word in edgewise because now she's going on about what studies she's read that support her thinly veiled insult.

As the boys back at my Irish stables would say, she was taking the piss out of me and before I could defend myself, Beckon sniffed me again and pinned her ears.

Ellie nods solemnly like she was expecting nothing less. "Incredibly interesting," she says, and walks off with the cranky mare trailing behind her.

"It's not interesting." I dash after them. "It's typical mare behavior. Everyone knows they're touchier than geldings."

It's mostly true, too. Geldings are, ah, gelded and the lack of testosterone makes them easier to handle. Stallions and mares, on the other hand, have full sets of hormones. Riders like to joke that "you tell a gelding, you ask a mare, and you negotiate with a stallion." Beckon seems to fall in the stereotype although judging by the arrogant way the mare sweeps up the drive, I would also guess Beckon enjoys people bowing and scraping to her as well.

Judging the way Ellie sweeps along next to her, I would bet she enjoys people bowing and scraping to her too.

The stable is already busy when we duck inside. Sam's lecturing a groom on something, but he eyes us as we pass, and my comments from earlier come back to me. If I want everyone to be professional, I should at least start by being professional myself.

I follow Ellie into the concrete wash stall we use for the horses, watching as she pulls Beckon's bridle and saddle. "So how are we going to do this?" I ask.

To her credit, she doesn't pretend to be confused. She kneels to un-buckle the protective boots on the mare's legs. "You could go away and let me handle the horses like I've already been doing for three years"

"Not going to happen."

"Look." Ellie stands, boots in hand, and faces me. "I know you think you know how to prepare upper level horses, but until you've done it, you don't have a clue. Leave the riding to a rider."

"Happy to do so, but there's more to this than riding. Sam said Mrs. Mar coming tomorrow and the Wesley party the day after that."

Ellie's eyes narrow—whether she's annoyed with me or with Sam though I can't tell. "So?"

"So I want to be here for the sales appointment and I'm going with you to the party. I'm your date."

She takes the water hose from the rack and turns it on, showering Beckon with cool water. After soaking the mare's left side (and both of my feet), she turns to me. "No, thank you."

So polite and yet she manages to pull the words into something pis-sy. "You need the help."

"I do? And how exactly are you going to help? Stand around with your hands on your hips and glower at her?"

"I don't—" Except I am. Right now both my hands are on my hips and yeah, I'm glowering. I shove both hands into my pockets. "Wow. Mature. What else would I expect from you?"

"Wow. Condescending. What else would I expect from *you*?"

We glare at each other.

"Fine," Ellie says at last, breaking our staring contest to start drying Beckon's soaked coat. "You're my date, and you're going to help. Are we done now?"

"Do you talk to all your bosses this way?"

"You're not my boss."

Yet, I think—and she's thinking it too. For all of Ellie's confidence, worry flitted through her eyes, shadow-quick. Guilt squeezes me and it shouldn't. I don't think anyone should be afraid for his or her job, but I have Aiden to think about and the farm's future.

"Look, you heard the Colonel, we're in this together. We've got to find a way to make it work."

"You're the one who wants me gone."

I can't fault her on that one.

Ellie arches a brow. "Haven't you ever made a mistake? I guess not, huh? Okay, try to stay with me here: what if you made a one-time mistake, but everyone thinks it's the sum total of you?"

I open my mouth. Close it. "You're right," I say at last. "I'm sorry, okay?" In terms of apologies, it's probably my worst ever. I make 'sorry' sound like something I pushed off a cliff, and Ellie's eyes narrow like she's unimpressed. "I overreacted," I add. "It's the effects of being home and I took it out on you. I'm sure you could tell my father and I don't really get along."

She grinds her teeth for a second, two seconds. "I'm sorry too."

"You already said that."

We eye each other. "I still think you're an ass," she says.

I blink. "Well, I still think you're a liability."

"Good, as long as we're both clear on that. Now if you'll excuse me, I have a sales appointment." Ellie's braid snaps as she turns toward a well-dressed family headed our way.

Ah, I think, following her, *these would be the potential buyers Sam mentioned*. The father and mother look nervous. The trainer and kid look excited.

"So glad you could make it," Ellie says and I can hear the smile in her voice.

It strokes something hot down my spine.

***

Ellie doesn't say a word to me as I follow everyone down to the riding arena, but I can tell she's seething. She shouldn't. Thanks to me she has back up now. Selling horses makes people crazy. It doesn't matter if you're in Europe, the United Kingdom, or the States, people are flaky and when it comes to horse people, they're generally the flakiest. I've always wondered if it's all the head injuries we sustain because it can't just be something in the water.

Or in this case, the Perrier.

The father—a land developer in his late fifties—keeps playing with the dark green bottle, passing it from hand to hand. The mother isn't much better. She holds herself completely rigid, attention glued to Bree, their daughter.

"I never relax during this stuff," Mr. Davis mutters, watching Bree swing her leg over our sales horse. She settles in the saddle, Echo dancing a little underneath her.

"'This stuff'?" I ask. "You mean the riding?"

"Absolutely. Other girls play tennis. It's loads safer—and cheaper." He takes a meaningful look around us, no doubt taking in the four rows of stadium seating, the high-tech footing in the arena, and of course, the stable itself, sitting high on the hill above us. I get it, but when he shoots me a dirty look, I smile anyway, shrugging my What-Can-You-Do shrug. "Why couldn't she have picked another sport?" he complains

"Keep reminding yourself of the amazing opportunity you're giving her," the trainer says quickly. She's probably early thirties with thick blond hair and a toothpaste ad smile always aimed squarely at Mr. Davis. "Riding is like nothing else in the world. This horse will be her wings."

My eyes bug. I can't help it. *What the hell is she—*

Ellie faces Mr. Davis, pulling her Jacks or Better ball cap a little lower to shield her eyes from the sun. "I don't think anything good comes without risk, Mr. Davis, but I can certainly understand your concerns. While no horse is perfect, we think Echo is wonderful. He's safe. He's kind. He knows his job. If you daughter makes a mistake, he can help get her out of it."

"*Every* time?" Mr. Davis asks. Next to him, Mrs. Davis shifts a little in her seat, fingers tightening around her purse. "Can you assure me she'll never have any difficulties with him?"

"You know I can't. They're horses. What makes the sport tough is also what makes it great." It's a tactful smack down and Ellie delivers it with a smile.

Mr. Davis continues to scowl, but I can tell he's thinking it over. Honestly? So am I, but for totally different reasons. The Davis's trainer is practically trying to sell them glitter and dreams, but Ellie tackled his concerns head on. I like it.

And as soon as I realize I do, I'm scowling too.

The daughter picks up a trot, steering Echo around the arena and getting used to his stride. Horses are just like people—they're all different—so it can sometimes feel disorienting. Luckily for everyone though Bree Davis has more tact than her father and she quickly settles into Echo. The gelding seems to settle into her as well. He's a nice horse—bright copper chestnut with four matching white stockings—but he never turned into anything special enough for the international stage.

But he has plenty of talent for riders like Bree Davis. The Colonel once said Echo could take a monkey around a three and a half foot course. It sounds disparaging, but it's a great asset. It means a wide, *wide* variety of people are looking for a horse like this.

And they'll pay dearly for it.

The trainer leans over the arena's fence, watching Bree and Echo closely and critiquing as they ride by. "Watch your shoulders," she tells the girl. "You're hunching again."

Bree straightens her shoulders and rides on. After another ten minutes or so of watching, Ellie asks if they'd like to try him over a few jumps.

Overhearing Ellie's question, Bree perks up. "Definitely," she says.

Good sign, I think, hopping to my feet to help Ellie and the trainer move poles around. Bree jumps Echo over a small course and it doesn't take long before the kid smiling. Actually, grinning is more like it. She likes the horse. A lot.

I glance at Ellie and catch her looking at me. I raise my brows ever so slightly and she answers with the world's tiniest nod and I know she's going to go for a pitch.

"Echo has competed throughout the East coast," Ellie begins. "His record speaks for itself and—"

Bree swings around the turn at a quick canter, cutting too close and putting Echo in tight to their next jump. It's a skinny vertical meaning not only is it upright, but it's narrow too. You have to ride accurately to keep the poles up and keep your horse from running out to either side, and at the last second, Bree panics, throwing her reins away.

Echo jumps anyway, but he hits the top rail with his knees. The force sends the pole flying and tosses Bree half up his neck. Echo stops, waiting patiently for her to shimmy back into the saddle. The girl's face has gone bone white under her navy helmet.

Her trainer rushes to her side. "Are you okay? Ohmygod!"

Bree shakes her head and my stomach sinks. It wasn't the horse's fault, but before I can open my mouth Ellie peels away from my side and walks up to Bree. "It's happened to all of us," she says. "Take a deep breath, okay?"

After a hesitation, Bree does. Ellie grins. "Try it again," she says. "This time, I'll coach you through it."

"No," the trainer says, shaking her head. "No way. I thought you said he was well trained."

I bristle, ready to argue about how the kid rode like crap and maybe the trainer should take some lessons herself, but Ellie doesn't engage. She looks up at Bree and I realize Ellie never needed me as back up. She's got this.

"What do you want?" Ellie asks Bree.

The girl keeps her eyes on Ellie, fumbling with her reins before saying, "I want to try it again."

"Great!" Ellie pats Bree on her knee and double checks that her girth is tight. "Now pick up your canter and this time, look for your turn as you're *passing* the gate."

They don't get it perfectly the second time, but it's better. Bree prepares for her turn, but she rushes Echo a bit on the approach and they take a flyer. Still, they don't drop any rails and the girl's smiling again as she circles back to Ellie and her trainer. The other woman has fallen noticeably silent and her face is stony. Bree hops off and passes Ellie the reins.

"He's really nice," she says.

"He is," Ellie says, patting Echo's shoulder. "He took good care of you. I like that about him. He's a good soul."

My first instinct is to say it's a line to get Mr. Davis and Bree's trainer on board, but I can look at Ellie's face and tell it isn't. She genuinely likes the horse and even seems to like the kid. I have the sneaking suspicion she'd nix the whole thing if she thought it wasn't a good match.

So she's good at her job and *honest*, I think. *What else is there?* Then Ellie turns, gifting me with the sight of her perfect ass and my fingers curl.

Next to me, Mrs. Davis stands, and I'm positive she's leaving, but she doesn't. She tucks her purse under one arm and her daughter under the other. "We'll take him."

A smile breaks across Ellie's face. "I think they're going to be a wonderful team."

Mrs. Davis nods once and then looks at her trainer. "Set everything up."

Red-faced, the trainer mutters an agreement and we all walk Echo back to the barn. Bree is telling Ellie some horse show story and Ellie is listening like the girl is fascinating. If I'd been watching the exchange even an hour before, I would've thought Ellie was just pretending, but now I know she isn't. She's genuine.

That's rare in the world.

We reach the barn entrance and Bree says something and Ellie bursts out laughing, head tilted back, dark braid swinging. I almost trip. It's the first time I've heard Ellie really laugh—and I want to hear it again.

Get it together, I tell myself. "Hey, Ellie?"

She turns, eyes narrowed. "Yes?"

"I need to head back. Pleasure meeting you." I shake hands with the Davises and their trainer. "Good luck, Bree. Let us know if you have any questions."

Bree nods, but I doubt she really heard me. The girl only has eyes for Echo. She leads him into the barn with her trainer close on their heels.

"Thanks for letting me sit in," I tell Ellie before she follows them.

Her mouth hangs open and I smirk. *Didn't expect me to leave, did you?* I think.

Ellie smirks back, thoughts crystal clear in her eyes: *Didn't expect me to be this good, did you?*

I nearly laugh. I can't help it—and I'm not sure which I dislike more: the fact that more and more I can't help myself around Ellie Lennox, or the fact that she's right: I didn't expect her to be anywhere near this good.

CHAPTER 10 | Caleb

While Ellie finishes up with the Davises, I catch up with Sam and the staff inside the barn. He's corralled everyone in the tack room and the guys stiffen when I walk in.

"Don't look so grim," I tell them, dropping into the closest chair. "This is just a meeting to introduce me to everyone and have a chat."

They sneak glances at each other. Can't say I blame them. I take a deep breath. "Let me start out, I'm Caleb Reese. I've been in the industry pretty much since birth thanks to my parents. Yes, I'm the boss's son. No, you won't have to worry about that."

Someone snorts, but I can't tell who. I grin. I know how this goes. "Yeah, I hear you. Now who wants a cup of coffee and a chance to tell me what we're doing wrong?"

The guys look at each other and then at me and grin.

About an hour later, I have a page full of notes and plenty to think about. Sam and the guys head back to work and as I follow them into the aisle, I spot Ellie leading Beckon out into the sunshine. I tuck my notes into my back pocket and hurry after her.

"How'd it go?" I ask after catching up.

Ellie slides me a cautious glance. "Good. They'll want a vet to check him, obviously, but I'm not anticipating any problems."

"Good." That's a relief. Generally speaking buyers always vet potential horses. The process can involve everything from X-rays to bloodwork to radiographs, but it's always been worth it to me. You want to know what you're riding, and if you have a kid, I would think that would be doubly true.

We reach the paddocks and Ellie opens one gate. She leads Beckon through, closing the latch before pulling the mare's halter off. Beckon trots off, shaking her head and swishing her tail.

"Aren't you worried about the heat?" I ask Ellie. Usually, our horses only went out at night during the summer. They spent their days under massive ceiling fans in the barn. During winter, we would switch them back to day time turnout.

Ellie hangs the mare's halter and lead rope on the hook by the gate. "I'll bring her in before it gets too hot. She'll be grouchy if I don't let her have some extra turnout."

"So this morning, that was Beckon being sweet?"

Ellie gives me the tiniest smile before she spins on her heel and walks off, and for a full three seconds, I'm distracted *again* by the sight of her curvy ass in those figure hugging breeches. I shake myself, and take off after her. "Where are you going?"

"Home. My sister is making me breakfast."

I fall into step next to her. "Yeah, I heard. Good thing, I'm hungry."

Ellie slows. "She *invited* you?"

"Tate did." I bump my chin toward Tate's red BMW. It's parked between the farm trucks and looking really tiny and out of place. He'd told me he was coming by and asked me to join them. "Think he's afraid you're going to finish the job, Lennox?"

Okay, now who's being immature? That would be me. I hold my ground and refuse to think about it. Instead, I grin at Ellie. She rolls her eyes and spins away, but not before her eyes dip to my mouth.

And linger.

It's heartbeat quick, but it's there and it makes my blood hum. I'm not the only one who feels this annoying attraction. Ellie strides off for the apartment, and I can't help but follow.

****

Ellie takes the spiral staircase stairs two at a time and when she reaches the top, she kicks off her boots, motioning for me to do the same. She opens the door, stepping inside and pausing. For a second, I think something's wrong and then I realize she's taking a deep breath of home. Just as quickly as I recognize it though she's off again, striding through the tiny mudroom-storage-laundry-room and into the kitchen.

I don't remember the last time I was in the upstairs barn apartment, but I don't remember it being quite like this. The kitchen smells like vanilla and coffee. There's a vase of wildflowers on the counter. Wren's at the stove, face screwed up with concentration. Dark hair swept into a braid. She looks so much like Ellie it weirds me out. Like the world *needs* two Ellie Lenoxes.

Tate's sitting at the tiny kitchen table, sipping coffee. "Hey, man," he says when he sees me.

Wren looks up, seeing me. Her eyes narrow.

"I hope you don't mind," Ellie whispers loudly, hugging her sister with one arm and swiping a piece of toast with her free hand. "It followed me home."

Wren's mouth does a weird little twitch, and I can't tell if she's trying not to laugh or trying not to tell her sister off. Tate shakes his head, passing me a coffee while Ellie goes to the sink to wash her hands.

"He did tell you I was coming, right?" I ask, glancing between Tate and Wren.

"Of course," Wren says, a strand of wavy dark hair falling in her eyes. "He tells me everything. So does Ellie."

Ah, so now everyone knows about my ultimatum yesterday. I eye Wren's hands as she flips the pancakes and wonder if she added ground up glass to mine.

"You should see the view," Wren says, waving toward the narrow hallway off the kitchen. Somehow I doubt it's a suggestion. I sip my coffee and wander through the apartment. The dining room and living room are pretty much the same thing: one open space with wide, inviting windows that look down on the stable's courtyard. Wren's right: the view is lovely. The apartment is nice too. It would be actually be pretty when fully decorated.

Or decorated at all.

Place is sparse, I realize, and then notice the moving boxes stacked in the living room's corner. It's sparse because Wren's moving out.

I frown. And if Wren's packed all her stuff, what does Ellie own? There are no pictures, no posters, no books, no anything. All that's left is the couch and coffee table. I'm about to sit down when I realize Wren's joined me. She's holding a coffee mug in both hands, her oversized cardigan slipping off one bare shoulder.

"Nice to see you again," she says. "Sorry we aren't prepared for guests."

"Don't worry about it. Please. It's minimalist," I say, gesturing to the surroundings. "I like it. I'm sure Ellie will fix it up later."

Her mouth tightens. "Everything Ellie needs is downstairs in the barn."

Which I threatened to take away. I frown. This was a mistake. "I should go," I say, heading for the kitchen when Wren grabs my sleeve.

"You can't go in there right now," she says. "Ellie's apologizing to Tate."

As if on cue, Tate bursts out laughing. I quirk a brow at Wren, but she isn't looking at me. Her eyes are pinned to the kitchen door and she's smiling this little rueful smile. The sisters really love each other. I mean, I know families are supposed to, but in my experience, they mostly just fight. Look at the Colonel and me. The accident of genetics is all that keeps us together. Ellie and Wren have something more and it tugs at me.

"Breakfast smells amazing," Ellie says, breezing through the living room, tugging her dark hair down as she goes. "I'm going to take a quick shower."

The word is like a kick to my gut: fast, hard, and utterly unexpected. Suddenly the thought of Ellie, wet, soapy, and naked is all I can picture.

Think of puppies, I tell myself. *Or kittens. Or Grandma Welly.*

Actually that one works. Really well, too. My body stands down. My blood rush slows. Nothing like thinking about an eighty year old yogi nudist to bring everything back under control.

Wren sniffs me and I tense. "You smell like horses," she says. "Go wash up."

Gladly. Anything to get moving. I start for the kitchen again, and she grabs me. "Use the bathroom. I have too many dishes in the sink."

"But isn't that...?"

Wren shakes her head. "Jack and Jill bathroom. She'll have the door to the shower room closed. You can wash your hands without interrupting her. Second door. Hurry up."

It's the same tone she uses with Ellie: light, but unwavering. There's zero point in arguing and I head down the hallway. As told, I open the second door, revealing a tiny bathroom—sink room really. There's a white painted cabinet to my right and a dark stained dresser converted into a sink on my left. A few strides ahead, there's a single door—closed—but I can hear the shower running.

Ellie, I think again. *Naked.*

It makes everything in me harden.

What is wrong *with you?* I wonder, turning the water to cold and splashing my face. I glance up, catching my reflection in the mirror.

And the crack between the door to the shower and the jamb.

The apartment's air conditioning unit kicks on and the slice of shower room opens a tiny bit more, revealing a slice of Ellie leaning back against the countertop, waiting for her water to warm.

She's naked.

And when she shifts, I can see she's touching herself.

My knees nearly give out. *Look away,* I think. But I can't. Her left hand has found her perfect breasts and she's squeezing them softly. Her right hand slides lower and lower, heading unmistakably toward the strip of dark curls between her legs. Her mouth opens on a puff of air, no doubt finding her clit. Her fingers stroke back and forth, finding a brisk rhythm, driving herself relentlessly.

She needs it. It's like another kick to my gut. My dick hardens and my breath rushes from me. Her head tilts back as she strokes. Enjoying it. Needing more. I'd love to give it to her.

Ellie moans softly, one hand playing with her pussy the other playing with her nipple. She's close—*so* close—and I'm spying on her like a pervert.

Go, I think, wrenching myself back a stride. *Get out.*

Ellie's eyes snap open. She looks at me and I expect a scream of outrage. Instead, she comes. Hard.

CHAPTER 11 | Ellie

The pleasure damn near shatters me. I want to scream and I can't. I have to settle for rubbing myself frantically, head thrown back. I can *feel* Caleb's eyes on me and realizing it washes another wave of pleasure over me. Slowly, it subsides, leaving me with shaky hands and knees. I wobble, grabbing the counter edge before I end up on the bathroom floor. I breathe in, out, again.

There, I think, everything in me centering.

I open my eyes.

Caleb's gone, and a tiny, *tiny* part of me is disappointed. Clearly it's the suicidal part—the same part that became excited knowing he was there. I mean, it's not like he was going to come in here and scoop me onto the countertop, spread my legs, and take me.

The very idea makes me wet again. *Get it together, Ellie*, I tell myself, leaning into the shower to switch the water to cold. I get in, gasping when it hits my overheated skin. I hadn't planned on any of this and now I didn't quite know where to have myself. Point of fact, I have sold almost a hundred horses over the course of my career and I have never *ever* left a sales appointment desperate for release.

There was just something about Caleb. All through the Davis appointment, I couldn't stop snatching glances at him—his easy smile, his focused attention, his *chest*. When he leaned back against the railing, his polo had pulled tight across his pecs and all I wanted to do was touch him. And when he looked at me and I knew he was thinking the same thing I was thinking? Goner.

If he weren't such a raging ass, we'd make a great team.

I turn my face to the icy stream. It should stop my raging body in its tracks. Instead, it makes it worse. My nipples tighten, my skin prickles. *He* made me like this.

Somehow, I knew Caleb was there even before I saw him. Was it because I felt him? Sensed him? Whatever it was, it should've panicked me. I hadn't shut the door. I was naked. I was touching myself.

But realizing he was watching, I couldn't stop.

I could feel his eyes on me. Everywhere they went, I heated. The harder I touched myself, the more intently he watched.

He wants you. It's a smug realization until another one follows it: *You want him too.* I scowl, grabbing my shampoo and working it through my air. *You actually want a guy who said he would fire you if given the opportunity.*

Now there's a damper. Talk about crappy taste in men. I rinse my hair, follow up with a metric ton of conditioner, and start scrubbing down with body wash. Minutes later, I'm done. I shut off the water and grab one of Wren's fluffy towels from the hook, wrapping myself up.

I feel...good, and there's just enough left of my common sense to know that's probably weird.

Okay, definitely weird.

Out in the kitchen, Wren turns on Frank Sinatra, croons of "fly away" drift through the air vents. Tate laughs and Wren joins him, and for a few seconds, I'm eaten up with longing. As long as I'm attracted to men like Caleb Reese, I will never have a relationship like Wren's.

Then again, if I had the opportunity for a relationship like Wren's would I even recognize it? It took me months to figure out James The Gigantic Tool was, in fact, a gigantic tool. Then again, I recognized Caleb as an asshole right away. Maybe I'm learning.

Right, I realize, *you're learning by playing with yourself in front of him*. I frown, remembering I never did that in front of James. I also never came that hard. There's just something about Caleb that's...

Irritating, sexy, and incredibly irritating.

And also incredibly sexy. I huff hard and strand of damp hair falls against my cheek. *Just because you want him doesn't mean you have to act on it*, I remind myself, pulling off the towel and running it over my hair.

In the mirror, my eyes are still a bit glassy, wild. Wren would be horrified if she knew what I just did. Hell, *I'm* a bit horrified at what I just did.

But I'm also incredibly pleased. Caleb Reese thinks he has one up on me? Fine. Because I have something even better on him. All I have to do is remember those intense eyes, how he couldn't look away.

The next time he infuriates me—which odds are good, is probably, like, twenty minutes from now—I just have to remember he wants me.

And I'd be lying if I said that didn't make me smile.

CHAPTER 12 | Caleb

I blow out of that damn bathroom like my hair is on fire. "Gotta go," I say to Wren and Tate as I hurtle through the kitchen. I wave my cell at them like I have important shit going on and Tate stares at me like I've lost my mind. For the record? I have.

I pound down the circular staircase and stride through the tack room. The grooms eye me as I pass. I'm not sure what they see and I'm damn sure I don't want to know. I find Sam overseeing one of the horses being groomed.

"You still want to take that ride around the farm?" I ask him.

Clearly surprised, the old man nods. "Absolutely."

We spend the rest of the day focusing on Jacks or Better. We start with the broodmares moved on to the young stock and finish with the undeveloped portions of the property. The farm sits on five thousand acres along the Chattahoochee River. At the moment, we're only utilizing a few hundred for barns, pastures, and housing. The rest is undeveloped farm land and deep pine forests.

Sam sticks to business and I try to follow suit, but when I look at the two new imported broodmares, all I see is Ellie's mouth rounding on her orgasm. And when I look at the fence line Sam wants to expand, all I see is Ellie's bold gaze meeting mine.

I shove that image away as quickly as I can, but it doesn't stop my dick from stirring. She is the hottest thing I've ever seen. I haven't been this hard up for anyone since...

Mandy, I realize, my gut sinking. You'd think I would freaking learn.

"Are you still up for this?" Sam asks, attention still fixed on the undulating terrain leading into the trees. "We could go back if you're jet-lagged."

81

"No, I'm good." And even if I weren't, there is zero way I'm letting a seventy-year-old outlast me. "Let's go."

Sam pops the farm truck into drive and we continue down the dirt road that winds through the property. "If you have the time," he says as we study the ground elevations leading into the trees, "we could drive further up and let you see how the surrounding developments have spread out. Some fancy neighborhoods have moved in. Loads of kids—and you know what that means."

I nod. It meant possible trespassers, probably the need for an updated liability insurance policy, and better protection for the horses. People do stupid things and the animals often end up paying for them.

"I have nothing but time," I tell Sam. After all, I had an excellent reason for staying away.

"You ride?" Sam asks me later.

I glance at him. "Like you haven't looked me up."

A wry smile tugs the corner of Sam's mouth. "Fine, yes, I looked you up. Just because you don't compete doesn't mean you don't ride."

"I used to when I was younger." In fact, it was all I did when I was younger. Riding was my life. When my mom was home, we rode together, hacking through the woods in the fall, horse shows in the spring and summer. It was our thing and after she died, well...I never sat in a saddle again. "I don't have the time anymore," I add. "My horses are better left to the professionals."

The old man raises one bushy, white brow. I know what he's thinking: I'm already interfering with the farm's current professional. To Sam's eternal credit, though, he lets it go and we drive on, rounding another bend in the road. The trees on either side of us give way to a sprawling pasture overgrown with wildflowers. If Beckon sold, we could develop the property into something else—barns for the broodmares or maybe for young horses in training. I roll down the old truck's window and stare out already able to see it.

"You have any questions for me?" Sam asks.

"Yeah," I say, taking a deep breath of damp, warm earth and grass. "I'd like your input on some upcoming changes I have in mind."

"And what would those be?" A guarded note has entered his voice and I turn to him.

"Pay. I've been reviewing the farm's financial statements and if we move some things around, we can afford to increase the staff's salaries."

Sam glances at me, eyes traveling over my face like he's seeing me for the first time. "Not that I'm complaining, but why would you want to do that?"

"Because if you want to keep good people, you have to pay them." The equestrian world is notorious for its low pay. I'd like to say it's simply an aspect of the higher end equestrian world, but it's rife in the lower levels too. Trainers and clients take advantage of the enthusiasm of young people or undocumented workers. Grooms, exercise riders, and assistants can end up working seven days a week for only a few dollars an hour. "I don't want to be the kind of business that doesn't appreciate its staff," I add. "I know what that's like. I won't do it to other people."

"Fair enough," Sam says, and I catch him studying me again. He's looking at me differently and it shouldn't make me feel better, but it does. "You have time for us to check the equipment sheds?"

***

Hours and hours later, I turn for home. Or what used to be home. Even in the dark, the old mansion is still beautiful. Moonlight turns the white columns almost silvery, makes my mother's climbing white roses bone bright. Ten bedrooms, fourteen baths, a kitchen that could cook for a football team, and an actual ballroom, the place was made for entertaining, which was probably why my mother loved it. She adored parties.

I can't remember the last one we had. A year after she died? Two? The Colonel had spent most of it locked away in his library.

A humid breeze stirs as I hike up the front steps, carrying the scent of roses with it. I kick off my work boots by the door and let myself in just as the ancient grandfather clock chimes eleven. Long day of work, even for me, but tomorrow will probably be longer.

I stand in our foyer, letting my eyes adjust to the dim, and suddenly remember Ellie taking that deep, happy breath because she was home. Have I ever felt like that?

Pretty sure you know the answer, I think, but I try a deep breath anyway, inhaling the faint scent of orange floor wax and an even fainter smell of dinner. Mary, our housekeeper since I was two, would've served it hours ago. I sniff again. Tomato sauce of some sort?

Let there be leftovers, I pray, padding across the polished hardwood toward the kitchen. Shafts of moonlight catch on the gold framed oil paintings and silver trophies that crowd our walls and side tables. I'm almost past the library when the door flies open and the Colonel appears. "You're late," he says.

"I was out with Sam."

With the lamp light behind him, my father's shadow is thrown long, like it's reaching for me. "Message for you."

He flicks me a Post-It Note, and I catch it, my father's handwriting standing out in bold, black scratches. Mandy Gibson, he'd written. There's a phone number beneath her name. She's changed it since we last talked.

"Is this starting up again?" the Colonel asks.

"No."

"Then why is she calling here?"

I shrug, pocketing the note. "Probably because she's curious or because I changed my cell number or because this town is too small for its own good and everyone talks. It's not a secret that I'm home."

And now Mandy's reaching out for me.

The Colonel's eyes narrow. I can tell the wheels in his brain are turning. He wants to ask something, but he doesn't. We stare at each other, saying nothing until it becomes uncomfortable.

Or more uncomfortable. Whatever.

"Getting dinner," I say at last, tilting my head toward the kitchen. He nods and to my total surprise follows me down the hall and into the darkened kitchen. I flip on the lights, illuminating the white cabinets and cherry stained butcher block counters. The sweep of windows usually overlooks the foal pasture, but now only reveal our shadowy reflections. I open the stainless steel fridge and find a huge pot sitting squarely in the middle shelf, another Post-It stuck to the front.

Eat, it says.

"God love you, Mary," I mutter, heaving the pot onto the counter before riffling through the drawers for a fork.

"What did you think of the farm?" the Colonel asks, leaning against the countertop.

I hesitate, almost unable to believe there's a note of insecurity in his question. I sit down on one of the stools that lines the breakfast bar and stab the pasta with more force than necessary. "You're going to need an updated insurance policy for those neighborhoods. They're so close people could walk through the woods to get to the horses."

He nods. "I can call our agent in the morning."

"The staff is fantastic." I pause, swirling pasta around in the pot and thinking about how they'd perked up when I'd asked them about Ellie and how things were running. Whatever I could say about her personal life, the woman was pretty much adored by her staff. "They like how everything's being managed."

"And Beckon?"

"The mare's brilliant," I say, catching the awe in my tone. "It's a good idea to sell her immediately."

"Actually...I've been thinking about keeping her. She'll be worth more after the Grand Prix."

"*If* she wins."

The Colonel eyes me. "You think she won't?"

"I think horses were born trying to kill themselves. Sure she could win on Sunday. She could lose too—or break a bone, or pull a suspensory. Anything can happen. If you get an offer, you should take it."

His mouth flattens. He agrees with me. He doesn't want to, but he does.

"I think the better question is why are you holding on?" I ask.

"The mare's special."

I pause, fork halfway to my mouth. My father has called his horses a lot of things: talented, hardheaded, once he said a stallion prospect swung "his hips like a teenage girl," but he's never thought of any of them as special.

I study my food so my face doesn't give away my surprise. People outside the industry—hell, even some people inside the industry—think horses are magical. They believe the right rider can tame any wildness, and *boom* that rider is off to the Olympics. Reality doesn't work that way.

The truth is, horses are a lot like people: some are born broken and some get broken, and often there's nothing you can do. Sure, once in a blue moon, you'll hear about a rider who brought a horse back from the brink and made it to the big leagues, but it's so rare the exception proves the rule. My father used to understand this.

I glance up at him. "You think the mare's 'special?'" You been watching horse movies or something? Catching up on some teenage horsey reads?"

A flash of annoyance crosses his face and I smile. I can't help it. Still got the touch.

"When you get to my age, you've seen a lot." He lowers himself heavily on to the barstool and studies his hands. The tanned skin's lined and cracked as an old paper bag. "But you haven't necessarily seen those special once-in-a-lifetime moments. I think Beckon could be mine."

I take my time chewing another mouthful of pasta, giving myself a minute to think. "Tall order."

"It's the truth."

I can tell. He's facing me dead on. His expression is grim and tired, but there's something else underneath it, something like longing and it knocks me speechless. I haven't seen the Colonel this raw since my mom died. Honestly, I don't like it. It changes our dynamic and I was happy—well, I was at least satisfied—with where our relationship was.

"I'll see you after my morning meetings," he says, pushing to his feet. His back pops and he winces.

"'Night," I say, listening to his feet shuffle away. I'm suddenly starving and I power through most of the spaghetti before I realize I'm barely tasting it. I slow down, forcing myself to actually chew. It's no good though. Slowing down makes me realize how tired I am.

I close my eyes, half-expecting to see my to-do list, but it isn't.

Ellie Lennox is instead. She arches her back, dark hair cascading down, and eyes on me.

I stab my fork into the pasta again and swirl it around. *What is* with *you?* I wonder. *Girl makes you act like a fourteen year old.*

It's the power of her. The confidence. It streaks through my blood better and hotter than whisky. There's nothing sexier than a woman who knows how sexy she is.

And Ellie Lenox knows.

I pass one hand over my face. This is beyond a bad idea. It must be the stress. It does weird things to people. Usually, I get more focused. Now...

Now I can't get Ellie Lenox out of my head.

CHAPTER 13 | Ellie

"Sit up!" I command, hands clenched around the arena fence's top rail so I don't cover my eyes. "Evelyn! You have to sit up!"

Evelyn doesn't sit up. In fact, from the looks of it, she doesn't breathe either as her cute, little paint gelding romps around the jump course I've set for them. They canter down the arena's long side with Evelyn's fists buried deep in his mane, and when she turns him toward the last jump, her shoulders slouch even more.

Henry, to his eternal credit, hops over the small gate anyway and trots toward me, ears pricked. "You're a good boy, Henry," I say as he skids to a stop next to me.

Evelyn pitches forward, slumping against his neck. "I thought I was going to die!" she pants.

I try not to laugh. "Nah, dismemberment probably, but not death."

Evelyn's eyes go wrinkly as she grins. "I don't know why you put up with me. Don't you have younger, skinnier riders to work with?"

I shrug. "I don't have any riders as brave as you are."

She sits up, adjusting her riding helmet's chin strap. "What are you talking about? Last time you put the jumps up to two feet, I about cried."

Now I do laugh. I can't help it. Evelyn looks like a stereotypical grandmother. She's all curly gray hair and wide smiles and hugs, but that day? That day, Evelyn had sworn a blue streak as she piloted Henry around. She'd been terrified and elated and even though they'd easily cleared everything, she still swore I was trying to kill her. "I mean it," I say, sliding off the fence. "Most of my students have been riding since they were little. You didn't swing a leg over a horse until you were sixty. That's impressive."

"Bless you. You're a sweet child."

"Ha! You know I'm not." I pat Henry's damp shoulder and he sniffs me for cookies. "Now do it again, but this time *sit up!*"

Evelyn nods determinedly, and nudges Henry into a trot. It makes me smile to watch them. I'm lucky. My dad never enjoyed teaching. He was a rider through and through, but I enjoy giving lessons. True, it's not as fun as riding, but it's so rewarding to see my students improve. I might be having the worst day ever, but seeing Evelyn's confidence increase or one of the younger riders finally grasp a hard concept? It feels like winning a championship.

A few minutes later, I wrap up Evelyn's lesson and leave her to cool down Henry. I head back to the stable, mentally listing everything I needed to finish. I rode Echo and Swing earlier, but the new four-year-old still need to be exercised. I need to follow up with the vet. The broodmares have to be—

I'm almost to the tack room before I realize none of the grooms will meet my eyes. Every time I smile at one of them, he skitters away. Something's up. I stop outside Echo's stall, surprising Danny and Tomas.

"Danny," I say and his shoulders hunch up around his ears. "What's going on?"

"Uh." When Danny turns around, his face is paler than ever. He points at the tack room. "You might want to look for yourself."

"Look at what?" I ask, and then suddenly I know. Caleb. Has to be. I don't know how I know, but I do and I'm furious. I spin on my heel and burst through the door. Sure enough, it *is* Caleb. He has my equipment strewn everywhere, and he's standing in the middle of it.

Behind Caleb, Juan bugs his eyes at me, clearly panicked. It would be funny, if I weren't so instantaneously and enormously annoyed. "What are you doing?"

Caleb doesn't look up from my equipment. He runs both hands over my laced reins like he's inspecting them for cracks and somehow that makes me think about how those hands would feel on me.

My skin heats, and now I'm even more annoyed. "Seriously. What are you doing?"

"Getting to know your program before Mrs. Mar arrives. This is everything you use?"

"Depends on the horse." I could elaborate and say not every horse is going to go in a snaffle, or I could say something about how sometimes we often try different bridle set ups until we find one the horse likes best. But I don't bother. It isn't like he's going to listen anyway.

Caleb puts the bridle back on its hook and glances around, brows drawn tight. "Where are your draw reins?"

"I don't use them. They're a gimmick."

"No way. They're a tool. Back in Ireland, both of my riders used them—not all the time, but on an as needed basis. The horses benefit from the deeper work. It helps them work through their backs. You should know this."

Blood thumps in my ears and I pause, trying to separate my indignation from my explanation. This isn't any different than when I explain my process to students. It just feels different because he's my kind of sort of boss.

And an ass.

"They're not a tool I'm interested in using," I begin, and then proceed to outline all the reasons I don't use them—links to spinal damage, fake headsets, poor training. Sure, plenty of riders use them, but plenty of us don't. "Tool or not," I finish up, "commonly used or not, I won't use them, and coincidentally, neither will you."

There's a squeaking noise behind me. Juan? Probably. I don't have to turn to picture his face: rounded mouth, huge eyes, probably looks like he's going to pass out. For several seconds—years?—Caleb and I glare at each other.

"Get out," Caleb snarls at Juan. The groom's brown eyes meet mine and I nod. He doesn't need to see us argue it out. If I could, I'd leave too.

"I'll catch up with you later," I tell him and Juan flees, slamming the door behind him.

Caleb leans into me. "We're supposed to collaborate. You can't talk to me like that. You have to support me."

I take a deep breath. *You can do this.* "I can't support you when you're being stupid." Okay, not the most tactful thing I've ever said so I hurry along my explanation: "Your father pays me for my expertise. It wouldn't be honest of me if I stood by and said nothing."

Caleb's mouth snaps shut. *He has nothing to say*, I realize, smothering a smile. Speechless is not a bad look for him.

Until he advances on me.

"You can't support me when I'm being stupid?" he echoes.

I retreat. "Pretty much."

"You think I'm stupid?"

"I think you're arrogant. You're far too worried about what other people think."

"You're not worried *enough* about what other people think."

My shoulder blades hit the wall and Caleb braces his arms on either side of me. I'm caught. That shouldn't feel so...delicious.

"You're not going anywhere," he whispers.

I bump up my chin. "And you're a fool if you think you can scare me."

Caleb smiles. Before, it had been a cold smile, a menacing smile, but now...there's a glimmer of actual warmth. Pushing back amused him. *I* amused him. For a second, I see the real Caleb and it lights me like a fuse.

"And you," he whispers, leaning close. "Have the most amazing body I've ever seen and I want to strip you naked."

My breath strangles. Caleb cocks his head, drags his gaze down my face...my neck...my breasts. It makes my nipples harden, makes my back arch. I can't help it.

"I saw you watching me," I whisper. "I knew you were there."

His inhale is a hiss. "The whole time?"

I nod, smirking. *I have the upper hand*, I think.

Until Caleb's warm breath coasts over my skin and I begin to shake. "I have an offer in mind," he says, "would you like to hear it?"

Say no! Say no! "Yes."

Another slow smile. It sends heat straight between my legs and Caleb's smile slides wider like he knows it. "I want you." He trails one fingertip along my jawline, and it streaks stars across my skin "You want me. Let's indulge."

My whole body clenches. I could have this. I could have this sexy, infuriating, *sexy* guy. I push out a long breath as Caleb lowers his mouth to mine. His lips skim so close, but they never, ever press. It makes my fingers curl into his shirt. I want him to press. I want him to crush me.

"Mmmmm, would you taste as good as you smell?" he breathes.

Another clench. I whimper and it makes Caleb's eyes go bright. "Say yes, Ellie. Say yes and I'll make it better."

His almost touching lips drift from the corner of my mouth up my cheek and curve around my ear lobe. Suddenly, there's a pinch of pain and all my joints turn to puddles.

He bit me. I shudder and Caleb kisses away the pain. *Imagine where else he could kiss you.*

Images of Caleb's hands on my ass and mouth on my nipples fill my brain. I could have it. I could have *him*.

Caleb nips me again and I rock onto my toes, following his mouth. "That's my girl," he whispers. "You need this."

I do. In fact, I need it so bad I indulge myself and lean into him. Caleb growls and drops his mouth to mine, taking me hard. I gasp. All my first kisses have been gentle, tentative, but there's nothing gentle or tentative about this one. Caleb's hands are in my hair, bending me back, his lips demand I open, and his tongue...

Oh my God, his tongue teases me until all I can do is hold onto him.

Until he pulls back. "Say yes, Ellie."

I hold him harder. Under his shirt, Caleb's chest is smooth, *hot* and I go wet in a rush. It's amazing...and terrifying. I stiffen. If he can make me this wet from just playing, how much control would I lose if we had sex?

All of it, I think, cold rushing down my spine. I open my eyes and push him away. There's a heartbeat of hesitation before he releases me. We look at each other, panting hard. I force myself to smirk. "An 'offer?' Seriously? Does that line usually work for you?"

He goes still. "Dunno, haven't used it before."

"Another line."

The tiniest smile lifts the corners of his mouth. "I promise you'll like it."

I know I will. I jerk my shoulders back and straighten my clothes. "And what will you be like afterward? Oh, that's right, you'll be the same condescending know-it-all. Only you'll think even less of me because I gave it up."

When Caleb's mouth thins, I know I have him, and yeah, it's insulting, but it...helps. I force myself to take a breath and then another. My body steadies a little. I can't give into this guy. As good as the sex might be, *he's* not good for me, and I have to remember that.

"Look," I say, "I might want you right *now*, but I've wanted to be a manager with Jacks or Better for *years*, and I'm not going to help you get rid of me."

I wait for his response, but there isn't one. Caleb's expression is inscrutable. He's thinking hard, but God knows what about.

"Well," I say in my best Polly Perky Pants voice, the one that helps me deal with everyone from two-year-old stallions and to two-year-old humans, "that was fun, but some of us have real work. Maybe you should come out and check Beckon with me." I force my gaze to lower, taking in Caleb's raging hard on. I'm trying for dismissive, but just looking at it makes my joints go liquid. James-with-the-too-fast hands might still be calling me, but it's been over six months since he's touched me—since anyone's touched me—and right now, I feel every second of it.

I glance up, and unsurprisingly, Caleb's glaring at me. "Oh, gosh," I say, grinning. "I guess you aren't going anywhere soon. Pity."

I spin on my heel and bounce from the tack room like my panties are damp and my nipples aren't aching. There are a lot of things about being a woman that aren't particularly enjoyable, but thank God we can hide when we're turned on.

Out in the aisle, I tug my hair back into its ponytail and stride toward the arena and my next lesson. With every step, I feel better, more in control. Caleb will never know how close I was to losing it.

CHAPTER 14 | Caleb

Ellie walks away with practically a spring in her step and it takes everything I have not to rush after her, pin her against the wall, and kiss her again.

Kiss *her?* I think, torn between a laugh and a groan. Like kissing her is all I want to do. I have a raging hard on and she knows it. Hell, she knew I was watching in the bathroom, knew I couldn't take my eyes off her.

She liked it.

Both of us did, I think and the realization nearly knocks my legs out from under me. The air conditioner kicks on, rustling a few papers sitting on the desk and I turn my face toward the cool breeze.

Of course, now she's playing like she doesn't feel the attraction. Gotta admit, relationship games usually turn me off, but this...doesn't. Why? Because Ellie's adamant she doesn't want me?

Other women's games were always to bring me closer. Ellie wants me as far away as possible.

Or so she thinks because the way she leaned into me? The way she practically panted? That's not the reaction of a woman who wants me to get lost. I grin, the memory of her warm breath against my skin washing over me all over again.

Outside the tack room, someone turns on a classical station and someone else, Danny probably, shouts a protest. The heavy door and paneled walls muffle the words, but I recognize Ellie's own shout among the guys'. Whatever she said makes them laugh.

I shake my head, instantly irritated. What the hell am I doing? Women usually come to me. I don't chase. I don't play games. I damn sure don't come onto an employee—coworker—*whatever* she is.

And yet everywhere her body touched mine is still burning.

Just thinking about it makes my dick harden again. This is starting to be a serious problem. I lean my head back against the wall and take a deep, *deep* breath. *Think of kittens*, I tell myself. *Think of puppies. Think of Grandma Welly.*

CHAPTER 15 | Ellie

As soon as I finish my last lesson, I head straight for Holly's place. She lives with her mom in the world's most adorable cottage. It's right next to the polo fields and every Sunday I'm off work, we sit on her back porch, drink mimosas, and watch the matches. Technically, I'm not off work today, but Holly doesn't question it when I knock on her eye-poppingly yellow front door.

"Tell me you have food," I say, holding up a bottle of champagne in one hand and a bottle of orange juice in the other. I hit the grocery store on my way and after dealing with Caleb freaking Reese I have never felt more in need of a drink.

"Do I have food?" Holly drags me inside, grinning. "Is the Pope Catholic?"

I laugh. A true southerner, Holly always has food in her house—real food too, not like what I lived on while Wren was in France. She makes her biscuits from scratch, gets her vegetables from the farmers' market, and has fifty bajillion ways to prepare a chicken. Luckily for me, the only thing Holly loves more than cooking is cooking for other people.

"Is your mom around?" I ask. Holly's mother is one of my all-time favorite people. She's like sunshine embodied in a person.

"Nah, she's at"—Holly makes air quotes—"Bunko."

"Aw, without us?" Mrs. Benson's Bunko club never actually plays Bunko. Instead, they go the racetrack, day drink, and on one occasion, went to a shooting range. They're the wildest old ladies I've ever met and I hope I grow up to be just like them. Sometimes Holly and I tag along for the fun.

"I know, right?" Holly shrugs. "God only knows what they're up to. Mom's driving."

"That's not good."

"Tell me about it."

We retreat to the cottage's rear kitchen where, as usual, something's in the oven. I take a big breath of cheesy, buttery goodness. She must've made ham and cheese croissants. My favorite. "Did you know I was coming?"

"After Friday night, I figured it was a sure thing."

"Wren and I made up."

"Really? That was fast. I would've thought she'd give you at least a week of silent treatment." Holly takes plates down from one of the high cabinets. We spent part of last summer repainting the whole kitchen. The ceiling is now the palest sky blue and the cabinets are the softest mouse grey. "You got lucky."

"Yeah."

"Mix up the mimosas. The first match is about to start."

I grab a Mexican glass pitcher, fix our drinks, and follow Holly onto her rear patio. Everything smells like lavender and fresh cut grass. Across the playing field, people are setting up their Sunday picnics. It's another perfect day in Atlanta.

"You heard from Parker?" Holly asks. "I've left two messages and she hasn't called me back."

"No," I say sadly. Parker is the other musketeer to our threesome. We've been best friends since high school, but don't get to see her much since she's moved to the west coast.

Holly takes the oversized swing and I grab the chaise lounge. Dress sketches are scattered all over the cushion and I paw through them, devouring the deep burgundy day dresses and vintage satin evening gowns.

"These are gorgeous," I tell her. "Even better than usual."

Holly frowns. "Maybe."

"I wish you would give yourself more credit." In addition to being the world's greatest best friend, Holly is also a fashion designer. She supplies a limited run of her own dresses to shops around the Southeast. The designs *always* sell out and Holly's *always* surprised. I'm not. We've been best friends since we were ten and riding our ponies around and even then I knew she was special.

I take a sip of my mimosa and carefully put the drawings in their folder. "I wish you'd think about that website again. You could sell the dresses through it."

She gives me a wry smile. "Did you really come all this way to pep talk me?"

"It's not really 'all this way.' It's more like fifteen minutes."

"Semantics. What's going on?"

It takes me the rest of my mimosa, but I tell Holly all about losing the manager job, making up with Wren, and most of all, Caleb's offer. She stares at me, stunned.

"I know, right?" I say. "And you know what's the worst part? The worst part is I'm such a troll for being hurt Wren's moving on. She's happy. I want that for her—and I want to stop annoying Caleb. It's like every time he shows up, I can't help but be..."

"Flirty?"

"I was going to say a bit hostile."

"Darling, you never learned to flirt. This is your abused and neglected libido crying out for help." The polo riders gallop past again and Holly watches them go, finger tapping against her glass. "You know what you should do?"

"Hit him with my truck?"

"Jump him."

I shiver. I can't help it. "What?"

"Take him up on his offer. Jump him." Holly pours herself another mimosa and settles back into the plushy swing. She sweeps the tips of her toes against the stone tile and sends herself swaying. "It would be good for both of you. Work off some of that edge."

"I don't have an edge."

Holly quirks one brow.

"Okay, fine I have an edge."

"And you don't want that right before the show."

I kinda hate that she's right. Tension and Beckon should never be combined. Unless I want a dirt facial (or worse), I need to get my head in the game. I focus on the field for a few minutes. The players are swapping horses, getting ready for the next chukka. "In that case," I say slowly. "Anyone could work off my edge."

Holly shakes her head. "I think you need to get Caleb Reese out of your system."

"He's not in my system. He's annoying."

"Oh, God." Holly stabs her foot against the floor, stopping the swing. "If you're really going to stick to that lie, I'm going to need more champagne."

"Fine, he's in my system. Fine, I have an edge. Fine, you're always right."

Holly lifts her glass in a mock toast. "Take advantage, Ellie. The man is gorgeous."

"Yeah, he's gorgeous—until he opens his mouth."

"So tell him to be quiet." Holly suddenly throws her head back in a fit of giggles. "Or keep his mouth busy doing other things."

My face goes nuclear. Actually...all of me goes nuclear. I just can't get rid of the image of Caleb Reese's mouth keeping busy. My nipples suddenly begin to ache as I think about what it would be like for him to suck them.

"He's gorgeous," Holly repeats. "He also wants you."

"He wants my job. He could end up being my boss."

Holly shrugs and leans down to grab a ham and cheese croissant from the coffee table tray. She takes a ferocious bite and points a finger at me. "Makes it even better as far as I'm concerned. Keep the situation on your terms that way you're in control."

I help myself to a croissant too. Partially because I'm hungry, but mostly because I don't have the words to properly explain how nothing about me is *in control* where Caleb is concerned. How would sleeping with him make it better? What if it made it worse?

Sudden heat turns my insides liquid. Since when has 'worse' sounded so...perfect?

And irritating.

And *perfect*.

Holly pulls apart the rest of her croissant as she watches the riders gallop across the field.

"What are you wearing for the Wesley party?"

"Huh?" I jerk my thoughts away from how my whole body is going warm. "Oh, I'll wear that black lace dress."

Holly frowns and flicks the mutilated croissant back onto the tray. "The black lace dress you wear to *every* party?"

She sounds so disappointed I can't help my laugh. "It's one of yours!"

"Hmmm. I have something else in mind." Holly jumps up and disappears inside, leaving me to enjoy the rest of the match and croissants. Moments later, she reappears, carrying a long garment bag. "I think you should wear this," Holly says, pulling the zipper down to reveal the dress inside.

I brush off my hands and lean forward as a waterfall of cobalt blue silk spills out. Holly tugs the dress free, revealing a stunning column gown with bare shoulders and an open back. I would need my highest heels to accommodate the sweeping beaded hemline.

"It's amazing," I breathe, standing up to better feel the fabric. "Is it vintage?"

Holly makes a face. "Sort of? The design is vintage influenced—totally the twenties'—but I made it myself." She holds it to my frame and I strike a pose, duck lips and all. "Stop being annoying," she tells me. "Yep, this is what I want you to wear. It's perfect for man catching."

I burst out laughing. It's the mimosas and the stress and, well, the very idea of 'catching' Caleb Reese. "You make it sound like I'll need to pack a hunting rifle."

"No one needs a hunting rifle when she's wearing one of my dresses."

"That's because we don't have anywhere to put it."

Holly arches one brow. "Darling, this dress was made for you—or should I say it was made for your situation?" I give her a questioning look and she grins. "It's easy to put on, and easier to take off."

CHAPTER 16 | Ellie

When I get back to the farm, I go upstairs to drop the dress off and change into work clothes. Wren is already there, packing up the last of her things and I smile at her like the sight doesn't kill me. "Want help?" I ask.

She shakes her head, smoothing down stripes of clear tape across the box tops. "Nah. I'm done. Have a coffee with me before you go back down?"

"Sure."

"I'll make it. You go change."

A few minutes later, we meet back in the living room, Wren barefoot and in a sundress, me in my usual polo and shorts uniform. My sister passes me a mug of coffee and flops down on the couch next to me. "You were with Holly, right? Did she tell you about going wedding dress shopping?"

"No, what happened?"

"She didn't like the dress, or the shop's seamstress."

I pause. "Holls has very...definitive tastes."

"Exacting is more like it."

I grin. "What happened?"

My sister's eyes drift upward as if she's replaying the scene. "Something about how if the pleating wasn't taken in correctly, it would interfere with the drape of the skirt. I didn't really understand much except Holly telling the poor woman the dress would look like a hot mess."

"Ouch."

"Yep. On the bright side, Holly's found another shop we can try. I'm going to try on a few more dresses and see if we can find something that will work better." Wren elbows me. "You'll come with me, right?"

"Wouldn't miss it. I just need to ride Beckon before we go and—" My cell buzzes with an incoming call. For a heartbeat, I'm convinced Parker's *finally* calling me back and what awesome timing she has too and—I check the screen, scowl. James. I send him to voicemail and turn my attention back to Wren. Her expression is something between worry and annoyance.

"How many times does this make now?" she asks

I think for a beat. "Probably six or seven calls in the last three weeks? I don't want to answer. He told me I would regret losing him. He's probably checking to make sure I'm miserable—and I'm not."

"Should you get another number? It would stop all of this."

I shake my head. "I don't want to. I've had it for years and all my contacts know me at this number. My own fault I guess for mixing personal and business on the same line."

"It's not your fault. It's his for being a disrespectful asshole. I wish you'd never dated him."

I smile. I can't help it. Wren rarely swears. "He'll go away eventually. He only wants me because I won't let him have me." I blink and then blink again as Caleb suddenly appears in my mind. James isn't the only guy who wants what he can't have. My stomach sinks like I'm disappointed and it stops me dead—because I *couldn't* be disappointed that Caleb Reese was only chasing what he can't have...could I?

I tuck my legs under me. "What was Caleb like back then? Before he left?"

"I didn't really know him. I mean I saw him at y'all's shows, but I was more focused on you." She thumps my arm hard. "And furthermore, 'back then?' I'm not that much older than you are."

"Sorry, I didn't mean it like that." I pause. "I saw him ride and even then, he was good—really good—and then he stopped riding at what? Seventeen? I know he partied hard until he walked off the farm at nineteen. And I gotta say for two years of partying to still be following him ten years after he left, it has to be good stuff."

"Good stuff?" Wren echoes, laughing.

"Yeah, I'm assuming like Animal House levels of partying, like monkeys swinging from the chandeliers and strippers with body paint."

She gives me a smug smile. "Maybe you should ask him if you're so interested."

"That would involve actually having to talk to him." My cell goes off again. This time, it's a text.

You know you miss me?

My stomach sours as I picture his handsome face. James never lacked for confidence. It was a total turn on, and then became super tedious. I'm half tempted to turn the phone off so I don't have to think about it, but if something happened at the farm, Sam or one of the grooms might need me. Besides, I'm not a coward. I can ignore texts and phone calls with the best of them.

"Are you sure you're okay with this?" Wren eyes the cell. "It just seems so weird that he would resurface after six months."

I shrug and show her the text. "It's not. It's just the way guys like him work. Trust me, I know the type now. They only want what they can't have."

Another image of Caleb Reese appears in my mind and I brush it away.

"Never heard you so definitive," Wren says.

"It's because I'm right." I pocket my cell. Right?

CHAPTER 17 | Caleb

It takes some doing, but I manage to avoid Ellie for a few days. I stay busy with paperwork and helping the guys. In fact, it works beautifully until our newest import, Grace—short for Grace Like Rain—tries to colic. Horses have amazingly, *frustratingly* delicate digestive systems, which basically means loads of stuff can set them off. A bad case of colic can kill them. Luckily for all of us, Sam spotted Grace's discomfort early on and had the vet out right away. The mare's going to be fine, but someone will need to watch her through the night to make sure she doesn't take a freak turn for the worse.

I told Sam that someone would be me. Again, there was that faint look of surprise that ghosted over his face, but I ignored it. Eventually, Sam—and the rest of the staff—will realize I'm not messing around. I'm here to work.

I double check our feed store order and make my way down to Grace's stall. The grooms are finishing up for the night and soon the whole place will be quiet except for the horses. I look over the stall partition and spot the top of Ellie's head. Her hair's swept up into a loose top knot, tendrils snaking down against cheeks pale from exhaustion.

She's waiting up with the mare? I catch myself doing a quick calculation. If she's been in the barn since six that means...I resist the urge for a low whistle. Wren was right. Ellie *is* a workaholic. She might even be worse than me.

I slide the stall door open and Grace pricks her ears with interest. She's a lovely Selle Francais mare. Impeccable jumper bloodlines packed into a sleek frame. She's leggy, but compact, and the loveliest seal brown color.

"No treats, darlin'," I tell her as she sniffs my hands. Grace deflates a little and goes back to her hay. "You can go on," I tell Ellie. "I'll take it from here."

She shakes her head, eyes still on the mare. "I want to be here—if you don't mind."

Our eyes meet and I consider telling her I actually mind. But if I admit it, she'll know she's gotten to me. No way am I letting her win.

"'Course I don't mind." I slump onto the straw-strewn floor across from her and for several minutes, we sit in silence, watching Grace munch her hay.

"How're the wedding preparations going?" I ask finally.

"Good. I've almost talked Wren into making you wear a banana hammock."

"I could pull it off." I smirk when Ellie scowls. "You're thinking about me in that banana hammock, aren't you? *Tsk tsk*, Lennox."

Her scowl deepens. *One for Reese*, I think. *Zero for Ellie.*

One aisle over, the last groom to leave flicks off the overhead lights and we're left in semi-dark. Everything smells like hay and horse and somehow I can still pick up the faint lemon scent of Ellie's shampoo. Moonlight coming through the stall windows casts her in silver and black.

The silence stretches between us and Ellie begins to fidget. She jiggles her foot, cracks her knuckles. After another minute, she starts into a round of small talk and I try to keep the amusement out of my voice when I answer her questions. So Ellie doesn't like awkward silences. For some reason, that feels like something I should remember. But even small talk has its limits and as we inch past midnight I hear myself saying, "I admired your dad. The way he handled your family's sales barn was spot on and the way he rode? It was like a master class in gentle riding and patience. He could've been one of the greats."

"He *was* one of the greats. He was amazing. I learned so much from him."

Now that she mentions it, she's right. That's why Ellie's riding seemed so familiar to me. She rides like her dad: almost invisible corrections, soft murmurs to the horse, and a thousand watt smile. Regardless of what I think about her behavior outside of work—and the serious case of blue balls she's given me—Ellie's poised to be just as amazing as her dad was. "He would be really proud of you."

She makes a scoffing noise.

"It's true—especially considering how much you had to accomplish after he passed. I know what it's like to lose a parent."

A hesitation and then, "I'm sorry, Caleb. It must have been really hard to lose your mom."

"Cancer sucks." I close my eyes and see my mom in the hospital bed, bones standing up like ghosts beneath her skin.

"You know, it's been years since my parents' accident and missing them still *hurts*. Sometimes it takes my breath away."

I roll my head toward Ellie only able to see the silvery outline of her profile. What's happened here? Is it the dark? We're spilling ourselves to each other. Somehow I doubt we'd do that in the daylight. I can't see Ellie ever admitting anything so personal to me.

Maybe it's leftover sexual frustration or maybe it's the shadows and the soothing sounds of Grace's soft breathing, but it feels like something's shifted between us. We can talk—really talk—and I want more.

"Have you and Wren always been close?" I ask.

She nods, a tiny smile playing at the corners of her mouth and her eyes going far away as she relives some memory. "It was hard losing her for the summers—she spent them in Paris with her mom—but after my parents died...well, it got really tough being without her."

"Have you thought about going with her?"

Ellie shifts in the straw, her boots making rustling noises. "No, not really. I'm needed here, and I wouldn't want to intrude, you know?"

"No."

She glances up at me, exasperated.

"I don't get it," I say. "Wren thinks the sun rises and sets on you. She would love to take you home with her."

"But it's the only time she gets to see her mom."

"Probably make it even better if you were there."

The mare snorts softly and we both freeze, watching her darkened outline. After a moment passes and nothing more happens, Ellie turns her attention to me. "And how would you know I would make it better for her?"

Because I can't imagine it wouldn't, I think. They're close. You can't be around them for more than five minutes before realizing they love each other's company. But saying that would make me sound like a stalker. I'm not even sure I like the fact that I *know* that.

Actually I'm sure I don't.

Ellie shifts again. "Why don't you ride anymore?" she whispers. "You love this world. Why would you quit?"

I pause. "You can enjoy horses and not ride them."

"Not for you."

"Oh yeah?"

"Yeah." Ellie's voice is so tired, but there's something unwavering in the word. Whatever she's about to say she believes with all her heart. "I saw you ride. It was years ago. I was still riding ponies for my parents. You were good, which isn't really that surprising. I mean with your background of course you would be, but even then I could tell it completed you...and then you quit."

I try to brush it off with a laugh and I can't. In some ways, it's completely cheesy. I mean how many movies and books have talked about completing yourself? It's overused to the point that it's meaningless except right now in the soft dark with Ellie so close and so far and the farm all around us, it feels right. I gave up riding, something that made me more, and traded it for distraction.

I swallow and my throat clicks.

A phone vibrates and we both check our cells. "Not me," I say, sliding mine back in my pocket.

Ellie stares at her screen for a long moment before setting the phone on the straw next to her, ignoring how it buzzes and buzzes. Whoever it is keeps calling back.

"You sure you shouldn't answer that?" I ask after the third call.

"Oh, I'm sure." The faint light from the screen catches her cheekbones. "It's my ex. He's decided six months of silent treatment hasn't brought me to heel so he's trying to pull that whole 'We were good together, baby. I miss you.'"

"Oh, one of *those* guys." I blow out a sigh. "Let me guess, he always wants what he can't have?"

She sits up straight. "Exactly! He—wait, what do you mean 'one of those guys?' You *are* one of those guys."

"I am not."

"You are *so*. Have you forgotten your little offer?" She smirks, proving I really might be 'one of those guys' because my dick suddenly hardens. I want to kiss that smirk away. I want to make her mouth round like it did before. I want *her*.

"Face it, Caleb," she says. Her voice has gone the tiniest bit shaky and I realize all over again I'm not the only one who feels this attraction. "You only want me because you can't have me."

"That so?" I give it a moment, letting silence do my work for me. Ten seconds later, she squirms and I smile. *Can't have you, Ellie? Think again.*

CHAPTER 18 | Ellie

The next morning, I drag myself downstairs and Caleb's already up. He stands next to the coffee maker, stretching his shoulders and it makes my mouth go dry. He's not football player bulky or rider lean, but something in between the two. Powerful, but not trying too hard. I watch how his polo pulls tight across his shoulder blades, remembering distinctly how they felt under my fingertips.

How he crushed me against him.

How I pulled him closer.

"Morning, Lennox," he says without turning around. "You going to gawk at me all day?"

Damn him. I breeze down the last few steps and join him. "I was just amazed a man could work the coffee maker. If you remember to clean out the filter, it'll be a miracle."

A smile tugs the corner of his mouth. He passes me a mug and I sniff. Damn him again. How did he know I like hazelnut creamer?

I narrow my eyes. Someone's been snitching, and when I find out, that someone is going to muck stalls for weeks.

"What do you have planned for today?" Caleb asks, leaning one hip against the desk. "I'd like to watch you school Beckon again, but the vet texted that she'll be here in the next hour and I want to meet her."

I nod, listening silently while he goes on to outline the rest of his morning. A few days before, I would've been annoyed, but things feel...different. I'd like to say we're totally relaxed with each other now, but we're not. There's something simmering between us.

Not 'something', I think as Caleb reaches across me to grab some paperwork and my heart double thumps. *It's not something. It's* want.

And he feels it too. His eyes keep lingering on my mouth...and lower.

My skin begins to tingle and warmth spreads through my stomach. We're too close.

"So," Caleb says, eyes still on my mouth. "Sound good to you?"

Good? What was good? I blink, super confused, and then realize he was talking about our schedule for today.

"Sounds great," I manage, voice Minnie Mouse high. "If you need any help with the vet or whatever, let me know."

I launch myself toward the door, morning heat and humidity slapping me in the face as I hustle down the aisle. I'm almost to Beckon's stall when my cell goes off, vibrating deep in my vest pocket.

Please don't be James, I pray. *Please don't be James*. My libido is running so high if he offered a quickie, I'd probably take him up on it. Thankfully though the universe is looking out for me because it isn't James at all. It's Holly.

Relief floods through me and I pick up. "Hey! What are you doing up so early?"

A yawn barrels down the phone line. "I wanted to get a few sketches done before the day gets crazy. I won't make it to the Wesley party tonight. I'm so sorry."

My flare of disappointment immediately dies. "Are you okay?"

"Yeah. Just struggling to keep everything together." She sounds like she's fighting back tears. "I keep thinking, what's the point, you know? I'm not in New York anymore. It's over."

I step outside the barn, walking toward the huge oak trees so we can have some privacy. I'm not sure how much Holly will want to talk. What she's going through...it's so hard. She takes care of everyone else and often there's nothing left for her. Sometimes it boils over and she'll talk to me for hours about how heartbroken she is over leaving New York. Other times, she won't talk about it at all and it seems like today is one of those times. I scuff my boots against the grass as we make small talk.

"You sound exhausted," Holly says after a few minutes.

"I am. We were up all night with Grace. She was colicky."

"*We?*"

I wince. I shouldn't have said that. "Caleb and me."

Holly cheers. "And did you jump him?"

My face goes hot. "*No.*"

"Why?"

No one's around, but I drop my words to barely above a hiss: "He could be my boss one day."

"You could get hit by a truck tomorrow."

"Well, that's *grim*. Thanks, Holls."

"Sorry." She giggles. "It totally was grim, wasn't it? Ignore me. It isn't even eight o'clock and it's already been a tough day. Look, I gotta go. You better kill it tonight in my dress. Don't let me—or that silk—down."

I grin. "I won't. I promise. Call me if you need anything? I'm really worried about you."

"Don't be. This'll pass." And Holly sounds so carefree when she says it, I can almost believe her.

"Love you," I tell her.

"Love you too—and Ellie?"

"Yeah?"

"Jump him. Use this for you."

She hangs up and I pocket my phone, standing in the shade to enjoy the last sips of my coffee before the day starts. *Use this for you*, echoes in my head and as if on cue, Caleb Reese strides out of the barn. He doesn't spot me under the trees, but I can't stop staring at him.

Use this for you. The idea is terrifying.

And delicious.

CHAPTER 19 | Caleb

If there's one thing horse people know, it's how to party, and if there's one thing the Wesley family knows, it's how to go overboard, and tonight is no exception. Their turn of the century mansion is decked out in enough white lights it's probably visible from space, and every room is packed with people. Not that I'm complaining. The booze is top shelf, the food is excellent, and the guests list reads like a Who's Who of the equestrian world.

I stand near the wall, and watch a trainer squire a few of his clients through the crowd. The clients look dazzled and the trainer looks worried. He should be. By my count there are four other trainers who would happily swipe his clients from him—and that's just in this room. People love to talk about how beautiful the horse world is. Mostly, they forget about the ugly underneath.

I check my phone. Ellie should already be here, but I haven't spotted her yet. We came separately. She was driving in with Evelyn, one of our older clients. Ever since taking care of Grace, things have seemed...different between us.

No, they *are* different. We're not sniping at each other, but we're keeping a careful distance too. If Ellie's at the desk during the staff meetings, I stay by the door. If I'm by the wash racks, she stays across the aisle. Not that it really matters for me. Every time Ellie's within three feet of me, I feel like the air between us goes molten.

Two women in black dresses sweep past me as the crowd shifts. Opens. A new set of guests have arrived and I know the outsized laugh before I see her. Mandy.

She's wearing a plunging gold gown, her black hair swept into an artful knot at the top of her head. From experience, I know she can loosen it with a few pins and well timed shake.

Our eyes meet and she gives me that slow smile I also know so well, the one that promises more, more, *more*. Now it makes my stomach sink.

You knew she'd be here, I remind myself. But, apparently, knowing and seeing are two different things and I turn for the bar, ordering a whisky neat to get me through this. "Thanks," I tell the bartender when he comes back with my drink. I slide my tip across the marble counter-top, already turning to go when I hear her:

"Hullo, Cay."

The nickname used to ripple through my bones. Not anymore. I glance down and Mandy smiles up at me. That smile is megawatt, and her gold dress isn't far behind. It shimmers over Mandy's graceful hips, hugs her breasts and ass perfectly. She's as beautiful as I remember, and different at the same time. It's something about how her moves seem ever so slightly forced, how my heart doesn't leap when she touches my elbow.

It must be the effect of coming home. Everything's the same, but it's also changed in this invisible way, like everyone else has moved an inch sideways and I'm still standing in the same place.

"I heard you were back," she says.

"Taking over Jacks or Better."

A wider smile. "I always knew you would. Does the Colonel appreciate you more now?"

"Something like that."

"I always said he should."

"You said a lot of things," I tell her. The party swirls around us and I ignore the sideways looks we're getting.

She makes a *tsking* noise. "Now, now Cay, are you still cross with me?"

"Not anymore."

"Then why didn't you call me back?" There's a note of excitement in her voice now. "Did the Colonel not give you my message?"

"He gave it to me."

Something—irritation or remorse or challenge—flits through her eyes, going too fast for me to label. *Another game*, I realize. This one isn't as fun as the game I play with Ellie though and I'm not sure what to make of that.

"Let's get out of here." Her eyes widen, *brighten*. "We could take a little trip down memory lane!"

"Yeah, no thanks."

She shimmies closer. "We weren't always bad together."

It's true actually. As much as I'd like to say she was the devil in-carnate, Mandy encouraged me to pursue my interests in showjumping breeding. "No," I say at last. "But we weren't great either, and at the end, we weren't anything at all."

Another *tsking* noise. "So dramatic."

Probably. I scowl and Mandy makes a low noise, deep in her throat. "I love that look on you." She pushes her lower lip out and gazes up at me through thick lashes. "Are you really over me, Cay?"

She's even closer now, leaning into me in a way she always did when she wanted something. "Because I don't think you could be over me."

Instant annoyance. I shouldn't engage. I know better and yet I can't stop myself from asking, "Yeah? Why's that?"

"Because I'm still me and you're still you."

***

Twenty minutes later and I still can't shake Mandy's words—or maybe I just can't shake how she's right. I am still me. Six years away and I'm *still* playing the Colonel's head games, *still* playing with dangerous at-tractions. I lose my head when Ellie's around—exactly how I acted with Mandy. It would be pathetic if it weren't so annoying.

No. Check that. It's still pathetic.

My cell vibrates and I check it again—it's a text from Sam about to-morrow's hay shipment. He'll be busy with the vet and he needs me to handle it. Fine, no problem. I'm actually glad he feels like he can ask.

Even before I left for Ireland, I made sure never to ask a staff member to do something I wouldn't do—or more importantly hadn't *done* myself. This means yeah, I'm the boss's son, but I've also mucked stalls, scrubbed buckets, cleaned equipment, mowed fields, repaired fences, and on a couple of occasions, I've helped our vets with colt castrations. Unloading a truck full of hair will be itchy, but not a big deal.

I text Sam back and pocket the phone as the crowd parts, revealing a dark-haired woman taking champagne from a waiter. Ellie, my brain registers. My whole body tightens. The dress's open back reveals the long column of her spine, and the vivid blue stands out against the other women's black silk and navy satin. She looks so...touchable. Like her skin would be as silky as the dress.

Shit. I bet it is. I shake myself. Ellie Lenox's skin is the last thing I need to be thinking about. I plaster on a smile and make my way through the other guests, nodding greetings as I go. A few feet away, El-lie notices me and smiles.

It kicks all the air out of me, and in my head, I hear Mandy chanting: "You're still you."

I scowl.

"About time," I tell Ellie, finishing my drink in one quick pull. "You're late."

"And you're staring."

Yes, I am. I jerk my eyes from her cleavage to her face and she lifts one brow. "Sorry," I say. I'm acting like an ass and I can't seem to stop. Even so the tiniest smile lifts both corners of Ellie's mouth. She's amused.

"Still staring." The tiny smile spreads, turning triumphant and everything in me pricks to attention.

More of that difference between us, I think. This thing we're playing at is changing, but I don't know where it's headed. The woman looking at me now isn't the clipped professional giving my father a farm update, and she isn't the rider who defended her training choices. It feels...closer to the naked Ellie, the one who needed release. The one who knows how much I want to give it to her.

"You look amazing," I say at last and I will forever be grateful my voice doesn't crack.

"So do you." Her eyes drop, taking in the tux and then drifting lower. I clear my throat, and glance away, eyes trailing around the room and falling on Mrs. Mar. Dressed in burgundy silk and tasteful gold jewelry, she's holding court in the corner of the Wesley's pale living room, the white walls and white furniture making her look even more vivid.

Okay, I think, taking a deep breath. *No time like the present to talk about Beckon.* I roll my shoulders. "How do you want to handle this?" I ask Ellie.

"What do you mean?"

"We have to play this Beckon situation right. Do you want me to go first? Do you want to catch her as she's leaving? Do you—"

"You're overthinking this."

"No, I'm *not*. This could be the biggest sale of our lives. It's already going to be the biggest sale in Jacks or Better's history and—"

Ellie's already moving, striding so quickly across the silvery grey carpeting I almost have to jog to catch up.

"What are you doing?" I hiss.

"You think too much," she says, just before we reach Mrs. Mar and her friends. "Mrs. Mar! It's so nice to see you!"

"And you!" Ellie and the older woman air kiss before Mrs. Mar turns to me, extending one hand, elegant as a golden age movie star. "We have a friend in common, Mr. Reese."

"Call me Caleb," I say, taking her hand in mine.

"Well, *Caleb*, my sister just bought two weanlings from your agent at Locheer. We hit it off, and he was very complimentary of you."

"I pay people to say nice things about me. I find it's easier."

She laughs.

"Did you see any young stock you liked?"

A glittery headshake. "I'm rarely in the market for young horses. I prefer them more established. Still, I found your bloodline selections to be quite interesting. My sister is quite thrilled with her purchases."

Outside, I'm sipping my whisky like this is no big thing. Inside, I am turning cartwheels like a damn cheerleader.

And next to me, Ellie Lenox has gone completely stiff.

Take that, sweetheart, I think, smiling at her. I'm prepared for Ellie to smirk back. I'm even prepared for her to flip me off. I'm not prepared for her to study me like she's making some sort of judgment. A decision. It's that same expression as before and it heats me up just the same.

Something's changed—not for me, but for her—and for the life of me, I can't figure out what it is.

But I desperately want to know.

"Adele! Dearest!" A woman with sky high hair and heels totters up behind Mrs. Mar.

Mrs. Mar's eyes faintly widen, but she smiles just the same. "I'll see you two later," she says, and turns toward the newcomer.

Ellie elbows me. "Take me to get something to eat."

I think it's supposed to be a question, but her tone doesn't leave room for argument. *Eating?* I want to ask. *Now? Are you* serious?

Her brows knot together like she's very serious and I blow out a sigh.

"Stop worrying," Ellie whispers.

I can't. She links her arm through mine, and briefly, we both freeze. "We're supposed to be pretending, remember?" she says, nudging me into the next room and toward an overflowing buffet table.

"Pretending," I agree, *pretending* like her soft grip on my elbow isn't threatening to give me a crippling hard-on.

Ellie frowns at a platter of meat and fruit skewers. "I have no idea what this is," she says, selecting one and popping it in her mouth. "Oh!" Her eyes go wide. "It's good! You should try it."

"You don't even know what it is."

She takes another two skewers and grins at me. "I don't have to know what something is to know it's good. Here. Try it."

I do. It's salty and sweet and I think it's some sort of prosciutto. "It's excellent. You're right."

"Mmmm." Ellie grins. "I *like* hearing that."

It lights me like a fuse. The satisfied noise. In another situation, it could mean so much more. My whole body goes hot and I focus on a piece of melon so I don't embarrass myself.

The string quartet launches into a slower piece, lending a dreamy quality to the scene. The trainer from earlier walks through the crowd again, only one of his clients with him now. He notices Ellie and nods. She smiles in return, but I can feel her sag a little. "He's having a hard year," she murmurs, studying her skewers' ends. "Most of his farm clients went with his husband—ex-husband—after the divorce. He's rebuilding."

I wince. Losing your partner and your business in one swoop? There aren't powerful enough words to describe the suck.

Ellie falls silent, watching the other guests like she's seeing them as something else entirely now. "Horses are a very hard way to make a living," she finally says. "But I can't see myself doing anything else."

I snatch a glance at her. She's staring into the crowd with a wistful expression that isn't meant for me to see, and it's crazy but she looks different tonight. It isn't just the hair or the make up or that banging dress, it's her.

And it's me too because I feel the same way—and I shouldn't feel the same as Ellie about anything—but there's something about horses that gets in your blood. It ruins you for everything else.

"There's ugliness underneath," I say. "That guy over there? He only hires illegals to work on his farm, and he pays them next to nothing—and that's when he pays them at all. Woman at the bar? She changes her horses, her saddles, her trainers, but no matter how many times she fails, she never changes herself. Ever."

Ellie faces me. "You're acting like I don't know these people."

I open my mouth and then shut it. "Sorry."

She shrugs, smiles. It hits me low again, curling something nameless through me.

"It's not all ugly," Ellie says, eyes lighting up. "The way I see it, you can look at life two ways."

I smile. Maybe it's the booze. Maybe it's the party. Maybe it's just Ellie, but I can't help it. "Yeah? Enlighten me."

She smiles back. "I will. You can look at life as if nothing is a miracle, or you can look at life like everything is." Pink tinges the tops of her ears and I know I'm seeing another version of Ellie, this one just as real and true as the girl from the barn apartment bathroom and the rider showing Echo to the Davis family. "Furthermore," she continues, "if you stay in the horse industry long enough, you'll see something amazing."

She turns toward an approaching waiter and, briefly, golden light coats her cheek. Something amazing, huh?

Chills climb my skin as I realize I might already be looking at something amazing.

CHAPTER 20 | Ellie

One of my favorite things to do at parties is people watch. Usually, the Colonel does the majority of the talking so I'm free to study everyone else. In some ways, it's like watching the horses out in their paddocks. You can get a feel for who's in charge, who's being bossed around, and in the case of one guy who's being bossed around by large woman in a pink fascinator, you get a feel for who enjoys being bossed around.

Over by the bar, a dark-haired woman in a gold dress throws her head back, hand going to her throat and calling attention to her breasts. The two men standing with her can't look away.

Mandy Gibson. It's not like I haven't seen her before. I just haven't noticed her—really noticed her—until now. I could say that's because she looks especially beautiful tonight, or I could say it's because she's turning everyone's heads, but I know it's because of Caleb.

This is the woman he loved.

This is the woman who ruined him.

Or so goes the rumor. Actually, there are a lot of rumors about Caleb Reese and I'm having a hard time reconciling what I've heard about him with what I've experienced with him. Yeah, he's a trust fund kid and will never want for anything, but he also stays up with sick horses, works on fencing, talks to the staff like they're peers and not servants—he's even working on getting everyone raises.

I was shocked when Sam told me this afternoon. Of course, we both know the quality of that raise will depend on Beckon's sale, and I'm not going to lie, that...hurts. I'll miss my girl so much it will damn near cripple me, but this is the industry. She was never mine and I have to remember that. Her sale could mean—will mean—a lot for the guys and for the farm's future.

Another moment and the crowd closes around Mandy and I'm staring at a man in a seersucker suit and a wine-reddened face.

Oh, boy, I think. He waggles his eyebrows at me and I struggle not to laugh. *How can he possibly think that's sexy?*

"Ellie!"

A satin gloved hand closes on my upper arm and I jump, spinning around. "Mrs. Mar!"

She beams, stepping to the side as a beautifully dressed couple squeeze by heading for their car. "Ellie, darling, could I have a word?"

"Of course." A fissure of unease winds through me. "Is it about Beckon?"

"In a way, but mostly it's about you, darling." She links her arm through mine, steering us deeper into the house and away from the crowd. We turn down an arch-ceilinged hallway and seconds later, Mrs. Mar lets us into the library.

I'm absolutely positive I shouldn't be here, but Mrs. Mar motions me inside like she belongs.

"I thought it might be better to have some privacy for our little conversation," she explains, shutting the door behind us. Instantly, the sounds of the party vanish, and the library gets an underwater hush. I have worked for the wealthy all my life. I have been in and out of houses like the Wesley's and the Reese's since I was tiny, but I will never get used to the way they can wrap themselves away from the world. It's remarkable.

And a bit terrifying.

No wonder the Colonel thinks I'm disposable.

Mrs. Mar drops onto a forest green couch studded with equally forest green buttons, and waves her hand for me to follow. I settle in next to her, plushy cushions sinking me so deep my heels almost leave the carpet.

Mrs. Mar plays with her wedding rings, twisting them back and forth. "I have to be honest, Ellie, I don't think Beckon would be the right fit for Beau."

My stomach hurls into my feet. Beau being Beau Kent, her lead rider. They've worked together for almost twenty years now. He's a legend. If he doesn't want Beckon—

"Don't look so worried, darling." Mrs. Mar puts her hand on mine. "Normally, I would pass since Beckon and Beau wouldn't be a good fit, but I can't stop thinking about her...and you."

My stomach shouldn't be able to get any lower, but it does. I stare at Mrs. Mar, unable to believe what I'm hearing.

Her gaze tracks back and forth across my face. "I think you have tremendous potential."

"Thank you," I whisper.

"I want you to come work for me."

It's like I'm in my body and outside my body and I *really* can't breathe. *Adele Mar* is offering me a job—and yet my first instinct is to put on the brakes. Jacks or Better is my home. I've put in so much time in there, with the horses, with the Colonel.

Who will let his son fire you if he gets the slightest chance, I remind myself. It's an excellent reminder. Too bad, it doesn't change that weird feeling in my gut: the one saying I need to think this through.

Mrs. Mar watches me like she knows it too.

I shake my head. "I couldn't leave Colonel Reese so close to the classic."

"Of course not, and I wouldn't want you to. I can wait. The classic is in what? Two more weeks? I can certainly wait until then. Do you think that would work for Colonel Reese and Caleb?"

Another flare of alarm hits me. I'm not just leaving the farm and the Colonel. I'm leaving Caleb. I pluck at my dress, mind spinning. Of all the things I should be worrying about right now, why on earth am I worrying about telling him?

Because you're panicking, I tell myself. And I shouldn't. "Two weeks would certainly be sufficient, but I don't go anywhere without Sam. You want me, you'll have to hire him as well."

Mrs. Mar's eyes brighten with interest. "I would love for Sam to join us. He's an amazing horseman."

"He is." I pause. I still can't believe this is happening. Do I want to work for Mrs. Mar? Would Sam want to work for her? On the surface, it's such a small decision. It's just switching jobs, right? One boss for another. But it's so much more, it would be leaving my home, everything I've built up. The idea makes me...panicky.

I pull my shoulders back. *Get it together, Lennox*, I think. "I'll speak with Sam tomorrow. Get his feel for things."

Like there would be any question in his mind. Odds are good, Mrs. Mar knows perfectly well Sam would be thrilled to work for her.

"Good," she says. "Let's get back to your friend."

We return to the party together. It's still going strong out here: The quartet is playing a waltz or something, waiters are breaking out champagne, and guests are spinning around. Some of them actually look like they know how to dance. Others...well, they're having fun. I watch one man twirl into a potted fern while his dance partner looks on and laughs.

"Oh, my," Mrs. Mar says. "They're both going to be hung over tomorrow. I'll see you soon, my dear." She squeezes my arm and smiles at me like I've already agreed.

I'd be an idiot not to, right?

"Complete and utter," I whisper to myself, looking up in time to see Caleb across the room, watching me. He's doing his gorgeous broody thing and he smirks when I catch him staring at me. It should be all kinds of annoying, but my mouth goes hot.

All of me goes hot.

He tilts his head, encouraging me to come to him and I'm moving before I even realize it, silk skirt swirling around my legs. What is with me? Maybe I do need to get him out of my system?

Or is that an excuse?

Caleb's smirk spreads into a smile as I draw closer. He looks me up and down like he's memorizing me, like he can't get enough of me and I love it. The rush of heat and power makes me grin.

"You look pleased," he whispers. "Anything I should know?"

I hesitate. Want and need and responsibilities all tangling up my tongue. If I accepted a position with Mrs. Mar, I wouldn't be sleeping with my possible boss. I would be sleeping with a competitor. The distinction suddenly seems like everything.

I slow, fingers knotting in the silk of my dress. Does that mean I've made up my mind?

Or does it mean I want him to touch me that bad?

We're toe to toe now and I'm far too aware of Caleb staring at me. Just like before, everywhere his gaze touches me seems to burn.

I want him.

So take him, I think.

CHAPTER 21 | Ellie

The party's dying down, but it still takes us almost an hour to escape. I get caught by some old clients who want to tell me how their horses are doing and then Caleb gets caught by someone who shopped one of his yards in Ireland.

I wait for him, watching, and catch Mandy Gibson studying both of us before hopping into her Range Rover.

It isn't over between them, I realize. Or it isn't over for her because I don't think Caleb notices. We walk to his car in silence and maybe it's the drink or the evening or my excitement talking, but the moment doesn't feel awkward for once. It's actually comfortable.

Caleb opens my door and asks, "Drop you at the barn?"

I pause. Am I really going to do this? "Actually," I say, gathering my dress into one hand before dropping into the car, "Sam mentioned you had revised contracts for the staff. Could we pick them up? I'd like to review them. See what you're thinking."

I look up at him, amazed I sound so calm when nothing about me *feels* calm. In fact, the longer Caleb studies me, the more I feel like I'm going to shake apart.

"Sure," he says, "they're at my place."

He closes the door and walks around the front of the car, stealing a glance at me through the windshield. I can't read his expression. Surprise? Suspicion? He hops in next to me, turns the ignition, and shifts the Rover into reverse.

"Your place?" I ask as he angles us into the stream of cars.

"Yeah, I moved into one of the cabins. It's easier."

I look out the window and wonder if that means it's easier because the cabins are closer to the barn or if it's easier because he isn't living with the Colonel. Working for Colonel Reese has been some of the best years of my life. They've been hard, for sure, but great in all the important ways. He's a tough boss, but I never considered what he would be like to live with. Looking at Caleb now, I have to wonder.

The dashboard lights edge his features in icy, electric blue. "Night went well. What did you think?"

I almost laugh. He sounds like the Colonel, but I know way better than to say so. "Went pretty well. Always hard to tell with these things though. Sometimes you don't see the benefit of chatting someone up until months or years later."

He turns toward home, stepping on the gas until the Rover purrs beneath us. "I could totally use a drink right now."

"Didn't have enough at the party?"

He smiles. "I had one. Going to need another to wind down."

I hesitate, his tension over speaking to Mrs. Mar coming back to me. Of all the people in the world who would get nervous about a deal, I would never have guessed Caleb would be one of them. Maybe there's more to it. "Is there anything I should know about? I mean, with Beckon's sale and all. Are we in financial trouble?"

He shakes his head. "No, there's just a lot of...personal stuff hanging on it."

"Stuff between you and the Colonel?"

A tight nod. "If I want to take over the farm, I need to prove to him I can do this."

I sit back against my seat, trying to think of something to say and coming up with nothing. No wonder he was nervous. He has a lot riding on this. I feel bad for him, and at the same time, it's kind of weirdly comforting to know someone else wants the farm to be as successful as I do. We're alike. In another situation, we'd probably be friends.

I'm not sure what to think about that, I realize. I bend down, reaching for my purse just as Caleb reaches for the A/C controls. Our hands brush. It runs a sizzle up my arm.

And Caleb snatches his hand back like he feels it too.

"Sorry," he says. "I'm going to fix a drink when we get to my place. Do you want one?"

I glance at him. *Is he thinking what I'm thinking?*

Doesn't seem like it. Caleb's eyes are on the road ahead of us. He's gripping the steering wheel lightly, all relaxed when I'm about to come out of my skin.

Surely if he was thinking what I'm thinking he'd be a little more...tense? The very idea of Caleb getting hard and tense for me again makes my pussy spasm. Tense. Hot. Wet. I can actually feel my nipples brushing against my bra's lace. It makes them harden.

"Ellie?" Caleb's voice jolts me. "Drink?"

"Definitely."

If he's surprised at my tone or my answer, it doesn't show. He turns the car toward his cabin and after another moment, it comes into view. 'Cabin' is probably the wrong word. It's more like a low country cottage, all wraparound porch and shutter framed windows. I can't decide if it suits him. The Colonel had four cabins built a few years before I arrived. Grooms and working students usually use them, but Sam has one to himself and I guess now so does Caleb.

He parks in front of the garden gate and gets out, waiting for me on the gravel drive. The night is extra warm and the jasmine overflowing the garden fence turns everything sweet. I follow him up the flagstone path. He fumbles with the door and then it swings open. I've never been inside any of the family cabins. Unsurprisingly, it's quite nice—a tasteful open floor plan carefully filled with antique furniture and modern art. But, it doesn't seem like him at all. I can't see Caleb Reese picking out a leather chesterfield couch, much less oil paintings of country landscapes. God knows I'm no decorator but this is like living in a hotel.

Caleb goes to his desk and swipes the papers off the top. He passes them to me and it's all very professional until I notice how his eyes are on my mouth.

I swallow.

Decide what you want, Mrs. Mar had said. *Use this for you*, Holly had said.

I will.

Caleb rubs one hand through his hair, making the dark strands stand up in spikes. "The contracts are good for another two years, but we have a clause that they can be changed if both parties agree. I doubt the guys would object to being paid more."

"I can't see it happening either." I tuck the contracts into my hand-bag. It's tiny and silver and the papers curl out of the top. "Caleb?"

He turns to me and for a moment, I'm struck speechless by the sight of him. Caleb Reese in a tux is something to be savored. My gaze traces his broad chest and narrow hips. I remember the length of him, the *hardness*.

I'm going to have that, I think, thighs squeezing together at the very thought of it.

"I considered your offer," I manage, wetting my lips.

"Oh?"

I stuff down a grin. He sounds awfully uninterested for a man whose hands have just tightened around the chair back. His knuckles stand up white.

"'Oh?'" I mock and push one strap of the dress off my shoulder. Caleb's whole body stills. I don't say anything. I don't look away. I slide the other strap down, and a slow, slow smile spreads across Caleb's mouth.

"I'm waiting," he whispers.

It makes me shiver. I reach behind me, loosening the delicate but-tons and letting the dress fall to the swell of my hips.

Caleb's eyes go bright. "Take it off."

Heat pools between my legs. I slide my hands behind my back once more and unfasten the last few buttons. The silk drops away and Caleb inhales. Hard.

Cool air makes my skin prickle with goose bumps, but it's *his* stare that makes my nipples harden.

"Keep going." He sounds half strangled, but doesn't move to touch me.

Drawing this out, I think, and it makes my hands run down my bare breasts that much faster. I skim my stomach and hips, reaching the edge of my panties. I hesitate.

"Don't stop now." There's a pinch in his voice that makes me whimper. I start to push them down and his breath leaves him in a rush. He grabs my wrist.

"On second thought, leave them." Another whimper from me and it makes him smile. "Come. Here."

Oh, God. I do. I step forward and he catches me by the arms, and then the waist. My knees crumble and I hold on to him—or is he holding onto me? Caleb drags me against him, his hard length already prodding my stomach.

He groans. "You feel perfect."

"So do you."

Another groan. I've said exactly the right thing and he rewards me with his mouth, lowering his head to mine, taking my lips with his. My aching breasts rub against his tuxedo shirt, reminding me I'm almost nude and he's dressed and he can do anything.

I go wet. I want him to do everything.

Pinning me against his hardness, his free hand finds my bare nipple, playing gently, and then tugging. I gasp and he covers my mouth with his, sweeping his tongue across mine as his fingers play with my other breast.

I sag, giving in to his hardness, his control. Seconds—years?—later, he sweeps me up, crossing to the bedroom in only a few strides and tossing me on the bed.

Yesyesyesyes! I can't wait. The coverlet is cool against my flushed skin, and the anticipation feels like the best thing in the world as I sweep my legs open, eyes on Caleb as he tugs off his clothes in frantic jerks.

"Please," I whisper, anticipating him falling into me, the hard ride.

He climbs onto the bed, grinning. "I like that. Say it again."

"Please," I repeat, torn between loving how I'm on my back and he's straddling me and being frustrated that I'm on my back and he's straddling me.

He bends down, sucking one nipple until I gasp and writhe.

"*Please.*"

"No." He licks me again and I moan. "I had to stand in that tack room for almost twenty minutes before I could walk normally. This is payback."

Another slow lick, always teasing, never touching hard enough. I arch my back and he pins my hips to the bed. "Ah ah. You can have exactly what you want..." His tongue skims my hardened nipple and I whimper. "You can have exactly what you want when *I* say so."

Oh, God, I knew he'd be like this. I knew it. The order leaves me panting, squirming.

Desperate.

The tiniest fissure of panic surges through me, coils in my gut. I squash it flat. I want him to be like this. It's pushing away everything except what's inside this room.

Everything except for him.

His thumb brushes over my panties and I jump—or try to jump. His weight presses into me. I can't move. I can only take what he's giving me.

Caleb's laugh is low and dark. "Wet already."

I nod, turning my burning face toward the pillows.

"For me?"

I swallow. *Admit it out loud?* It feels even scarier than stripping for him—at least then, I could tell how excited he was. Now, admitting I ache for him feels like I'm giving away a secret.

His thumb moves to where my panties meet the inside of my thigh. He caresses the soft skin and the soft lace, tugging it back just enough to make me writhe.

He's waiting for an answer. I bite my lip as Caleb teases me. Back and forth. Back and forth. *He can wait.*

I can wait.

Or I can until he starts exploring higher, finding my clit through the silk. Caleb rubs slowly, maddeningly, and I can't stop how my body jerks, how I can't help but grow wetter.

"For me?" he repeats.

"For you."

His laugh at my ear again. I shiver.

"Good," Caleb whispers. "Because I'm constantly hard for you."

His thumb skims under my panties and up to my clit once more. More touching. More circles. Caleb's mouth moves down my throat and across my collar bone. He kisses the swell of my breast...and the very edge of my tightened nipple...and then...and then...his lips close over it. Heat. Moisture.

Bliss.

I'm writhing in it. I can't stay still, and suddenly Caleb's looming over me. "How you move," he breathes, sounding in awe. I freeze, our eyes meet. "Don't stop, Ellie. I love watching you."

My mouth goes dry. Stripping in front of him was nerve wracking. Telling him I was wet for him was scary.

Knowing he's watching me enjoy this? I can't. It's too much. It's too...close. And, as if he knows what I'm thinking, Caleb starts playing with me again. His fingers play with one nipple, then the other. It's so soft and then he pinches me and it summons another rush of wetness.

I moan.

"Please?" he asks. It's a whisper, but his fingers play me like it's an order.

And I cannot help but obey.

I let the pleasure take me over, let it make my back arch and my legs drift wide. He rewards me with a firmer touch, lets me grind against his hand. One finger slips inside me then two, stretching me, filling me. I press my cheek against the pillow as he finds a rhythm, every stroke finding my clit and spiking me higher.

"Ellie." He sounds so far away and I'm so close. So. Close. "Ellie." His hand slows and my eyes fly open, meeting his.

He gives me a lazy smile. "Look at me."

"I am." Only as soon as his hand moves again, I'm lost, lids sliding shut. His hand slows once more and I squirm beyond frustrated.

"Look at me," he says and I do. His fingers begin again. I want to relax into it, let myself slide away, but he won't let me.

"I can't," I whisper. "Not like—"

Except I can because he's taking me higher, faster. He drives me to orgasm without ever letting me escape. At this moment, I'm his. At this moment, I will obey. The realization breaks something inside me. I explode in wave after wave, coming down only to have him urge me higher.

I scream, planting both feet against the mattress as my hips lift. I feel like I'm floating, and then I feel Caleb again, impossibly hot against me. He rolls me beneath him and my legs open.

"Again," he whispers and I moan.

CHAPTER 22 | Ellie

"God yes," I answer. "Again."

He chuckles, tightening his grip until each of his fingers brands me. His cock brushes the inside of my thigh and I gasp. It's even hotter than his hands. There's a brief moment of hesitation as he smooths on another condom and then he's between my legs again, spreading me. He enters me in a swift thrust.

I gasp as Caleb goes still. "God, you're tight," he murmurs, breath pouring into my ear. I moan against his shoulder, enjoying the fullness, the stretching. He pulls back and pushes forward, wringing another moan from me.

Then Caleb rolls, and takes me with him. Suddenly, I'm on top, balanced on my knees. His hands find my hips. "Take what you want."

I shiver. Heat pools low in my stomach and my joints begin to loosen. Caleb nudges me up and I gently lower myself down. "There," he groans, eyes closing. "There."

A wave of pleasure sweeps over me, and this time, I lift and lower, riding him the way I like best. His arms flex hard, making his chest stand up and all the muscles go rigid. "God, you're *perfect!*"

It lights me up, heat running everywhere. *I'm doing this. It's from me.*

"Never...seen...*anything* so sexy." Caleb flexes again, and power makes me wetter. I lift and lower, lift and lower, finding my rhythm as his thumb finds my clit again and he begins to rub. The initial discomfort slides into pleasant stretching and then into satisfying fullness.

My head rolls back. Nothing relaxes me like this. Nothing. He touches me like he could do this all day, and suddenly I need him to. I need him to push everything away until I'm only in this moment.

"Look at me." He bumps his hips, driving me harder, the reminder unmistakable: do as I say. My eyes flash open. Caleb smiles. His hand goes to my breast, gently twisting my nipple until I squirm. "What do you need?"

"This." I've gone boneless, legs spreading even further so I can take him deeper. "I need this."

His thumb traces down my stomach and I squirm. It finds my clit and I gasp.

But I do not look away from him.

"Good girl," Caleb says appreciatively, making me shiver and my pleasure spike. He flicks my clit, just hard enough to make me gasp again. The earlier relaxation disappears, swallowed up by a growing desperate need and Caleb plays with me like he knows and intends to make me wait for it.

"What do you need?" he repeats, this time smiling that smile that makes me wet.

"This. More."

He lifts his hips and I bounce, grinding hard against him. "You are the *sexiest* thing I have ever seen." It escapes on a groan, but his eyes never leave mine.

He means it.

Caleb Reese is staring me down like I am the most beautiful thing he's ever touched. This was supposed to be about stress release and unwilling attraction and *hell*, just having a good time, but now it feels like it's becoming something more.

He bumps his hips and I gasp. "Stay with me, beautiful."

Another one of his orders that isn't an order because I'm so willing to comply.

"Do you know what I need?" His fingers dig into my ass, lifting me up until I whine and then pulling me down—agonizingly slowly—until I gasp. "I need you like this: desperate."

He rolls his hips and I squirm, the pleasure making my toes curl and my nails claw his chest. Another roll. Another roll. My legs go loose around him.

He chuckles. "I know what you need, Ellie."

My name sounds delicious in his mouth. My hips jerk and he groans. "I know what you need too," I say, smiling as I lift myself up and settle on his shaft again. Lift. Settle. I'm controlling everything and both of us are shivering now.

Caleb twists beneath me, expression dark with want, eyes only on me. *I'm doing this*, I think and it's so erotic my pussy clenches.

I gasp. "I'm going to come."

Another stroke, and I feel the first wave.

And so does Caleb. His grip tightens until I feel each fingertip branding my skin. "Look at me," he says and I do. I can't help it. I look at his beautiful face and realize he's looking at me like I am everything he's ever wanted.

It pushes me over the edge all over again. I'm screaming his name like I'm drowning.

Like I'm lost.

CHAPTER 23 | Caleb

My breathing has barely returned to normal before Ellie's fallen asleep. She lies on her stomach, perfect bare ass curving out from under the sheets, tanned arms stretched beneath her pillow.

My pillow. The realization makes my stomach do a weird flip, and I ignore it, taking the time to savor a closer look at her. A strand of dark hair curls across her cheek and I brush it away. She's stronger than I thought, and the way she gave as good as she got?

I turn on my back, my dick going hard all over again. She looked at me like she owned my ass. Hell, she *did* own my ass.

Does own my ass? It seems entirely likely because all I can think about is taking her again.

And again.

She sighs in her sleep, feet rubbing together under the covers, and turns over, revealing her equally perfect breasts. The pale pink nipples seem to pucker as I stare at them, begging for my mouth, and I'm tempted to lick them, sucking her until she screams with pleasure, but then Ellie make a tiny huffing noise. Her body sags as she falls deeper into sleep.

Exhausted—and not just from me, but from the week we've had. I think it's the first time I've ever seen her look relaxed. I stretch, my muscles tingling, and realize that makes two of us. All my limbs have gone heavy and I feel like I could sleep for a week.

I lie back, pressing my forearm across my eyes as Ellie shifts again, my heavier weight causing her to slide a little closer. She fits into my side like we were made for this and I can't help but touch her again. I run my knuckles down her smooth cheek and along her jaw. She murmurs something in her sleep, turning so her throat is exposed. It's unbelievably soft. *She's* unbelievably soft.

And at the same time I hear Mandy whisper "You're still you" in my head.

"What the hell are you doing, Reese?" I whisper and it would be easy to tell myself I have no idea, or I could say it was just for fun, but it feels like a lie. Ellie's more than just fun. She's confident and funny and works as hard as I do.

She's amazing.

My bedroom grows darker as the moonlight fades. Morning's coming and with it is a laundry list of things to do. The farm is a seven days a week, every week. I hook a strand of hair behind Ellie's delicate ear.

You need her to pull this off, I remind myself. It's maybe the truest thing I've ever known and it's almost a relief until I realize: *You can't be with her.*

My hand stills. It's true. I can't. People will think we're boss and employee. They'll whisper about how she can only make it on her back—no matter how many wins she had before me. Pursuing this thing between us could really hurt her.

Not to mention it would just remind everyone of *my* past. The Colonel would be furious. I would look like I haven't learned a thing since Mandy, and even though it's different this time, I'll still look like the guy who can't keep his hands off the staff.

You are *the guy who can't keep his hands off the staff,* I think with disgust. Except it doesn't feel like it. I fell for Mandy because I was young and stupid and I thought she was what I wanted. I fell for Ellie because she's everything I admire.

Fell? Just thinking the word covers my skin in goosebumps. I slide deeper under the sheets and stare at the ceiling. I can't have fallen in love with her. I *can't.*

In the morning, we'll get things back on track. I'll apologize again for the way I acted when we first met. I'll offer her a partnership. We'll be working *together*, not as boss and employee.

It's the right thing to do. I have zero doubt about it, but I can't shake the feeling I'm making a mistake. Then I remember how her face lit up when I talked about giving the guys' raises, how her eyes met mine when we both knew she had the Davises exactly where we needed them, we're good together. I can't screw that up.

Ellie sighs in her sleep, one leg sliding up mine until her knee rests above my thigh. Maybe it's her breathing: slow and deliberate. Or maybe it's the weight of her: warm and firm. But for the first time since I've come home, I actually sleep.

CHAPTER 24 | Ellie

This early in the morning, Jacks or Better is almost magical. It's how the sunrise slants pink and gold across the fields, how I can ride Beckon past a herd of deer and they don't run away, how everything is quiet. It gives me plenty of time to think, my thoughts straying from the upcoming competition to Caleb to the chores I need to do.

And then return to Caleb.

I'd slipped out of his bed just as the light edged around his window. He'd briefly stirred, but fallen back asleep almost immediately. I wasn't surprised. Even while resting, Caleb had looked exhausted. His face was pale and there were half-moon shadows under his eyes.

It hadn't surprised me really. He'd been pushing as hard as I had been—harder—but I can't shake the memory. I squeeze my calves against Beckon and we move into a swift canter, slicing across the lower field.

I wish I *wouldn't* think about Caleb. After last night, I was expecting to feel, I don't know, guilty or relaxed or proud for being so bold, but I don't.

If anything, I want to do it again because that edge? It isn't gone. It's sharper.

We cross the dirt road in two huge strides. Beneath me, Beckon tenses and rattles her bit, sensing my distraction. I force myself to breathe, to focus. Horses read their riders frighteningly well. They know when we're scared, when we're happy. A trainer once told me, "the worst ones will take advantage, but the best sense our dreams and take us to them." I think he's right. Beckon knows I'm somewhere else today.

I angle us along the tree line, checking the timer on my watch before settling in for our gallop. "Six minutes, my love," I tell the mare.

She tosses her head like she already knows, playing with the bit, eager to get going. The timer beeps and Beckon surges forward, galloping up the tree line.

I knot my fingers into her mane and hold on. We do trot and gallop sets twice a week to build her stamina and it shows. The mare's barely broken a sweat by the time our six minutes finishes and I pull her up to check her heartrate and breathing.

"You're spot on," I say and Beckon's ears swivel back toward me.

Even when she's *not* spot on, Beckon still thinks she's perfect. The mare's arrogance is one of the things I like best about her. She knows she's good. I smile and pat her shoulder. "Next set," I say, squeezing my calves against her sides.

We spend the next twenty minutes working in silence. There's only my breath and Beckon's hoof beats as we work our way around the farm's perimeter. The grass galloping track runs between the tree line and the paddocks, arcing us gently back toward the barn. A couple of the young horses play alongside us in their paddocks, but Beckon ignores them. The track slopes up as my watch timer goes off again, and I slow the mare to a walk. By the time we reach the barn, she'll be cool and ready for a bath.

We cross the gravel lane that leads into the woods, and glide through the grass toward the barn. The roof and towers cast uneven shadows, dipping most of the entrance into dark, but I can still see someone standing by a pillar, waiting.

Caleb.

Beckon's head snaps up, watching him as he steps away from the shadows. She dances for a few strides, trying to decide if she's going to spook, and I briefly wonder if she'll dump me in a heap at Caleb's feet. It would almost be funny.

Almost.

Then he steps into the pink morning sunshine and glares at me in a way that kinda makes me want to run for the hills. But *really* makes me want to get closer.

I'm going to have to make a decision about Mrs. Mar's offer. Soon too. It's the professional thing to do.

So why does it feel weird? Almost like I would be making a mistake?

I stop Beckon at the barn entrance and slide down, taking a moment to adjust my stirrups and loosen the girth and pretend my hands aren't already trembling.

And ready for him.

Caleb scrapes up next to me, boots heavy against the gravel. He crosses his arms and continues his glower. Except his eyes keep dropping to my mouth. Is he working up to say something?

Or kiss me?

My stomach twirls. "Morning!"

His eyes flick up, meeting mine. "What changed?" he asks at last. "You're different."

I roll my eyes and lead Beckon into the barn. "How many times do I have to tell you—"

"I'm not talking about the club." He catches up and falls into stride next to me. "I'm talking about last night. You're different. What's up?"

I walk Beckon into the closest wash stall as the most curious shiver climbs my spine. He doesn't know about the job offer and he certainly doesn't know about Holly advising me to jump him, but he can tell I made a decision about it. It's funny too because I felt the difference in me as well.

I just wouldn't have expected Caleb to see it, and I'm not sure what to think about that. I focus on Beckon instead, slipping off her bridle and slipping on her halter. Caleb steps in to help, unbuckling my girth and putting the saddle on a nearby rack. For several minutes, we work in silence.

"Ellie?" he prompts.

I take a deep breath, ignoring the pinch in my chest. I'm so nervous. "I've been offered another position."

Caleb blinks, twitching like he's taken an off step even though he hasn't moved. "Adele Mar," he says at last, putting it together.

I nod.

He whistles low. "That would be...amazing for you."

"I—" My shoulders relax. I didn't even realize I was holding them so tightly. What had I been expecting? Anger? Resentment? Yes, either—both—but he understands and it makes me so damn grateful.

"It would be amazing," I finally manage, turning on the hose so I can rinse Beckon. "I wouldn't leave until after the Grand Prix—and please believe I will still be giving you everything."

The corner of his mouth spasms and my face goes hot. "I didn't mean like that. I meant with Beckon and the farm and—"

"I know." He grins at me like we're sharing the same inside joke. It makes my insides even hotter than my cheeks. "And I know you wouldn't let anything slide. It isn't like you."

My face goes even hotter. I concentrate on rinsing away every last bit of sweat from Beckon's coat so I don't have to look at him, but even so, I can feel him watching me. "What is it? I can tell you're thinking."

"I don't know if I should tell you now."

I glance up, confused. Caleb's only a few feet away, looking as broody and gorgeous as ever, but there's something more there too. Something in his eyes I can't name.

"I wanted to offer you a job here," he says at last.

"I have a job here."

"A different sort of job—a partnership, not an employee position."

"That would be..." Amazing. Wonderful.

Incredibly tricky.

I frown and Caleb nods. "Exactly," he says, beginning to pace back and forth in long, ground eating strides. "The way I see it, we can't have both. Either you work with me and we're hands off, or you work for Mrs. Mar and..."

"And I have you whenever I want?"

Bold move, I think, barely able to believe I said it. Caleb's struggling too. My question made him stutter step and I realize delightedly it's because I've turned him on again. He stares at me like he wants to strip me naked and I like it.

Love it. I tremble. It's the power making me bold. It's the way he makes me feel. Like I could conquer the world.

"Is that what you want?" he asks at last. "To...have me whenever you want?"

"Yes." There, I said it. My face still burns up though and I turn off the hose, focusing on drying off Beckon so I don't have to watch how the admission hits Caleb. Will he be excited? Turned off?

Ugh, please don't let him be turned off. After last night, I was supposed to be satisfied and I'm not. I want him again. I grab a fluffy towel from Beckon's kit and kneel, rubbing the cloth up and down each of her legs until the skin is damp and no longer soaked.

"If we continue like this," Caleb says quietly, "people will make assumptions."

I nod. I know they will, and I also know this is the part where I'm supposed to say I don't care what other people think.

To a degree, that's true. But the horse world is small around here and even if *I* don't judge someone for sleeping around, other people do. It could hurt my reputation. My wins should be enough for clients, but it's always more complicated than that.

And Caleb knows it. Even more, he's looking out for me. It's another unexpected side of him and I almost don't know what to say.

"I understand if you want to join Mrs. Mar's team. She's everything we want to be here." Sunlight forks through the skylights, catching in his hair and on his hands. "It would be huge for you."

I frown. There isn't even any animosity in his voice and now I *really* don't know what to say. Just when I think I have Caleb Reese all figured he out, he does this stuff.

Beckon paws the concrete, impatient to get going. Now that she's clean, she wants to be fed breakfast. I might be making the biggest career decision of my life, but as far as my girl is concerned, it's still all about Becks.

"Yes, yes, Your Highness," I mutter, snapping on her lead rope. The mare jigs along next to me as we head for her stall. Caleb follows up behind, watching silently as I check Beckon over one last time. She's in great shape, no nicks or cuts after the ride, and I give her one last pat before letting myself out of her stall.

Caleb's so close, I brush right past him. He catches my arm and chills rush across my skin.

"I know we both *want* to keep doing this," he whispers. "But *should* we keep doing it?"

"Guess it depends on what you have in mind to keep doing?" I throw him a teasing smile, and Caleb's eyes brighten. He pushes into me and I smile wider. *This* is footing I'm more secure on. *This* is what I want.

"What would you like me to do?" he asks.

Let me climb on top and grind on you, I think, biting down a whimper. *Pin me to the wall and take me hard. Anything. Everything.*

And now Caleb's smiling even wider, like he knows what I'm thinking, like he wants to give it to me. His hands run up my forearms, meet my elbows and grip. He turns me around, pulling me back against him, my shoulder blades into his chest, my backside into his hips. "Because you know what I would like to do?" he breathes. "I want to bend you over and take you from behind. I want to make you beg."

I whimper. I can't help it. The idea of my hips being pinned as he enters me nearly undoes me.

"Sounds like you're begging already," Caleb whispers.

"Sounds like you love it."

His laugh is low, curling against the back of my neck.

I rub my ass against his dick, feeling it harden even more. My knees go a little weak. "Feels like you love it too," I add.

Another laugh. "You're right." He takes a deep, deep breath, his chest brushing my shoulder blades. "So I guess this is your answer? You're leaving?"

Answering him feels impossible. Maybe it's because he's holding me like this, or maybe it's because the farm is laid out beneath us, morning fog making it look magical. I take my own deep breath. "Yeah, I'm leaving. Consider this my two week notice."

CHAPTER 25 | Caleb

I knew it was coming and it *still* almost knocked me on my ass. She's leaving. A huge part of me understands, even applauds her. It's a huge opportunity. I love watching her rise to it. There's nothing sexier than Ellie Lenox squaring up in front of a challenge.

No. Strike that. Ellie Lenox peeking at me from over her shoulder while begging to be taken from behind is definitely sexier.

Too bad I couldn't take her up on the offer. Not even two seconds after she told me she was leaving, Danny drove up. Thank God for knocking truck engines because we would've been totally busted. Instead, Danny walked in on two people having a conversation outside Beckon's stall.

After a few minutes of small talk, Danny wanders down to check on his horses and Ellie sneaks a glance at me. "How do we want to handle this? Should I wait to tell everyone?"

"No way. This is a great opportunity. Tell them whenever you want."

Her smile's so damn grateful I have to turn away. I mean, *yeah*, I'm glad she's taking the chance on Mar's offer. But there's still another huge part of me that wishes she'd stay. It's the same part that doesn't care if people whisper about us. We make a great team.

In more ways than one, I realize. The idea pastes me to the floor. *She wouldn't just be a good business partner. She would be an amazing...*

I don't let myself finish the thought. She'll go her way, I'll go mine, and this thing between us will eventually die. It's safer that way. Better. We would've been good together. Maybe even great. But we would've eventually crashed and burned. Sneaking around would only get us caught and no one survives the kind of scrutiny we'd get if we let everything out in the open. The whispers, the rumors, I don't want that stuff around me anymore.

"See you around," Ellie says, already striding toward her next ride. The brown gelding hangs his head over the stall, happy to see her.

"Yeah, see you." I sound like it's no big deal, but I can't stop myself from watching her go. Yeah, this is definitely for the best.

CHAPTER 26 | Ellie

I finish my last rides right before lunch, and briefly, I think about inviting Caleb out for a sandwich or something, but he's already gone.

"He's somewhere on the property," Sam says as he helps Tomas shovel Grace's stall. "Don't know exactly where. Why?"

"Thought I'd start going over what he'll need to look for in their next rider." It feels *so* weird to say. "I can catch up with him later."

Sam nods, smiling. He's been smiling ever since I pitched the idea of us leaving for Adele Mar's team. He likes the farm, even gets along with the Colonel way better than most people, but I think he's been ready for a change. Or maybe he just couldn't resist the opportunity. Either way, Sam's on board. It's a huge relief.

"I'm going to go return my dress to Holly," I tell him. "I'll be back after lunch. You need anything before I go, Tomas?"

"Gatorade. I'm dying."

I grin. "You got it."

About thirty minutes later, I hurry up Holly's front step, purse and dress bag in tow. She opens the door before I even have a chance to knock, sweeping me into a huge hug.

"Hey! Mama's lying down," she whispers, pulling me inside. "We have to be quiet."

I tense. "Is she having another bad day?"

"Hard to say. I think she's just tired." Holly's tone is bright as ever, but worry creases her mouth. She takes the dress bag from me and hangs it on the foyer's coat rack—alongside two ancient raincoats, a fur cape, and some sort of Venetian mask.

"Ignore the mess," she says, waving one hand at the piles of fabrics lying around the room. To anyone who doesn't know Holly, it looks like a fabric shop threw up, but I know she's studying the color and pattern combinations, putting them in sunlight and shadows to see how they look.

I step carefully around a stunning rose pink silk piled on top of an army green damask and nearly collide with a stack of teal saris. There's definitely a method to Holly's madness, but it doesn't mean the method isn't also a tripping hazard.

She swings into the kitchen and grabs two bottled waters for us before walking out to the back porch. No polo games today, but a couple of people are riding in the distance. A humid breeze carries their laughter.

Holly flings herself onto a chaise lounge and cracks open her water. "Why didn't you call me last night? I wanted to hear all about how my dress slayed the party."

I grin. "Your dress totally slayed at the party. I got so many compliments. Seriously, Holls. You made me look amazing."

Holly sighs like this is only to be expected, but I can tell she's pleased. "Tell me something I don't know," she says. "Seriously though I want to hear all about it. What did people say? How did people react? And what did Mrs. Wesley end up serving because I heard her caterer quit at the last minute and—" Holly's cell vibrates, skittering around on the coffee table as a text message comes through. She picks up the phone and studies the screen with a frown.

"Everything okay?" I ask.

"Yeah, it's just Scott."

I pause. Scott is none other than Scott Ricio, a designer who's worked for everyone from Ralph Lauren to Alexander McQueen. He's enormously brilliant and a huge asshole and was Holly's boss for four years while she studied in New York.

"What's he want?" I ask, tamping down a sudden flare of panic. Scott's been after Holly to come back pretty much ever since she climbed on the plane to Atlanta. "Is he still pressuring you to come back?"

"Yeah." She flips the phone onto the coffee table and scowls at it. "He's gone from promising me the moon to predicting I die poor, alone, and unfashionable."

It would be funny if Holly didn't look so despondent about the idea. The cell goes off again with another text message and she slumps lower on the couch.

"You could never be unfashionable," I say. It's true too. Today, Holly's paired a gorgeous white pencil skirt patterned in delicate blue vines and flowers with a vintage Rolling Stones T-shirt. Her pale hair is loose, swirling around large hoop earrings she bought on a trip to South America. It's the perfect mix of high end and casual and it's classic Holly.

"I mean look at you," I continue, "you're working from home and you still look amazing."

She smiles at my compliment, but her eyes stay trained on the cell. There's something wistful in her expression.

"Holls, do you ever think about going back to New York?"

"No."

"Why not? Because of your mom?"

"Sort of."

I frown. Holly is never this cagey. Usually she's the definition of an over-sharer and I almost don't know what to say. Then Caleb's point about me going with Wren to Paris and sharing what you love with the people you love comes back to me. "What if we figured out a way for your mom to come with you?"

She shakes her head, blonde hair swishing around her shoulders. "Not a good idea. No way could I afford a place with an elevator and she doesn't do well with stairs and..."

"And what?"

"And I can't do it."

"I've never known you to back down from anything."

"It's not backing down." Holly blows her bangs out of her eyes. "It's more like realizing what you want. I go back to New York, I will be designing clothes for tall, thin women."

"Well, yeah."

"Models represent, like, less than one percent of the female population, but we use them as representative of all women. I don't want to do that."

"Oh," I say, finally catching up. "You want to design for normal women."

Her face screws up like she's tasted something sour. "Except I hate looking at it like that. You're normal—and the thing is, those models are normal too. I mean, don't get me wrong, I met a lot who had eating disorders because of the industry's expectations, but I knew a lot who were also just naturally tall and thin. I'm tired of expressions like 'real women have curves' because models are real women too."

"Holls? The point?"

"My point is New York refuses to design clothes for average sized women and if I go back, I'll be designing for models." Holly takes a deep, deep breath before her gaze meets mine. I don't know that I've ever seen her so serious. "But the rest of us deserve pretty, flattering clothes too. I want to design for women who are beyond a size 2."

"Did you tell Scott?"

"Oh, yes." As if to underscore her point, the phone vibrates again with another text message. "Hence his dire predictions."

"I'm sorry."

Her blue eyes flick up. "Don't be. I worked for that asshole for years and it was worth it. He showed me what I don't want to do and *definitely* who I don't want to be. I'm not going back to New York. I make it here or I don't make it at all."

"How can I help?"

She gives me a tiny smile. "Listen to me whine?"

"Goes without saying." I pause. "You know you can do this, right? If anyone can pull it off, it'll be you."

"There's more to it than that. I need financial backing, exposure, the right production team..." She groans. "Everyone thinks fashion is such a dream job, and parts of it are crazy amazing, but it's still tough. So many moving pieces. So many people you have to prove yourself to."

"Yeah, horses are the same way."

Holly sighs. "At least my clients don't try to bite me. Or kick me. Or—"

"I get the point."

Another dramatic sigh. "Why couldn't we be normal girls who have normal jobs?"

"Lucky, I guess." I pick at the pillow's tassel as her phone goes off again.

"OhmyGod!" Holly leaps to her feet. "If I have to put up with him, we're going to have a drink. Can you stay for dinner? I'm making baked chicken."

Cereal at my place or baked chicken at Holly's? That's a no-brainer. "I would love to, but I can't. I'm supposed to be back at the farm for the afternoon."

"Ugh, fine. We can just have lunch. Work interferes with everything, you know that?"

I grin, flinging myself into the chaise cushions as she disappears inside. Above me, the overgrown pecan trees sway in the breeze, scattering sunlight like gold coins over my hands and legs.

Holly comes back out carrying her favorite blue painted tray. It's loaded with snacks, champagne flutes, and a huge glass pitcher.

"Lemonade," she says, handing me a fluted glass. "It makes it fancier this way."

We clink glasses and I take a drink. It's lovely. If sunshine had a taste, it would be this. My mouth tastes like sweetened lemons and my blood is already buzzing because I know what I'm about to say. "I took your advice," I tell her.

Holly glances at me in confusion before her eyes bug. "You *slept* with him? So that's why you look so relaxed! I want to hear every detail!" She bounces down next to me and for a second, we're in high school all over again. "Seriously. Every. Detail."

I laugh. "You are so twelve, you know that?"

"Whatever. I was right. You needed this."

"Maybe."

"'Maybe?'" Holly cocks her head. "What is it?"

I look down at the pillow, tugging at the tassels. "It's just not what I expected."

"What do you mean?"

I take a deep breath. Am I really going to say this? For all of five seconds, I can't decide. Yes, this is Holly and I tell her everything, but it's also this thing between Caleb and me. "I think I like him. We...connected or whatever at the party. He's not a jerk—not completely anyway." I grin at Holly expecting her to grin back, but she doesn't. Her eyes are shiny with worry. She leans back against the chaise cushions and waits for me to finish.

"He's driven," I add, thinking over all the things I've noticed about Caleb. "He's uptight and he wants to prove himself and he gets in his own way because he wants it so badly."

Holly nods slowly. "He has an amazing smile." She grimaces. "When he chooses to exercise it."

That makes me smile. Holly's trying to see him as I see him. "And he has an amazing laugh—when he chooses to exercise it."

"And he has great taste in horses. All the time."

I look at Holly and feel like everything inside me funnels to a single point. "He touches me like I matter."

We go quiet because even though the words are small, Holly knows just how much it cost me to say that. "You do matter," she whispers at last.

"I know, but it's been a long time since I've been with a guy who agrees. Remember James the Gigantic Tool?"

She looks like she's stifling a gag. "Quite well."

"He's calling again." I'd been meaning to tell Holly for ages, but between Grace getting sick and the party, I didn't have time. "I'm ignoring him, of course."

"Good." Holly goes quiet, eyes still huge.

"It's a lot to take in, isn't it?"

"No kidding! I mean..." She hesitates. "Do you really think this thing with Caleb is..."

More than what it is? Special? "It's something," I say at last. "But I can't see it going anywhere. I don't want more with him."

Except as soon as I say it, I realize I think I kind of sort of do.

I swallow. "He made me feel like I was the most beautiful woman he'd ever seen—let alone touched."

Holly's eyes go even wider, and for a long time we sit quietly, watching the riders canter long, lazy circles in the distance. "I don't want you to get hurt," Holly says suddenly.

"I don't want to get hurt either."

"I don't want you to miss out on the real deal either. I want you to have what Wren has."

"We don't know Wren has the real—"

Holly shoots me a death look and I fall silent. "Yes, fine, I agree Tate is amazing, but trust takes time."

Holly rolls her eyes. "You seem to be trusting Caleb pretty fast."

I start to argue and stop. She's right. Oh my God, she's right. "We're alike," I say at last.

She arches one brow and reaches forward to take away my drink. I scowl and hold it out of reach. "I'm not drunk. It's true. We're both crazy about horses and riding and making the farm something wonderful. I get him."

"I'm not sure if I should feel sorry for you or for him"

"You're not funny."

"Meh, it was kinda funny." She pauses. "So what are you going to do?"

"About what? Caleb or Mrs. Mar?"

"Both. Either." She thinks about it. "Both."

"I'd be crazy not to take the job. She's launched so many successful riders."

"But?"

"But Caleb offered me a partnership and I've put so much time into Jacks or Better. It feels like where I belong. It's the closest thing I've had to home since...well, home."

Holly nods, but when she bites her lower lip I know she's about to say something that will hurt.

And yet I know I'll need to hear it. "Elle, the farm might feel like home, but it belongs to someone else—and so does Beckon. I'm scared if you pass up on Mrs. Mar's offer, you'll be passing up on something good for you and let's face it, you've been good for the Reeses and look how the Colonel treated you."

I nod, miserable as my dad's advice never to fall in love with things that don't belong to you comes back to me and then to make matters even more miserable, Caleb's words come back to me about the ugliness underneath the horse world. I might have helped make Jacks or Better's name, but it isn't my farm, and I might have made Beckon into the jumper she is today, but she doesn't belong to me. Everything I love can be taken away. Usually, I try not to think about it, but now I can't stop.

I wonder if this was always my destiny. I can't stop putting my heart into everything I do.

CHAPTER 27 | Caleb

As everyone expected, Echo passed his vet check with flying colors. The Davises were thrilled and wanted him delivered right away. Since their home barn was in Virginia, we arranged for professional transport. This was great because it meant I didn't waste a full day driving back and forth, but it was annoying too because the driver was running late after getting lost on the Atlanta perimeter and I had to spend thirty minutes on the phone with him, trying to figure out where the hell he was.

After hanging up and muttering about some people going through their elbows to get to their assholes, I went to find Ellie. She was in Echo's stall, preparing him for trailer ride. Some people prefer for their horses to travel with bare legs. Others wants padded bandages and lightweight blankets to protect them. The Davises belonged to the latter group and Ellie was carefully wrapping the gelding's legs with fluffy pads.

"Hey." I lean over the stall door and Echo gives me a sniff. "Morning, old man," I say, unwrapping a peppermint and giving it to him. While he crunches it, I look at Ellie. "Driver's running late. He got lost."

"How late?"

"About thirty minutes."

She frowns, finishes off the last bandage and stands up. "Do you have time to hang out until he's here? I'd rather have another witness while we load up."

I nod. It's a good idea. Weird—and sometimes horrible—things happen during transport. Horses panic and hurt themselves. Humans do something stupid and hurt themselves. I would rather have another staff member on hand in case it turns into Ellie's word against the driver's if something happens. "Yeah, sure," I say. "Coffee?"

158

For a heartbeat, she looks like she's going to say no then she smiles. "I never turn down caffeine."

We walk down to the tack room together and I pour both of us a cup. It's bitter after having been sitting in the pot for hours, but it's better than nothing. I kick out a chair and drop into it, watching Ellie from the corner of my eye. It's not even lunchtime and she's already ridden four horses.

All that time crammed under her helmet has left her deep brown hair wet with sweat, but she's twisted into a loose knot on top of her head, making the whole thing look effortless instead of bedraggled. Her polo's unbuttoned, revealing a hint of cleavage, and of course, she's also wearing breeches. The pale gray fabric hugs every single one of her curves.

"Did you lose something, Caleb?" Ellie asks sweetly as she sits down on the next stop. She swings her legs back and forth and eyes me in a way that goes straight to my dick.

I shift, suddenly uncomfortable. "How did you and the Colonel start working together?" I ask.

She blinks. "Oh. Well, I needed horses to ride and he had horses that needing riding. You know how it goes."

Well, yes, I do, but there's more to it, I think, staying quiet to draw the explanation out of her. The tack room's air conditioning kicks on as Ellie fidgets. She picks at her cuticles, the seam of her breeches, and finally huffs in exasperation.

"My parents died in a car accident," she explains quietly, eyes distant and glassy like she's living it all over again. "Without them, we couldn't keep our farm going. We had to sell the horses, the property. I had always known I wanted to go pro, but after they died, I knew I couldn't wait any longer. Wren was still in college and her degree meant everything to her. I couldn't ask her to quit so I had to make money. Fast. I declared professional status and started reaching out to the best barns I knew. In the end, your dad called me. He said he wanted to give me the chance to prove myself."

Huh. I concentrate on my coffee. Pretty story. Insert winning Olympic gold and she could be a Lifetime movie. "Did he know about your situation before he hired you?"

Ellie frowns. "I'm sure. Everybody did. I'd like to say that wasn't the reason he asked me to take over his rides, but I'm pretty sure it was a big factor." Her voice skews up in defensiveness: "I earned my keep later though. I sold all four of his jumpers by the fall. We were doing pretty brisk business within a year."

"I know. I saw the financials. Even more impressive considering how young you were."

Her frown deepens. "I didn't feel that young. Wren was barely nineteen when our parents died. She would've given up everything to take care of me, but I couldn't let her."

"So you made it work."

"Don't feel sorry for me."

"I don't." I sound totally honest too, but Ellie gives me a look like she knows I'm lying. It makes the back of my skull prickle.

"Sometimes the best way to learn to fly is by falling," she says.

"That's..." Scary. Reckless. *Probably the bravest thing I've ever heard,* I realize. I couldn't do that. Leaps of faith are not my thing. I believe in planning, drive, more planning. I can't imagine hurling myself toward what I want and trusting I would stick the landing.

It's amazing that she did, I think.

Ellie shivers a little like the past has brushed too close for comfort. "Anyway. Here we are and we're in one piece." She glances at me, something calculating in her expression. "You don't get along with the Colonel much, do you?"

I stiffen. "You're swift."

"And you're an ass."

I pause, shake myself—just talking about the Colonel makes my shoulders tense. "Yeah, I deserved that. Sorry." I take a sip of coffee and try again: "No, we don't get along. The guy you're describing? I can't even reconcile that with the man I know."

Ellie nods slowly. "Sometimes it's like that. You can't see the side of the Colonel I do. I can't see the side of him you do."

I give her a long, *long* look.

"Okay, yeah," she amends, "I can see that side. He was perfectly ready to fire me if you could find someone who could do a better job, *but* he gave me an opportunity—a huge opportunity—and I made good on that for him."

Yeah, you did, I think, my tinge of admiration turning into something more. She would've been just seventeen when she came to work for him. Talk about pressure. The learning curve would've been huge. Even with Sam coming to help out, she would've been held responsible for everything. I don't know a ton of twenty-five year olds who could do that, let alone teenagers.

I pause. I really like that about her. In fact, I really like...her. It's more than just Ellie's amazing body and gorgeous smile, I admire *her*. I can't remember the last time I was with a woman I admired. She isn't just better than me. She's embarrassingly better than me.

And the realization actually makes me grin.

"So." Her tone goes serious and I feel my grin vanish. "I have a very important question to ask."

"Yeah?" I ask. She gives me a sudden, eager smile and it goes straight to my dick. *As usual*, I think, making a mental note about how I should probably always wear my loosest pants when I'm around Ellie. "What's your very important question?"

"What was Ireland like?"

I laugh. "Amazing. I think it's one of my favorite places in the world. They live for their horses. It's a way different culture than here.

The public is more knowledgeable. A lot of people have grown up riding. Makes a huge difference in how the industry is perceived."

"You mean it isn't seen as a bunch of uptight, rich traditionalists who prance around?"

Now we're both laughing. "Isn't that a bit hypocritical coming from someone who rides a horse insured for a cool million?" In fact, if Beckon wins her first Grand Prix she'll be worth even more. It's kind of frightening to think about.

"It isn't hypocritical," Ellie tells me, glancing at the wall clock. We probably have another few minutes before the driver arrives, but she still slides to her feet, ready to go. "It's honest. You have to see things for what they really are—the good and the bad." She hesitates, huge brown eyes going large and shining. "Why don't you and the Colonel get along?"

"Happens in families sometimes. My mom was the glue that held us together. Now that she's gone..."

"But you came back."

"Because Jacks or Better is everything to me."

She nods, and I realize with a sickening pang that she gets it. She gets *me*. Chills climb my spine. I'm not sure what to do about that.

"Gotta make a call before the driver arrives," I say suddenly, standing up and putting my coffee cup in the sink. I don't have a call, but I need a moment. Maybe more than a moment. "I'll see you in a few."

"Sure." Ellie strolls back outside, and needing to move, I follow. She goes right. I go left. I tell myself I can spend the afternoon checking the north pastures and afterward, I can check the east pastures. Busy would be good for me right now. Really busy would be even better.

I reach the stable's double doors and snatch a glance back. Ellie's gone, but I feel her warmth like she's lingering at my side.

CHAPTER 28 | Ellie

The next day, I have barely enough time to finish putting away Beckon before Holly pulls in, ready to pick Wren and me up for the wedding shop appointment. She angles her vintage orange Bronco in next to the farm trucks and jumps out, looking like a million bucks in a tight mini skirt and loose tank. Her blond hair looks almost white in the sunlight.

"Coming!" I yell to her, running up from Beckon's paddock. My boots crunch across the gravel parking lot. "Like five minutes! I swear!"

"Dude." She pulls her tortoise shell sunglasses halfway down her nose to eye me. "You better take longer than five minutes. I am not spending all day with you when you smell like a goat." She takes a whiff of me and makes a face. "A dead goat."

"I feel a tackle hug coming on, Holls."

Her blue eyes go wide as saucers. "Don't you dare!"

"I can't help it! I feel it coming on!"

She shrieks and I feint grabbing her a few times, laughing so hard my stomach hurts. Then Holly pulls up straight, eyeing someone behind me. "Oh, hello Caleb Reese, I thought we weren't going to meet again."

Cheeks flaming, I turn around, ready for him to blast me for more unprofessionalism, but Caleb actually looks embarrassed. He rubs the back of his head. "Yeah, sorry about that, Holly. I was out of line." His eyes flick to me and I hate it but my cheeks go even hotter. Ever since we slept together, my body responds to him like it's starved. "Have a good day off," he says and hops into one of the work trucks, pulling out before I can think of anything to say.

"I could roast marshmallows on your face right now," Holly mutters.

"One more comment like that and I *will* tackle hug you."

She smirks and puts her sunglasses back on. "Hurry up or I won't be able to stop myself."

***

Thanks to surprisingly light traffic and Holly's lead right foot, we aren't even late to Wren's appointment. Although we are a bit windblown. I take a couple minutes to untangle my hair before following Holly and Wren inside. The boutique is fabulously cool and smells faintly of floral perfume. I take a deep breath and briefly wonder why on earth I chose a job where it's always hot and it *never* smells like perfume.

"Hello ladies!" One of the saleswomen steps forward. Against the boutique's pastel and spare backdrop, her navy suit stands out like a slash. The diamonds around her neck are huge and her heels give Holly's a run for their money. "I'm thinking tulle!" she says, beaming. "I'm thinking cream lace and silver accents!"

I smile. And *that* would be the reason I couldn't work somewhere like here. I don't think I've ever thought of tulle anything. The saleswoman leads us through the store to the private viewing room. Back here, it's all about opulence and comfort. There's a huge curved back velvet couch surrounded by coordinating chairs. High end magazines are stacked on the coffee table and the shop owner has already poured champagne.

"Look at bridesmaid dresses," Wren tells me before disappearing into the dressing room. "I want you to have something you like," she shouts.

The shop attendant frowns and I stuff down my giggle. If she thinks we're going to be demure or whatever, she's in for a rude awakening.

"Less talking. More dresses," Holly says, breaking out her camera and notepad. She's wearing her highest heels and is ready to camp out all day if that's what it takes. I'm just glad to be away from the farm—which isn't usually like me. I blame Caleb.

"Bridesmaid dresses through here?" I ask the attendant and she nods. I wander closer to the dress racks and start my search. *Gorgeous stuff*, I think, fingering a stunning lace sheath with some sort of draped bodice, *not as pretty as what Holly can do though.*

My cell vibrates with an incoming call and without thinking, I answer it. "This is Ellie!"

"This is James!"

My skin prickles. Even if he hadn't identified himself, I would know that mocking tone anywhere. James the Gigantic Tool. Six months of him giving me the silent treatment and now he's back. "What do you want?"

"Aww, Ellie, don't be like that." I turn, facing another rack of pastel dresses. I concentrate on their lace trim and satin sashes, but it doesn't distract me. I can still see his gorgeous face, picture exactly how he's amused because I'm still mad. It always made me feel so small and inconsequential. "I missed you! I want us to be friends again."

"Ellie?" Holly joins me at the dress rack brows in a what-the-hell gesture. She has huge veils draped over both arms and is struggling to keep them off the floor. "You okay?"

I shake my head. "Seriously, *James*, what do you want?" I ask him and Holly's expression goes stony.

"Give me the phone," she says through gritted teeth.

Ah, negative on that one, I think and quickly back up. Holly's been dying to give James a piece of her mind and her stiletto up his ass. If I pass her the phone, she will swear a blue streak at him and all of us will get thrown out of here.

"Holly there?" James says breezily. Technically, James always sounds breezy, in control, confident. It's one of the things I really liked about him and it takes me back to months ago when we were together. "I can tell she is from the way you say my name. Did you even *try* to tell her my side of the story?"

"What would that be? You cheated."

"But the rest of the time we were really good together."

"I'm hanging up now." Only I'm not. I can't seem to bring myself to. My brain is stuck on how sometimes we *were* good together. Sometimes I dared to let myself think he might be The One.

James laughs. "Face it, Ellie, you're not over me. I'll call you later." He hangs up and my face goes nuclear. He beat me to it. I *let* him beat me to it. Why do I always do that?

Because when it comes to him, you make terrible *decisions*, I think, scowling. Holly eases her arm around my shoulders, trying (and failing) to keep from crushing the delicate veils.

Furious tears sting my eyes as the dressing room curtains part. Wren steps out, voluminous white skirt whispering around her legs. The dress was lovely on the mannequin, but looks even more beautiful on my sister. The gauzy skirt is balanced with a fitted long-sleeved lace top that dips just low enough to show the sweep of her collar bone and a hint of cleavage. She's paired it with a thin jeweled belt and a white veil and it's so perfect I forget all about James.

"Wow!" Holly whistles low. "That is *stunning*!"

"Agreed!" I wipe a tear from the corner of my eye as Wren does a small circle, showing us the whole look. "It's my favorite."

She laughs. "It's only the first one I've tried."

"Still my favorite."

"Hard to improve on perfection, Wren." Holly drops into the closest chair and helps herself to the champagne the attendant poured for us. "Your figure is meant for that kind of cut." Holly then goes on to explain in agonizing detail why that dress works and how the boutique's seamstress will need to tweak a few details. It would be easy to say she's just caught up in the excitement—and she is—but I also know she's giving me a few minutes to get myself together. This is Wren's moment. I will *not* screw it up.

"Actually," Holly says, hopping to her feet. "Let's go ahead and get their seamstress in here now. I want to talk about alterations and turn-around times." She strides out of the dressing room like she's on a mission and Wren grins at me.

"That poor woman."

"I know, right?"

"Is everything okay?" Wren studies me, concern wrinkling her brows. I could tell her. She would be suitably enraged and we could spend the next two hours plotting all the horrible things that should happen to James, but that would turn the day into mine and I want all of this to be about her.

"It's nothing," I say, grinning at her. "You look so beautiful. I'm so happy for you."

CHAPTER 29 | Ellie

Holly drops me off at Jacks or Better just before dinner. The farm's quiet. The guys are gone and most of the horses are already out in their paddocks, enjoying the break from the heat of the day. I watch two of the foals play together and feel my shoulders unlock inch by inch.

Freaking James. He has that effect on me.

Luckily, Jacks or Better has an effect on me too. I take a deep breath of cut grass and horse and home and know I'm going to miss this.

And because James ruins everything, my cell goes off again. I check the screen. Yep, it's him. I send him to voicemail and tell myself it doesn't matter, but I can't shake the irritation.

Maybe I'm not over him?

It can't be true, but then again he can play my emotions whenever he wants, twist everything around so it's my fault. It is not my fault he cheated. It is not my fault my job was intense and I couldn't see him as much. He chose to cheat. I didn't drive him to it.

So why am I still so angry?

I pocket my phone and stomp through the silent barn, hearing Caleb's voice seconds before I open the tack room door. He's on the phone, long legs stretched out in front of him, twirling a pencil around and around in those long, elegant fingers.

He really is gorgeous and when he smiles at me, my whole body clenches. I'm angry. I'm worried. I want...to climb out of myself. He's a distraction I could use. He's a distraction I *need* to use. I just have to find the words.

"Earth to Ellie? Hello?" His smile is half mocking, half promise. I was so tied up in thinking about him, I missed him actually talking to me.

I smile. *All you have to do is tell him what you want*, I think, mouth going dry.

What you need.

"Come have dinner with me?" I ask suddenly.

He points to the phone. "Give me ten minutes."

"Sure," I say, looking him up and down. I grin. "I'm going to shower first."

"I'll be there in five."

In the end, it's almost twenty minutes before I hear the apartment door open. I'm already showered, bare feet, damp hair, and standing in the kitchen. *I hope he doesn't actually expect dinner*, I think, studying the nonexistent contents of my fridge, *because I don't have anything to cook.*

I turn as Caleb comes through. He stares at me like I'm some sort of revelation and I'm suddenly and stupidly shy.

"Hi," I say softly.

"Hi, beautiful," he says, crossing the space between us in a few strides. His hands cup my face, bending me back so he can take my mouth. His lips press mine, tongue edging my lower lip and begging for me to open. I can't help it. I do. I open my lips to his, sagging against him as his hands roam my hair and face, gasping as his tongue teases me.

The kiss is almost tender.

Then he lifts me onto the counter and settles himself between my legs. Another smile coasts across his mouth and it pools heat in all my joints.

Oh *my*. I clear my throat.

He smirks. "Spread your legs wider for me."

For about half a second, I consider denying him, making him work for it, but it's like my body's on autopilot now. It's *his*. My legs open, and he smiles.

"Wet for me?" His fingers play with the edge of my panties, a promise of what's to come. "I haven't been able to stop thinking about you."

"Thinking about me doing what?"

He rubs his thumb over my clit and I jump, gasp. "That." Another rub and then a circle. I'm squirming. I can't stop. "And that."

A teasing pinch, and I cry out. He soothes me with another circle and I go weak. It isn't fair how easily he plays me, but I love it. He leans in, his whisper rough in my ear. "And I definitely can't stop thinking about how you're going to moan when I take you from behind."

My stomach clenches and I go wet in a rush. I can't get my legs wide enough and I can't get his touch firm enough. My back arches, pushing my nipples toward him.

"Say it," he breathes.

"Please."

"Please what?"

"Please...suck them."

He makes a satisfied noise. "How could I not when you ask so prettily?"

I gasp again as he tugs me closer, my wet heat rubbing against him as he drags me upward. His hands find my ass, lifting until my nipples feel his breath. He balances one forearm beneath me, takes his other hand and uses just the tip of one finger to tease. I squirm, panting, *lost*.

And then he draws me into his mouth, and my head drops back. He presses me into the wall and I go boneless.

"You taste so good," he whispers against my skin. "One day, I'm going to lick and suck you as long as I like." And as if in promise, he tugs my hardened nipple into his mouth again, pulling a moan from me. "And you'll pant and beg and plead, and I'll just push you higher. Would you like that?"

"Yes! No!"

His laugh is low and dark and makes me shiver.

He sits me on the counter edge and I go for his pants, unbuckling his belt and tugging his jeans down. He's barely tugged on his condom before I have him in both hands, drawing his hard length inside me. The contact makes him hiss.

"Yes," he mutters, eyes sliding shut.

I go even damper. I'm in control. He's mine.

His thickness spreads me, stretches me. I hook one hand behind his neck and prop the other against the countertop, legs tightening around his waist. He gasps. "So hot. You're so hot."

And that makes me hotter. I move, sliding up and back down, letting his length drive me out of my mind. Faster. Harder. His hand dig into my ass, grinding my clit against him.

Close. So close. I arch against him, desperate for release.

He holds me still and I cry out. "No!"

"Yes!" There's that dark laugh again. He spins me around, pressing my back to his chest before bending me over the counter and nudging my legs apart until I'm completely exposed. Completely his.

"I want you," he whispers and the whisper crawls up my bare spine, leaves me trembling. He enters me with a single brutal thrust. My back arches, my knees buckle, and suddenly I'm only held up by his hands and the countertop's ledge. Another deliberate thrust. Another arch. I can't help myself. He's taking me exactly how he wants and all I can do is enjoy it.

"Please," I moan and I'm instantly rewarding. Caleb finds the rhythm I love and I give into him, agonizingly sensitive breasts swaying, legs gone boneless.

An orgasm rushing to the surface.

I squirm against him, desperate for it, knowing if I beg he'll tease me and I'm still unable to stop myself from crying: "Yesyesyes!"

"Mmmm," he murmurs, cock growing harder. "I do like hearing that from you. Say it again."

My pussy clenches and he groans. "You like being ordered around. Say. It. Again." Each word punctuated by a delicious thrust. I arch and squirm and cannot get away.

"Yes!"

"You want this?"

"Yes, please!" If I don't come now, I think I'll go out of my mind. I grind against his hardness and he rotates his hips, driving me higher, and then...

Hard thrust. Harder. "Come for me. *Now.*"

I do. I come in a black out rush, clenching and unclenching, unable to do anything but give into his grip and his thrusts.

"So good," he pants. "You feel amazing. Ah!" His release pushes me higher. My pussy spasms around his cock, needing more, and he gives it to me, thrusting until I'm shuddering and overly sensitive.

He holds me carefully as he pulls out, making sure I'm steady on my feet before pulling off the condom. I'm only vaguely aware of him leaning to the side to throw it away. Seconds later, his arms are around me again. He presses light kisses into my hair.

"Ellie," he breathes into the back of my neck. "Ellie."

I shiver. It's only a whisper. It scalds me like a brand.

CHAPTER 30 | Caleb

Once I'm sure Ellie can stand, I slip away from her, discarding the condom and grabbing a bottle of water from the counter. I open it, offering her a drink. Ellie takes it distractedly. Her eyes are glassy and wide. Her damp hair is tangled. I love that look on her.

I love knowing I *gave* that look to her.

"Stop smirking," she tells me, taking another swallow of water.

"No."

Pink spreads across her cheeks and she won't look at me as she passes me the bottle.

"Ah ah." I lean in close, making sure my whisper walks across her skin. "*Look* at me." More pink, but she does. Her eyes swing up to meet mine and I go hard in an instant.

"Why do you always make me do that?" she breathes.

"Because I like it—and so do you."

She grins. I grin. It turns the moment all sorts of cheesy and sexy and...more somehow. I look at Ellie and feel something snake through my chest.

You're in trouble, Reese, I think and turn away, pulling my T-shirt over my head. "What was all this about?" I ask. "Not that I'm complaining."

She hesitates. "Ex-boyfriend trouble."

"The guy who was calling you before?"

"Yeah."

"Glad I could be of service."

She smiles like I'm funny and even though I meant it to be funny and I meant for her to smile, my post-Ellie contentment fades. This didn't mean anything. It was just working off some steam. It's exactly what I wanted.

So why am I suddenly annoyed?

Silence stretches between us. "Don't look at me like that," Ellie says at last.

I stiffen. "Like *what*?"

"You're irritated."

"No, I'm not."

She spends several seconds untangling her hair with her fingers, waiting. I scowl and catch myself. She's right. Worse, she *knows* she's right. I don't really know what to do about that.

A smile pulls at her mouth. "Are you going to glower at me too?" She looks dangerously close to laughing. "Putting your hands on your hips and staring me down doesn't really work when you're..." Her gaze dips, taking in my loosened jeans. They're hanging off my hips. We'd been in a hurry. "The glowering thing doesn't really work when you're half naked," she finishes, eyes going half-lidded. She's turned on again and I grin.

"I think it's working quite well actually—or are you going to tell me you're not wet?"

She gasps, outrage making her mouth round.

"I know you are. You could admit it or..." I glance back at the countertop. Never thought I would be so happy to have a near empty kitchen at my disposal. "Or I could toss you up there again and find out for myself."

Her eyes flicker. Christ, I love how much she loves dirty talk. The possibilities of teasing her are endless.

Ellie licks her lower lip. "Are you hungry?"

I know what she means, but I still take a moment to drag my eyes up and down her. Naked Ellie is even better than Riding Pants Ellie. She's toned, but hasn't lost her curves: muscled thighs, graceful hips, and the world's most perfect breasts. The longer I stare at them, the more Ellie's nipples peak.

"Very hungry," I tell her, enjoying how she's getting more and more turned on by my stare. "What do you have?"

"What do you *want*?"

I go instantly hard. Ellie always gives as good as she gets. I might be able to make her wet with a dirty comment or dirtier look, but she can turn the tables just as easily. I study her perfect body, wondering where on earth to even begin and then realize I'll take it all. I reach for her, fisting my hand in her hair and easing her head back so she arches against me, nipples rubbing my chest.

She moans, eyes drifting closed. I'll let her. For now. "Caleb?"

"Hmmm?"

"This *is* what you wanted, right?"

For a heartbeat, I think she means something more than my mouth on her. For a heartbeat, I think I'll tell her the truth.

But when I open my mouth, all I can say is, "Of course."

CHAPTER 31 | Ellie

Sometimes, I think I could get used to using Caleb. Now that Wren's staying with Tate full time, he comes over every night. He's about as good at cooking as I am so usually he brings takeout or something his housekeeper has made him. Sometimes we finish.

Sometimes we don't.

Okay, most of the time we don't. I have a lot of tension. In some ways it's worse now that I have him regularly and in other ways it's better. Usually, Caleb leaves to crash at his place. We don't want Sam or one of the guys spotting him coming down from my apartment, but last night he fell asleep next to me. It felt so good I just...didn't wake him up to go.

No way would I admit it to anyone, but I slept great. His warmth and hardness and closeness was like a sleeping pill. I crashed hard. Sometime around five AM, he woke up anyway and slipped out.

But not before kissing my cheek.

I'm not sure what to make of that. In fact, it's almost lunchtime and I still haven't made up my mind about it. Our arrangement is starting to feel like something more and—

Sam elbows my side, bringing me back to the tack room and the sales videos I'm supposed to be watching. "Ellie?" he asks. "Are you with me? What about the colt?"

"Sorry. A lot on my mind." And none of it has to do with work. I mentally kick myself. I've got to get my head in the game.

Sam looks like he quite agrees. His bushy white eyebrows are knitted together like fuzzy, furious caterpillars and his mouth is all scrunched up.

"Let me run it back," I say, reaching for the computer mouse. We make it through the rest of the sales videos without any more interruptions, but as I'm emailing the buyer for additional information, Caleb comes in. He's in jeans and work boots and is somehow still pretty.

I stare at him as he chats with Sam, wondering how he does it. Good genes? I look like a hot mess after painting the fencing.

Caleb turns to me and smiles. "Favor to ask. I need to pick up Aiden. Drive me?"

It's something any coworker would ask, but the way Caleb asks it? Looking at me with that lowered chin and those intense blue eyes? It feels...borderline indecent. My thighs begin to tremble.

Stop it, I tell myself and give him my best Nothing To See Here Smile. "Sure thing."

I grab a set of work truck keys and we pile in. As I'm buckling my seat belt, I glance at him. "Why do you need me to drive?"

He grins. "Wanted your company."

Oh, I think. *Well, that's...*

Nice? How about kind of sort of awesome? I'm way more excited than I should be about driving to the airport. Then Caleb's hand finds my thigh and my happy excitement turns into a very different kind of excitement.

My breath dries up. Is he going to tease me while we drive? The idea is a bit alarming and quite delicious, but his fingers don't move. He's touching me just to touch me.

Like the kiss from this morning and wanting my company, I don't know what to think about that so I decide I'm going to enjoy it.

"How long have you known Aiden?" I ask.

"It's been a few years now. I think you'll like him—everybody does. He's a good guy. Just needs a chance to shine. Opportunities are hard to come by when you don't know the right people."

I nod, chest warming. I want to reach across the console and squeeze Caleb's hand. Part of this is because he's absolutely right, it *is* hard to get ahead in the horse industry unless you're well connected. The rest of it—okay most of it—is because he's kind enough to see that.

He wants to help other riders. Our earlier head-butting hadn't entirely been because of what happened in the club. He was trying to be loyal to Aiden, and keep the promises he'd made. That means a lot to me. More than I maybe realized until now.

Then Caleb launches into a rambling story about taking Aiden to look at some unbroken four-year-old in an Irish farmer's back paddock and their car's engine overheated and the four-year-old dumped Aiden and Aiden's kids scared off their babysitter, and then Caleb's laughing and I'm laughing and it feels like we make it to our exit in no time.

The Atlanta airport, Hartsfield-Jackson, is always busy. Lines of cars snake three and four deep around the pickup zones, and it takes us several minutes to wind closer. Even then, we have to linger, craning our heads to look over the crowds of people milling around on the side-walk. Someone honks behind me and I'm about to drive around the loop again when I see a tall, wiry guy stride out of the double doors like he owns the place. I've never seen Aiden Macken, but I'm guessing we've found him.

"There?" I point. Caleb takes a second to search the crowd and then nods.

"Yeah, that's Aiden," he says, glancing at me before getting out of the truck to wave down our newest rider. "How'd you know?"

"It's the build."

A scowl ghosts across Caleb's mouth.

"I don't mean like that," I say and now I'm scowling too. Why I'm defending myself? It *is* the build. Most male riders are built like swimmers, not football players. They're usually all muscle and no bulk and furthermore, I wasn't ogling Aiden

And so what if I was? I think, shoving back against my seat and flicking the steering wheel. Aiden makes his way to the truck and tosses his bag in the backseat, hopping in after it and giving me a jaw dropping smile.

Holy shit, the guy is hot. Where Caleb is all dark hair and moody swagger, Aiden is blond with bright blue eyes and a smile that promises mayhem.

"And you must be Ellie." He slides his hand between the two front seats and we awkwardly shake. His palm is warm and calloused. "Nice to meet you."

"I'm glad you're here."

"Me too."

I check my mirrors and slide us back into traffic while Caleb and Aiden make small talk about the flight and jet lag. But I'm not even to the interstate before the conversation's turned to horses. Aiden's complaining about some stallion prospect back in Ireland and Caleb's agreeing with him.

"He's an asshole," Caleb says. "Damn thing nearly took my thumb off when I was leading him."

Aiden leans between the front seats, giving me a glimpse of his perfect profile and a whiff of some sort of evergreen cologne. "I have to say," he tells me in a skin-tingling Irish brogue, "our friend here has been holding back. He said you were an accomplished rider, but he didn't say anything about you being beautiful as well."

"Oh, you *are* smooth," I say, changing lanes. "Maybe next you could tell me I'm stirring feelings you've never felt before."

Aiden laughs. "Well, now that you mention it."

I grin. I should be so interested right now. Aiden rides, makes me smile, and he's as pretty as Caleb.

Too bad he doesn't make my stomach swoop the same way.

"Try charming her all you want," Caleb says to him, stretching his long legs out in front of him. "She's immune to bullshit."

He's kidding, but I feel my cheeks heat all the same. I like Caleb thinking I'm immune to bullshit. Then again, I like Caleb thinking about me *period* and that's a huge problem.

"Immune to bullshit?" Aiden sounds disappointed. He leans back into his seat. "Well that's a bloody shame. I'm almost entirely made up of bullshit."

I laugh. "Is this your first time in the States?"

"It is. Don't really know what to expect, but I'm looking forward to it."

"What do you like to ride?" I check my mirrors and change lanes. "What's your type?"

"Type?" I can hear the sleepy smile in the Irish rider's voice. "Fast. Sensitive. Not afraid of anything."

I shake my head. This guy is going to kill it around town. If Caleb wants to go all professional, I'm not sure Aiden Macken is the guy to help. He's going to have women flinging themselves at him.

"And what do you like to ride, Miss Lennox? I saw video of that mare of yours. She is *nice*. How was she to break?"

"Only got me off a few times. The trick was making her think everything was her idea." I pause, considering Beckon again. "Actually, that's still the trick to her."

"Had a few of those myself." Aiden twists back and forth in his seat, trying to see everything around us. "They're great horses once they bond to you, but getting there?" He makes a noise halfway between a groan and sigh. "It can be a tough road."

The rest of the drive home is just like that: easy. The guys talk about people I don't know, but they're quick to explain background to me. I don't even have to ask for clarification. Caleb's thoughtful about asking after Aiden's family and friends, and Aiden eagerly tells him about everything from his Mam's recent foray into competitive baking to his niece and nephew's attempts to drive him into an early grave.

Aiden really likes him, I think. It's not really surprising. Caleb's plenty likable when he's not glowering or stressing out, but I like the realization all the same. I make a mental note: next guy will be someone like this, someone other people genuinely like.

As we turn into Jacks or Better, I meet Aiden's eyes in the rear view mirror. "Do you want me to drop you at your cabin? You could crash for a while."

He shakes his head, blue eyes somehow even brighter. "If it's not any trouble, I'd like to see the barn first."

Spoken like a true horse person, I think, turning toward the stables. We sweep around the final bend and Jacks or Better comes fully into view. Aiden whistles low and Caleb and I exchange a grin. Can't blame him. You can see the towers...and the horses...and the guy leaning against a fire-engine red convertible.

My stomach sinks. What the hell? That's *James*.

"Friend of yours?" Caleb asks. There's something in his voice that I can't read, don't want to read. I park as far away from James as possible and give Caleb my brightest grin. He doesn't return it.

"Not a friend," I say. "I'll get rid of him."

"Wait." Caleb tenses, looking out the window again. "Is that James the Gigantic Tool?"

Behind me, Aiden makes a small noise, like he's fighting down a laugh. Great. Just freaking great.

"Yes," I manage through clenched teeth, "that is the Gigantic Tool."

"You needed her to identify him?" Aiden asks Caleb, leaning forward. Blond hair falls in his eyes. "Man, he's wearing loafers with no socks. I'm fresh off the boat, er, plane and I can tell he's a tool from here."

I like you Aiden, I think. Knowing I'm glaring at him, James straightens. He pulls off his black Ray-Bans and gives me his best 'Well? I'm waiting' expression.

I hop out of the truck and stride toward him not stopping until we are toe to toe. "What the hell are you doing here?"

"You're ignoring my calls." James eyes Caleb and Aiden as they head for the barn entrance. "Every time I see you away from work, you're with Holly and we all know how that goes."

My stomach flips. "You've been following me?"

Distaste flashes across his face. "Hardly, Ellie. You're just predictable. Showing up here..." He looks around and shrugs. "What else was I supposed to do?"

"Respect the fact that I clearly didn't want to talk to you? This is my workplace. It isn't the place for your..." I want to say 'bullshit,' but Caleb is within earshot and I don't want this to look anymore unprofessional than it already does.

And why isn't he going inside anyway? I grind my teeth until my jaw aches and try to pretend he isn't there. It makes the whole thing even more embarrassing.

"This isn't appropriate," I say finally.

James gapes. "I'm being romantic, isn't that what women always want? I'm showing up. I'm making the effort—you know, what? I don't know why I bother with you. Yes, I made mistakes, but you had a hand in that too. I wouldn't have gone to her if you hadn't driven me."

It's the worst and best thing to say to me. Instantly, everything becomes crystal clear. Again. Because this is the thing about James: he makes you feel like you're the problem, like you're *always* the problem and he has to put up with you. I can't even express how much I hate that. Even when he's in the wrong, he'll still maintain it was your fault.

I inhale hard through my nose and reach for him. It would be easier just to kill him. More cathartic too.

A hand clamps down on my wrist.

Caleb.

I look up at him and he shakes his head the tiniest bit. Do not kill the guy, he's telling me. He freaking read my mind.

"Hey, darlin'," he says, that southern accent a little thicker and a little sweeter than it usually is. "Problem?"

"Oh." James's eyes dart between Caleb and me. "Are you with him now? Is that it?"

I open my mouth and Caleb cuts me off. "Yeah, she's with me. What's it to you?"

"Nothing." James raises both hands in a surrender gesture all the while shaking his head like it's one more failing on my part. "She didn't tell me, man. Sorry about that."

"Pretty sure by telling you to stop calling her, she was *telling you* she wasn't interested. I don't see why it's suddenly real because I'm saying the same thing."

"And now you've found another person to poison against me." James shakes his head, backing toward his car. "I wish you well, Ellie. I hope you don't wake up one day and regret this."

I start forward and Caleb holds me tight. Briefly, I think about struggling, but Caleb's grip is iron clad. I slump and he chuckles. "Wave, sweetheart, or I'll kiss you in front of everyone, and they'll know I love to fuck you senseless."

For a nanosecond, I can picture that kiss. Everyone wouldn't just know Caleb loves fucking me. They would know I'm desperate for him to do it. "You wouldn't," I whisper.

He pulls me a little closer and I squeak, waving to James with a big Screw You grin on my face. It actually feels pretty good too.

"You're so right," Caleb says. "He *is* a gigantic tool."

I nearly laugh. My heart's pounding and my hands are shaking, but suddenly the whole thing feels funny. It's a relief too. James is excellent at making everyone think he's the victim. Holly saw through him, but she's the only person who did and it feels unbelievably good to know Caleb sees him for what he really is too.

"Are you okay?" Caleb turns, grasping me gently by my upper arms. "You're trembling."

I swallow and my throat catches. "He gets to me, and I hate that he gets to me."

"I know a way to relax you."

I grin. He's trying to make me laugh—distract me—and it works. Suddenly, everything I am is consumed with Caleb: his grip on my arms, his hard chest inches from me.

It's more than that, I realize, but I push the thought away before it can go any further. I look up at Caleb and ask, "Take me?"

His eyes darken. "God, yes."

"My place?" I keep my tone teasing as I back away, but I'm already wet—and getting wetter—as he follows me. "Ten minutes?"

Caleb looks me up and down. "I'll give you five. And Ellie?"

I'd started to turn away, already heading for my apartment. "Yes?"

"When I come in, I want you naked and spread for me."

CHAPTER 32 | Ellie

Naked and spread. The words are stuck on repeat in my head—a serious problem since they make me wetter and wetter every *single* time. I drop my shirt in the kitchen, kick my shorts off in the hallway, and shimmy out of my bra and panties in my bedroom.

The A/C is on, but my skin still feels overheated. I'm *so* ready to go. I loosen my ponytail as I look down at my bed and nearly moan. Normally, I love when Caleb undresses me, but the idea of being naked and waiting for him has captured me completely.

I sit down and lean back, lifting my heels to the bed's edge and letting my legs fall open. My clit is already begging for attention and my fingers drift toward it, playing as I hear my apartment door open and close. My nipples tighten. Ache.

Seconds later, there are footsteps in the hallway. A shadow stretches into my room, and then Caleb's there. His breath leaves him a whoosh, and I reach for him.

"Ah ah," he says, peeling off his shirt and staring me down. "Keep going. I love watching you."

My pussy clenches, and my fingers turn frantic. I love him watching me too. He drops his jeans, his boxers, and pads silently to me. For one whole minute, he stands between my spread legs and watches me, growing harder and harder. I can't take my eyes from his cock. I don't think he's ever been this hard before and it's for me.

All for me.

"You're so damn beautiful," he grates and then leans over me. His heated length rub the inside of my thigh and I moan. "Do you know that?"

My face goes hot. Right now, I don't feel beautiful. I feel desperate for release, for *him*. "Please?" I whisper.

He swears. "Christ, I love that."

And he enters me with a hard stroke. I gasp, and he swears again. "So fucking wet. So fucking *perfect*."

I agree. My pussy stretches around him as pleasure surges through me. My legs tighten, and he increases his rhythm, hitting my clit so every stroke sends me higher. I moan.

"I love doing this to you," he breathes.

My eyes open. "I love it too," I whisper. I love...him.

Our eyes meet. Hold. His fingers find my aching nipple and twist. Sensation bolts through me and I melt. He's in control. I love it. I love how he plays with me.

I love how I look in his eyes. Caleb watches me like he can't look away.

"Come for me." It's supposed to be a question, a prayer, but it's Caleb and it's us and all I can do is obey. He strokes me hard, and I come, screaming and screaming until his kiss drowns me.

***

Screw work, I think, my bones (and most of my brain) gone mushy. *I'm never moving again.* I lie in Caleb's arms, slowly coming down and realizing there's no where I'd rather be. My cheek is pressed to his chest and my heartbeat is matching his. He presses a kiss to my hair, lingering like he feels it too.

"I can't get enough of you, you know that?"

I snuggle closer so he can't see my smile. "You know I have to get back to work."

"Well, technically, you're banging the boss's son so you can do anything you want." He curves so we're face to face. I can't look away. "What *do* you want?"

It's teasing, I tell myself. *He's not serious.*

I laugh and sit up, tugging the tangles from my hair. "'Banging you' makes me feel like I can suddenly take on the world. Get dressed."

"Yes, ma'am."

I swing my legs off the bed and start searching for my panties. Did I actually *fling* them when I came in? It looks like it.

"I can't believe you wasted a year on him," Caleb says.

Everything warm from our earlier moments drains from me. I stiffen. Embarrassment stings me, and I turn toward him. Caleb isn't looking at me though. He's checking his phone.

Let it go, I tell myself, but I can't. I yank on fresh clothes, fuming. It's that comment, the "I can't believe you wasted a year on him" that infuriates me—mostly, of course, because I agree with him. Still, there's an arrogant undertow to Caleb's words that flies all over me. I'm suddenly, enormously pissed.

"I can't believe you said I was just like him," he adds, glancing up.

It's like my bedroom shrinks. Suddenly, I feel too large and the space is too small and everything is wrong. I did think that, and I was wrong. Caleb isn't James. I thought he was in the beginning, but now I know better. But still, that comment lingers with me. I made a mistake—just like at the club, but also way worse because it took me a year to figure out I was being an idiot.

And now Caleb knows I was an idiot too.

Even worse, he just talked to me like I'm one.

I duck out from under his arm, and glare up at him. "Pretty boy with loads of money, women lining up to be with him, and an arrogant, antagonistic streak? Yeah, I'd say the resemblance is pretty striking."

His voice drops to barely above a whisper. "That used to be me. It isn't anymore."

I swipe a loosened strand of hair out of my eyes, anger and embarrassment squeezing me. "James would say that too. If you want to follow it up with a round of It's Your Fault I'm Like This Anyway, I know that song and dance too."

There's a pause and it stretches out for so long I dare a glance at Caleb. He's watching me with that thoughtful expression again, the one where I feel like I'm being pulled apart. Sometimes I love that, but this is *so* not one of those times. I don't want him to see me like this. I don't want *anyone* to see me like this.

"Let me get this straight," he says at last, "you expected me to over-look your mistake at the club, but my mistakes *before we even met* define me?"

Yeah, he's got me on that one, but now that I've pointed how they're alike, I can't stop wondering if it's true. I have crappy taste in men. Did I replace one James with another? Yeah, Caleb isn't like him in *some* ways, but they share a condescending streak. No one is going to talk to me like that. Not anymore.

"Why does it matter that it's before we met?" I ask, yanking my shirt over my head.

"Because it does. Because I haven't been that guy with you."

"You haven't? Because I'm pretty sure I just heard you talk to me like I was the dumbest three-year-old on the planet—"

"Ellie—"

"You acted like a huge ass to me. You wanted to get me fired."

"And I apologized." Caleb doesn't raise his voice and somehow I al-most wish he would. It would be easier to take his anger than the tight-ness running through his words now. He's trying to be Mr. Perfect Pro-fessional and it just infuriates me more. "I was wrong," he continues. "I said so and I changed my behavior. When's the last time Gigantic Tool did that?"

My cheeks heat. He never has. I mean, James has apologized before, but it took me months and months to realize he didn't mean a word of it.

"I'm not the same guy," Caleb says, glaring at me.

I glare right back. He has a point. In fact, he might even be...right.

But right now when I look at Caleb, I can't see anyone other than James.

CHAPTER 33 | Ellie

It's surprisingly easy to avoid Caleb for the rest of the day. He's tied up with Aiden and farm stuff, leaving me to ride horses and stew. Have I traded James the Gigantic Tool for another version of him? Of course not. Now that I'm calmer, I realize that.

But the way they both speak to me? That arrogant tone? That's exactly alike. I'm *not* putting up with it again—and I keep repeating it to myself all through my rides, all through my chores, and all the way up the stairs and into my apartment.

The last of Wren's boxes are gone, leaving our kitchen extra white and extra empty. It turns my bad mood even worse. I toss my baseball cap onto the counter and consider painting the whole kitchen green. Or maybe yellow.

Or maybe I'm kidding myself because when am I going to have the time? My two week notice is almost up. Soon, Caleb and Jacks or Better will be someone else's problem.

I ignore how that makes my heart squeeze and wander to the cupboard. I pull out a box of Cheerios, eating the cereal in handfuls over the garbage can. No point in dirtying plates and I'm too tired for anything else. Tomorrow's another long day plus I'm heading over to Mrs. Mar's place to drop some equipment. It's my last chance to arrange personal stuff before we leave for the show.

My cell rings and it makes my breath catch. I check the screen. Holly. "Hey."

"Hey yourself. What's with the bad mood?"

"Everything. Nothing. I'm sorry."

"Do you want to talk?"

I hesitate. Honestly? No. I'm too embarrassed and too upset and too raw to talk about any of it—and that's a first for me. Usually, I tell Holly everything. "Not yet. I'm still...working through it."

"Do I need to kill someone?"

I laugh. "Possibly. Can I think about it and let you know?"

"Premeditation. I like it. Of course, you can think about it. Call me tomorrow?"

"Definitely." I hang up feeling ever so slightly better. I can't be completely horrible if I have a friend like Holly, right?

There's a noise on the stairwell, and I pause, dreading and hoping it's Caleb and we can talk about what happened. But the doorknob doesn't turn and everything goes quiet again. I stuff another handful of Cheerios into my mouth.

You're not over me, James whispers in my head, and I flinch. What if he's right? What if I went looking for someone else just like him?

Maybe our pasts define us.

Worse, maybe our pasts predict our future. Maybe I'll always gravitate toward entitled dickheads.

Now there's a terrifying thought. I swallow my Cheerios and glance at my phone. It's after nine. If Caleb were coming, he'd be here by now.

"Of course he isn't coming," I announce to the empty, shadowy kitchen. My voice cracks and I clear my throat. "That isn't the way guys like them work. He doesn't see a problem talking to me like that."

He doesn't, but I do. The thought pulls my chin higher. I'm right about this and I know it, but too much of me keeps listening for Caleb, hoping he'll come through that door. He doesn't.

I shouldn't be disappointed, but I am.

CHAPTER 34 | Caleb

The morning staff meeting will be done by now, I think, sinking into one of Tate's plushy leather armchairs while I wait for him. Ellie will be off riding and doing chores and heading for Mrs. Mar's any time now. Even if I wanted to catch up with her, I couldn't make it back in time.

Not that I want to catch up with her.

"Hey," Tate says as he opens his office door. We're supposed to do lunch today, but I've been waiting for a half hour and from the looks of it, Tate's been busy. He has a handful of file folders in one hand and is unbuttoning his suit jacket with the other. "Glad you're here. I'm starving. What do you want for—" He stops and stares at me. "You look like hell. What'd you do last night?"

I think about my possible responses, running through everything from "It isn't what I didn't do, it's *who* I didn't do" to "I didn't sleep. At all." I was up obsessing over Ellie.

"I'm having an argument with someone," I tell him at last.

Tate sits down, sliding his file folders into a desk drawer. "Let me guess, that someone is Ellie Lennox?"

"She thinks I'm an asshole."

"You do have your moments."

I give him the finger. "Doesn't everyone? But I wasn't being an asshole yesterday. I was *helping* her. Her ex showed up at the farm and was hassling her. I intervened and he left. You would not believe this guy. Total dick. I told her I couldn't believe she wasted a year on him."

"Bet that went over well."

I pause, feeling like a cartoon light bulb just went on above my head. Oh, *shit.* He's right. No wonder she was angry. I was pissed at James and I took it out on her. I never should've said that. Ever.

I scowl, pissed at myself for saying that and pissed it took me so long to catch on and embarrassed because Tate's studying me like I'm a moron.

And he's right.

I slouch lower in the armchair. "She thinks I'm an asshole because her previous boyfriend was an asshole and we share similar characteristics."

"Do you?"

"Possibly." In fact, if I think about it, maybe more than possibly. We might be alike in the way that really counts: how we treat Ellie. I spoke to her in the same manner James did. I never should've done that. Again, I was angry.

Again, I shouldn't have taken it out on her.

Tate smirks. He leans back into his chair, both hands propped behind his head. After almost ten years of friendship, I know what this means: Tate's going to give me some advice. Normally, I wouldn't mind. Tate's one of the most put together guys I know and his advice is usually spot on, but right now I'm not in the mood.

"What's really going on?" he asks.

I lift both brows. "I don't know. I thought you were going to tell me what to do. You had that look about you."

Now Tate gives me the finger. "How can I give you advice when I don't even know what's going on."

"Never stopped you before."

"Okay, yeah, fine." He pauses. "Wren and I had some suspicions. Are you with Ellie or whatever?"

"I'm not *with* her. We're..." Complicated? Over? The best thing that's ever happened to me? I clamp my mouth shut. I'll be damned if I say that to Tate. It's bad enough that I feel like Ellie's burned down the best parts of me.

"I get it."

I hesitate. "It wasn't supposed to be like this."

My best friend nods and somehow, I think the agreement has more to do with Wren and him than Ellie and me. "Does she make your life better?" he asks.

I hesitate again. For such a simple question, I have a dozen answers and images flitting through my head: Ellie making me feel at ease during the Wesley party, Ellie making me laugh, Ellie making me proud. The way she handles the clients, the staff, hell, the way she handles herself, it leaves me in awe. She's amazing.

"Yeah, she makes my life better," I say, and the answer sounds even more confident out loud than did in my head. "She makes my life *way* better."

"Then that's your answer."

"No, it's not."

"Because you're being an asshole."

"I'm not—"

"You're right. You're being chicken." Tate waits like he thinks I'm going to argue and when I don't—because it's slowly occurring to me that he may have a point—he continues, "She's what you want, and you're too chickenshit to admit it. So she's like Mandy? So what? Big deal. So you're like her ex? You can make her see past it."

There's a knock at the door and a younger guy sticks his head in. "Uh, Tate, we're going to need you in the conference room."

Tate groans. "Seriously?"

The younger guy looks a nanosecond away from a freak out.

"Yeah, yeah, coming." The door shuts and Tate looks at me. "Sorry. We're having some issues with a new client. Can we do lunch another day? We still need to pick up tuxes for the wedding."

"No problem. I should be heading back anyway."

I start to stand, but Tate doesn't move. He stares me down, seriousness making his whole body go tight. "I didn't expect Wren to be The One, but it happens when it happens."

I nod, acting like I agree because it's easier and Tate will feel helpful. Thing is, none of this shit really applies. It doesn't matter if Ellie's The One for me because I'm not The One for her. She saw it yesterday when I ran my mouth. There's no going back.

CHAPTER 35 | Ellie

Caleb misses the morning staff meeting, texting Sam and me about a meeting in Atlanta. It's not a lie. He'd mentioned the meeting with another local breeder before we fought, but my heart still sags a bit when I walk into the tack room and he isn't there.

You should be grateful you're done, I tell myself. *You want more with Caleb, and it would only end in disaster.*

Well, perhaps 'disaster' is a touch melodramatic. He would eventually treat me like a three-year-old kid, and after getting royally pissed off, I would act like one. There was one bright side to all of it: If being with James taught me to stand up for myself then being with Caleb has taught me I'm a relationship girl. I want the real deal.

"That's why we date," Holly said after I told her everything this morning. We were sitting in my practically empty living room, eating the leftover Cheerios for breakfast, and I was trying not to cry. "By seeing lots of people and staying open-minded, we figure out what we want—sometimes by rubbing our noses in everything we don't want."

It made perfect sense. Of course, that didn't make the situation any easier this morning

And it doesn't make it any easier now.

Luckily, there's plenty to keep me busy. I still have four more days as a Jacks or Better employee so that means riding, chores, paperwork—all the usual stuff. But I'm also supposed to drop off some of my things at Mrs. Mar's place today. Holly's coming along because she's awesome, and probably, because she felt sorry for me.

"It'll be fun," she said as I walked her to the Bronco that morning. "Mom's terrorizing the church ladies today so I actually have some free time."

195

I laughed. Mist still lingered out in the paddocks, making the horses look they were stepping out of some kind of fairy tale. It was going to be another beautiful day of riding horses and taking care of the farm. "I don't know," I tell Holly. "Watching your mom talk about the time she smoked up with some artist or went skinny dipping in the Indian Ocean would be way more fun than watching me unload my gear at Mrs. Mar's place."

Now Holly was laughing. Her whole body shook as she no doubt pictured the old ladies' expressions. "I know, right? But no. I want to see where you're going to work. I'm excited for you."

She slings one arm around my shoulders, and for a moment, we lean into each other, watching the horses wander around in their paddocks. "I'm excited too," I say at last and realize I mean it. The excitement of the new opportunity outweighs the fear of the unknown. I love getting to share it with Holly.

But I'd be lying if I said part of me still didn't want to share it with Caleb too.

***

It's not a bad drive to Mrs. Mar's place, maybe thirty minutes if a normal person is driving. Since Holly's behind the wheel, we make it easily within twenty, and only nearly die twice.

"Oh, please," Holly tells me as we make the final turn. She hits a pothole and the Bronco leaps. "We only nearly died once—and that wasn't my fault. That guy didn't check his blind spot."

"He probably *did*, but he wasn't expecting someone flying up on his left side doing ninety."

"At best, I was doing eighty-five."

"Ninety."

"Seventy-five."

I can't stop laughing. It's gotta be nerves because Twelve Oaks' huge, front gate has loomed up in front of us. We're here. This is happening. The stone wall on either side of the gate stretches on and on, bits of dark green ivy climbing over the top. Holly presses the buzzer and someone on the other end releases the gate, letting us in.

After that, it's only a few more minutes before the driveway leads us up to the main barn. It's...huge. I mean, I knew it would be, but still.

"Oh. My. God," I mutter as Holly and I stare up through the windshield. The sweeping slate roof, the wide gleaming windows, the acres and acres of paddocks stretching out around us—it's pretty much my definition of heaven.

My hands begin to tremble.

Holly parks us next to Mrs. Mar's pocket-sized silver convertible, and looks at me. "Don't chicken out now," she says, and grabs my gear bag from the back seat and slams the door.

"I'm not chickening out. I'm...appreciating the moment." Or possibly chickening out because right now, sitting in the shadow of Mrs. Mar's three-story stable, my hands are definitely shaking and stomach is sloshing around my feet. All my earlier excitement has evaporated and I'm annoyed with myself. It's not like this is a surprise. I've known I'm doing this for days now.

But now it's real.

Our boots crunch across the gravel and we step inside, eyes adjusting to the light. Two rows of wrought-iron and brass accented stalls stretch out ahead of us with polished crystal chandeliers hang above the aisle. Most of the horses are dozing, but a few stick their heads out to see us and I recognize one grey face immediately.

"That's *Arch*," I tell Holly, rushing across the aisle to stand in front of his stall. The gelding looks at me and I feel the irrational need to giggle. Or maybe pass out. "I'm standing in front of Arch, Holls. *Arch*."

Arch snorts, flicking horse snot onto me. "I'm close enough to Arch he can snot on me. I've been snotted on by a gold medalist!"

"I say this with love: you are crazy." Holly's smiling though. She isn't so far away from the riding world that she's forgotten how special something like this is. We grin at each other and I have the irrational urge to grab her by the arms and jump up and down. I'm so glad she came with me. The moment is so much better because I can share it with her.

Speaking of moments, I think, slowly taking in the stable aisle once more. *What the hell is going on here?*

I'd been so caught up in the stable's beautiful architecture and horses, I'd almost missed how deserted the place was...and cluttered. Somehow I doubt Mrs. Mar would be okay with half cleaned water buckets sitting outside the stalls and a bag of feed slung on the brick inlayed floor. If one of the horses got into it, they could eat themselves sick.

"Where is everybody?" Holly asks, dropping her voice even though no one's around. I get it. There's a hush to the barn like someone holding their breath.

"Dunno. Should we look around?"

She shrugs. "I wonder where Beckon will be stabled. Do you think she'll be on this side or—"

A side door opens and a tall, wiry guy spills out. He limps across the aisle and collapses in a heap on one of the wrought iron benches that sit between stalls, head between his hands.

He does not *look good*, I think, exchanging a glance with Holly. Her light brows have climbed half way up her face. Clearly, she agrees. Then the guy shifts, throwing himself back against the bench and lifting his face to the sunlight streaming through the skylight. He's *gorgeous*, but even from here, I can smell the booze on him.

"Um," Holly whispers. "What do we do?"

His head slowly lifts, turning in our direction. "Hello, lovelies."

Ah crap, I think. That guy isn't just drunk. He's Beau *Kent*. Two time gold medalist, once upon a time number one in the world, and Adele Mar's best rider. He's a legend.

He's also about to puke.

"Ah," I manage at last, "hey...Beau." I can't believe I just used his first name. I clear my throat. "Mrs. Mar around?"

He blinks at us for several seconds and Holly rolls her eyes. "Pro riders, I swear."

"I agree completely, sweetheart," Beau tells her and Holly rolls her eyes again.

The side door swings open once more and Mrs. Mar rushes out. I've only ever seen her in party clothes and the sight briefly jars me. She's wearing work boots and *jeans*. I didn't think billionaires owned jeans. Nevertheless, she's rocking the hell out of them. Her dark hair is carefully swirled into a French twist and her finger's jammed in Beau's direction.

She's about to rip him a new one, I think.

"We have guests," Beau says quickly, motioning in our direction.

Mrs. Mar swings around and her face pales. "Ellie!" She hurries toward me, hands clenching and unclenching. The sunlight streaming through the skylights splashes across her face, highlighting the dark shadows under her eyes. "I'm so sorry, dear. I should have called. I've had a setback. Beau's assistant quit and she took almost the entire staff with her and, well, we're in a bit of a turmoil."

Beau leans into a bronze-colored flower planter and vomits. Twice.

Mrs. Mar winces and I consider him for a long moment. That's a 'bit of turmoil?' The elegant older woman looks close to tears and it makes my heart hurt. I hate feeling out of control and right now? The whole place is approaching chaos.

"How can I help?" I ask.

"I don't even know where to begin."

"I do." Holly steps forward, passing my gear bag to me and propping both hands on her hips. "He needs to get his act together. I had a boss just like this. You have to stay on top of them."

"I'd love you on top of me." Drunk or not, Beau's smile is the stuff of legend. In fact, with his dark hair, muscular build, and the kind of face that belongs to Greek marble statues, he *knows* his smile is the stuff of legend. His attention—and that thousand watt grin—switches to me and briefly, I can actually feel a little heat rise in my cheeks. He winks and then glances to Holly. His eyes drag up and down her. "Why don't you come over here and try it?"

Mrs. Mar glares at him and Beau dissolves into shoulder shaking laughter. He's not so wasted he doesn't realize his sponsor is ready to kill him. It's odd really. I mean, technically, the whole thing is odd, but his disregard is especially weird since Beau is known for his focus. He has the career *everyone* wants, and right now, he seems determined to throw everything away.

Holly shakes her head with disgust. "Why do you put up with him?"

I blanch. Because he's number one in the world? Because he's a living legend? Because he's been Mrs. Mar's top rider for over a decade?

But the older woman surprises me because she doesn't say any of those things. She tilts her head, considering Beau for so long I almost think she won't answer. "Because he always comes through in the end," she says.

Next to me, Holly stiffens, and I don't have to look at her to know she doesn't believe a word of it.

"I don't suppose you know anyone who could properly manage him?" Mrs. Mar asks me.

"I—"

"I could," Holly interrupts.

I blink, turning to Holly in confusion. "Holls...?"

"I could," she repeats, and Mrs. Mar's mouth turns into a tiny O.

"Darling," the older woman says, taking my best friend's arm and tugging her to the side, "the thing is, Beau needs an assistant who can, pardon my French, kick his *ass*. Is that something you feel up to doing?"

"Is the Pope Catholic?"

A slow smile spreads across Mrs. Mar's face.

"She's really good at kicking ass," I say. "You should have met her previous boss."

"All jokes aside, I need the job." Holly tosses her hair back and faces Mrs. Mar. I've always known she was amazing, but right now, I'm seeing the Holly who took on New York fashion scene, the Holly who will make her dreams happen through sheer force of will. "I want to start my own dress line and I need a job in the meantime. Taking care of him won't be a problem."

Mrs. Mar looks from Holly (standing up straight and looking like she could conquer the world) to Beau (slumped in half and looking like he's going to puke again), and takes her hand. They shake as Mrs. Mar says, "I think this is going to be perfect."

CHAPTER 36 | Caleb

By the time I get home, Ellie's long gone. She'll probably be at Mrs. Mar's until five or six. Maybe later if the older woman asks her to stay for dinner. I'm not sure what to do, and for a long moment, I sit in my car and stare up at her apartment windows.

Does she make your life better? Tate's voice is so clear he could be sitting next to me. I think the better question would be *Do I make her life better?*

Because I'm pretty sure I didn't by being an ass to her. I was just so...*annoyed* at James.

No, it was more than annoyance, I realize, getting out of my SUV. I was jealous and feeling protective *and* annoyed. I slam the SUV's door and stomp through barn, heading for the tack room and the import paperwork waiting for me. But even after three hours of burying myself in tax forms, Ellie still hasn't returned.

I check the horses once before flipping the lights off and driving home. There's a pinch in my chest that won't loosen and I keep telling myself it isn't worry or regret or *missing* her, it's exhaustion.

It's also knowing I need to drop off the grooms' contracts with the Colonel. He'll probably want to review them while I wait and I don't have the energy. My nerves are on edge. I'd rather punch something than have a conversation about whether we need to pay our people more.

But, like always, I make myself go in there anyway. I park out front and let myself in. This time of night, Mary's long gone and the house is shadowy and too quiet. I pad down the hallway toward the office and something moves to my right.

"Caleb?" the Colonel limps in from the dining room, book in one hand and his cane in the other. The pain must be bad if he's using it.

I hold up the contracts. "Brought my proposed groom contracts. I wanted to leave them for you."

The Colonel nods. His grip wobbles on the cane and now that he's closer, I can see how pale his face is, how hard he pinches his lips together. He's definitely having a bad night. "Can you put them in the library?" he asks.

"Yeah." I hesitate, not sure if I should offer help or pretend I don't notice he's suffering, but the Colonel moves on without saying another word and my decision is made for me.

Down the hall, the library is exactly as I remembered it: dark wooden desk with coordinating bookshelves, fox hunting paintings in thick gilded frames, and *silence*. The heavy furniture and thick carpeting swallows all sound. It's like sitting in a tomb.

Almost fitting considering the Colonel has every picture of my mother he could find lining his desk top. I pick up the closest—a silver framed picture of her with Jacks or Better's first filly. Her smile overreaches her face and for a second, I'm pasted to the floor. Losing her...we missed out on so much. That's the thing about death: it isn't just one horrific day of loss, it's all the days that come after. You don't lose your loved one once. You lose her again and again.

The Colonel shuffles in behind me and shuts the door. "Glad you came up. We need to talk."

I try not to frown. "No offense, but it's been a long day. I wanted to bring you my proposed new contracts for the grooms, but I need to crash."

My father stands a little straighter. "It won't take long. Ellie's departure made me realize some things and I need to tell you now before..."

"Before what?"

"Before I make another excuse about why I shouldn't tell you."

I go quiet. I have no idea what to say and for all the Colonel's talk, he doesn't seem like he knows what to say either.

"I owe you an apology, son. I...manipulated you to get you to come home and then manipulated you again to get you to stay." He eases himself into the leather armchair behind the desk and his eyes go straight to my mother's pictures. "I was...hard on you long before you left and I want to apologize. I want us to be...more."

His gaze lifts to mine and I still don't know what to say. The clock on the wall ticks three times before he rubs both hands over his face, slumping lower in his seat like all the air's been kicked out of him.

"You look just like her," he continues, looking at his upturned palms, "and after she died, it was impossible for me to look at you and not see her. I took it out on you. I made mistakes—things I can't take back and I can't fix. I can only move forward and try to do better." His hands drop to his lap and he stares at me. "I want us to do better. I don't want the next six years to be as silent between us as the past six years."

I open my mouth and nothing comes out. We've never been this honest with each other. Ever. And even though there's plenty more to say, I can see all of it in his eyes: a metric ton of pain, a lifetime of regret.

"Your father doesn't know how to love," my mother had once said. It wasn't quite right. It wasn't that he couldn't love. He didn't know how to express it. Not that I can judge because clearly I can't either.

There wasn't a manual to this stuff. We didn't know how to love and we didn't know how to grieve, but we knew how to punish each other. We're good at that.

Were good at that? I'll need to make that choice. "Okay," I manage at last. "I don't really know what to say to that, but I want things to be different too."

He nods. "Good. That's good. I want to try again. I don't want to keep making the same mistakes—and I don't want you to make the same mistakes I did."

I go still. "What does that mean?"

"You think I haven't seen the way you look at her?" He watches me closely, disappointment in his eyes. "The way she looks at *you*? It isn't your fault. You don't know what to do with her. You never really learned. We aren't men who know how to love."

And once again, I think about what my mom said all those years ago—and something about the way he said it makes me realize he's thinking the same thing.

I cross my arms, everything spinning through my brain. "Is that what you meant when you said I couldn't keep Mandy still?"

To his credit, he actually winces. He focuses on the paperwork scattered across his desk and plays with the edge of a receipt. "Yes, but you also have to remember Mandy Gibson wasn't ready to be committed to anyone. She wanted to have her fun—she still does, no matter what she thinks when she looks at you. Ellie's different. I don't want you to make my mistakes with her."

We may be on our way to trying again, but I'm not ready to have this conversation with him. I shrug. "What are you talking about?"

"Your mother was my everything, but I didn't know how to love her—not as she needed to be loved. She was so different from me, from anything I knew." The Colonel's looking at me, but his expression is faraway. He isn't in his library, but somewhere in his past and I suddenly realize how easy I could turn into him. This could be my future. "In the beginning, it was thrilling," he continues. "Later, it damned us. I damned us. I didn't treat her like the gift she was. I didn't support her."

I swallow. So *that's* the reason behind his drive to make the farm the best in the world. He's honoring her now—honoring her with Jacks or Better, with Beckon, with helping Ellie reach her dreams. I stop, fingertips resting on the picture frame. That's the real reason he wants Beckon to become a star. The mare is the living embodiment of everything my mother—his wife—worked for and wanted. This farm, that mare, what he did for Ellie, it was all for my mother.

I glance up and the Colonel won't look at me. I'm actually glad. I can't name what I'm feeling and I don't know what he'd see in my face.

Maybe recognition? Maybe determination? Because I don't know how I'm going to tell Ellie what I feel, but I'm going to try. I'll apologize for my stupid comment. I'll promise to talk to her in the future instead of pulling away. I won't be my father.

But by the time I reach her apartment, there's no answer. Her truck is gone. Her equipment is gone.

She's gone, I realize, standing in the stairwell's darkness. I'm already too late.

CHAPTER 37 | Ellie

I spend the night at Holly's even though it means I have to get up extra *extra* early the next morning. It just seems easier that way. No Jacks or Better to remind me that I'm leaving. No empty apartment to remind me Wren's already gone. No Caleb.

Funny how he isn't here, but I feel him everywhere. I miss him. I shouldn't, but I do.

Dawn comes bright and humid. It might technically be fall, but in Georgia the temps don't really drop until late October, and since I don't like to trailer my horses in the heat of the day, Sam and I leave the farm just as the sun is starting to edge pink light across the horizon. Aside from the traffic we hit on the interstate, it's not a bad drive. The horse park is maybe forty minutes outside of Atlanta. Built for the equestrian portion of the 1996 Olympics, the original park spanned hundreds of acres but is now reduced to the main barns and arenas.

The fall classic stretches across two weeks with hundreds of horses and hundreds of classes. Clients will fly in and out of the local airport while the trainers and horses stay in town. At the end of the two weeks, everyone will pack up and head for the next venue, which is usually the fall series at the Tryon International Equestrian Center, but some will head south to Wellington. It can be a nomadic existence, chasing championships and wins. Some riders compete forty to fifty weeks a year, others considerably less. Mrs. Mar and I have really discussed those details yet, and driving past the horse park's huge sign, I feel a surge of excitement that this could be my new life.

I maneuver our truck and trailer around some of the huge rigs unloading in the stable yard while Sam checks the barn assignments. All the stalls are assigned by the show office, and I'm hoping we've scored something quiet, away from the riding arenas.

"We should be the next stable block," Sam says, peering at the paperwork in his hands. I pull into one of parking spots, glad to see Beckon scored an end stall. She'll get to look out at the sights and not antagonize her neighbors.

I shut the truck off and hop out. The show's in full swing—has been for two days now—and the air crackles with shouts and neighs and loudspeaker announcements. There's an energy to it that makes me grin every single time. I walk back to the trailer, slipping inside with Beckon and spending a moment getting her ready to unload.

"Ready?" Sam calls from outside.

"Ready!"

Sam lowers the side door and Beckon tenses, ears pricked. She nickers deep in her chest like she's welcoming the competition. Probably she's just glad to be getting out of the trailer.

I lower the chest bar and walk her down the ramp. When she hits the parking lot's gravel, Beckon neighs—well, screams is more like it. She glances imperiously around the stable yard, looking half a second away from exploding. I would be concerned if she didn't act like this every time we took her to a competition.

"Yes, yes," Sam grumbles, limping around to join us, "everyone knows you're here now."

Beckon snorts as if to say that's just as it should be and I laugh.

"Hussy," Sam says, smiling. "I'll start unloading. You take care of the mare."

I nod, the next three hours passing in a pleasant blur of setting up for the weekend and keeping an eye on Beckon. For all her bluster, she settles in beautifully, drinking deeply from her water buckets and picking at her hay. I've just finished hanging up her bridle and saddle when Sam comes through with the farm's curtains and valences. Done up in Jacks or Better deep green and gold, they'll add a bit of polish to our makeshift space, providing a little privacy while also announcing our presence. They're a pain to put up, but the Colonel loves them.

For him, everything has to coordinate—from the curtains to the tack trunks to the indoor/outdoor rug I always throw down in the tack room. To the non-horse person, it probably looks insane.

And they might actually be a bit right.

"There," I say when we've suspended the last valence. "I think set up is officially done."

"Thank God for that." Sam slouches against Beckon's travel trunk. "I'm getting too old for this."

"Sorry." I jump down from the ladder and fold it up so I can drag it back to the horse trailer. "I would've been happy to ask Tomas or Danny to come."

He waves one hand. "I didn't want them here. This is our moment, kid. Last show as Jacks or Better staff. Your first Grand Prix. Moving on to other opportunities. I want a chance to savor it."

We grin at each other and suddenly I can see what Sam must've looked like when he was my age. His eyes are actually twinkling and there's an air of excitement all around him. Horses can do that. They make you feel like something amazing could happen at any minute.

"Then let's savor away." I drop onto the trunk next to him and we sit in silence, watching Beckon chew her hay and the grooms down the aisle care for their charges. I take a deep breath. Sam's right. This *is* a big moment and I want to remember every second of it.

Too bad I keep remembering Caleb too. I need to focus on what Holly said: our mistakes can lead us to the right answer. By knowing what I *don't* want, I now know what I *do* want.

I want Caleb. I stuff down the thought, bury it under everything else around me. Beckon leans over her stall door and snuffles the back of my neck, tickling me with horse whiskers and hay bits. I lean back and smile up at her. No matter what's going on in my personal life, I'm the luckiest woman on the planet right now. There's nowhere else I'd rather be.

"Is this what you call working?"

Sam and I straighten, looking down the aisle at Holly who's power walking our way. She's wearing a floaty dress, enormous floppy hat, and battered combat boots, striding along like she's on a runway.

I grin. "Is that what you call a barn outfit?"

"Please." She stops in front us, hands on hips. "Some of us had work this morning. Video conference call with an investor," she adds.

Sam lifts one bushy eyebrow. He's known Holly almost as long as I have, and he adores her, but he's never really understood the fashion scene she works in. He thinks she should wear buttoned up suits and style her hair into a tight bun.

"We've been up early too," he says, rubbing his faded cap against his bad knee. "You two want lunch? I'm buying. We need to celebrate."

Holly brightens. "Celebrate with greasy burgers from the concession? I'm in."

"Me too."

Sam nods. "Good. Let me lock up the rig and we can walk down. Give me five." He slouches off toward the parking lot and Holly turns to Beckon. The mare is hanging over her stall door, watching us with interest—only as soon as Holly gets close, she wrinkles her nose.

"Hello to you too," Holly says, rolling her eyes. She pauses, looking over Beckon with a critical eye. "Is she a bit off? That seems snarky even for her."

"Nah." I pat Beckon's neck. "It's just her. She's actually being rather sweet."

Holly laughs, leaning one shoulder against the stall wall. "*This* is Beckon being sweet?"

"Okay, fine. She's not sweet." I manage a smile even though everything in me goes back to that first day Caleb watched us ride and said almost the same thing. "But she didn't bite you so there's that, right?"

"Totally—" Holly's mouth snaps shut, her whole body going still. "You have a visitor," she says through gritted teeth and I know without even looking it's Caleb.

My mouth goes Sahara dry. I turn, feeling like I'm underwater, and instantly spot him coming down the aisle. He's still a good thirty feet away, but he's spotted me too and when our eyes meet, his expression darkens.

Chills rush across my skin and I smooth one hand down Beckon's neck again. She sniffs me, and when she realizes I don't have any treats, goes back to dunking her hay into her water bucket.

I look at Holly and feel all the blood rush from my face. "I don't know what to say. He looks pissed. What do you think—"

"Ellie, can we talk?" He's at my side now and I can see how cool, calm, professional Caleb is gone. I almost don't recognize the man standing in front of me. His face is pale and his eyes are bloodshot. He looks like he's been up all night.

"I..." I trail off, and Caleb glances at Holly

"Can you give us a minute?" he asks.

She pretends to think it over. "Uh, no."

"Caleb," I begin, "I don't think—"

He catches my hand. Briefly, I think he's going to pull me to him, but he doesn't. He holds me like I'm fragile. Precious. "I owe you an apology."

"I'm sorry...what?"

"What I said the other day? I was out of line. It won't happen again."

I waver, remembering all of James's promises and how they meant nothing—and Caleb can tell. I can see it in how his jaw sets.

"Ellie," he begins, looking down at my hand like he can't believe it's real, "I can't promise I won't fuck up again, but I can promise I'll make it right."

"Why would you do that?" My voice comes out helium-high.

"Because you're worth it."

I open my mouth, close it, open it again, and I can't think of any-thing to say. Caleb's thumb skims my palm and he leans closer to whisper, "You said, I could look at life like nothing was a miracle or that everything was a miracle, and I didn't get it. I didn't get *you*. Not yet."

My heart trips. "And you're saying you do now?"

"Yes! I mean, no!" His thumb skims on, finding the back of my hand, the top of my wrist, and I realize he isn't holding me like I'm precious, not exactly. He's entreating me to come to him.

And I want to.

"I don't always understand you," he continues, "but I *want* to understand you. The point is, Ellie, I never thought I'd have someone like you. I'm too cynical to see everything as a miracle, but I see *you*. I see nothing but you. You're my miracle."

It feels like the world tilts under me and then rights. I gape, vaguely aware Holly's doing a slow clap. It brings me back even as my smile just can't stop.

"Not bad," Holly says, holding up one hand to tick off her observations. "You showed you learned something. You showed you listened. Most importantly? You basically said Ellie was right. How many times did you practice that little speech?"

"All last night and all this morning." Caleb's eyes never leave my face. He looks at me like I'm everything and I'm still gaping like an idiot. I probably look like a goldfish. He steps close, so close all I can see is him: his gorgeous face, his intense eyes. "Ellie, we both have pasts and we've both made mistakes, but when I apologize I'm making a promise to change, a promise to do right by you, and if you let me, I'll do right by you today and every day after. I love you."

My breath hitches. I can't believe I'm hearing this. I can't believe—"I love you too!"

Relief makes him sag and then he jerks me against him. We hug. Hard. He holds me close and I pull him closer. "Caleb?"

"Yeah?"

"You do realize you pretty much promised to always agree with me?"

His laugh curls into my hair. "Not quite."
And then he kisses me.

EPILOGUE | Ellie

Three days later...

There's an energy to Grand Prix day. I always feel like the air is humming and my skin is charged. I'm sure it's just me being overly excited, but I love the feeling. It propels me through the day—even though that day starts at five in the morning because Beckon needs to be walked to stretch her legs and then fed breakfast and then walked again.

Holly shows up a little after eight and because she is the world's most amazing best friend, she also brings coffee. "Oh my God," she says, "if you could see your face right now. Settle down, tiger. The coffee isn't going anywhere and neither am I." She passes me the cup and I take a long swallow. "I'm not even sure I should be giving you this stuff. You already look wired for sound."

I grin. "Grand Prix day!"

"Is it?" Holly smacks one hand against her forehead. Per usual, she looks amazing in skinny jeans, a floppy hat, and tall boots. Her blond hair blows around like she has an invisible wind machine following her. "I didn't realize. You hadn't mentioned it *at all.*"

Next to me, Beckon snorts, dancing on the end of her lead. I've been hand walking her since seven, but she's still wired. I think she knows what's coming too. I grin. "No one thinks you're funny, Holly."

"Whatever. I think I'm plenty funny."

We circle the showgrounds perimeter in silence, enjoying the held breath quiet before the storm. Beckon's stride has a joyful swing to it. She's happy and relaxed and it makes me happy and relaxed.

Or relaxed until we turn back for the barns and I see a stoop-shoulder older man shuffle down our aisle. He pauses in front of Beckon's stall, checking the stall nameplate, before nodding to himself and continuing on.

"Isn't that Dan Emerson?" Holly whispers.

I nod. Dan's a living legend. Not only did he ride for the United States in international competitions, he also coached the last four Olympic teams. These days, he's retired from teaching, but he still works as a scout. There's only one reason he could be looking in on Beckon and me, and briefly, my stomach swings into my mouth.

Holly grabs my arm and squeezes. "You deserve this."

"I don't. We haven't won anything."

"Anyone with eyes can see what you two have." She glances at Beckon, and the mare tosses her head like she agrees. "Now hurry up. We have things to do before you win the whole damn thing."

I laugh. Holly's ridiculous, but she's sort of right too. There's Beckon's stall to clean and water buckets to be scrubbed. I'll need to hand walk the mare several more times before our class, not to mention I want to wipe down all my equipment again. I want it to shine. Then there's the bathing and braiding and...yeah. Everything needs to be perfect.

Then again, everything is pretty much already perfect. The weather's shaping up to be gorgeous. Beckon is in great shape. Holly's here.

And Caleb's coming.

Holly walks back to the barn with us while I list out what I want to do next. "I think I'll braid while she's eating breakfast. Less chance for me to get bitten."

For competitions, I always weave tiny, individual braids into Beckon's mane. It's an industry tradition and while enormously fiddling, it looks amazing when you're finished.

Unfortunately, Beckon always disagrees and usually spends most of her time trying to nip me. Breakfast will help distract her, and hopefully, the mountain of hay I'll add to it will occupy her until I'm done.

"You need a hand?" Holly asks, opening our stall door so I can lead Beckon inside. Though the stall is only ten feet by ten feet, the petite mare is completely comfortable in it. I've banked shavings up on all the sides and the sweet smell of hay greets us.

"Nah. I'll only be a minute," I say, leaving her to wait with Beckon while I run back to the rig for my braiding kit and the mare's feed. I drop the grain into Beckon's bucket and grab my braiding supplies from their kit, stuffing my pockets full of yarn before sticking a stool by Beckon's shoulder. This way, I can better reach her mane—and I also spot Caleb heading our way before he sees me. He strolls down the aisle looking as alert and excited as I am.

"Down girl," Holly murmurs, sipping her coffee and smirking.

"I don't think I can," I murmur back. In fact, I don't think I'm ever going to get tired of looking at him, and it's more than Caleb's gorgeous face and amazing body, it's his energy and how he's exactly where he wants to be right now. He loves the horse show scene.

So do I.

"Morning," he says to Holly, coming closer. "I was hoping you'd make it."

She gives him a cheeky grin. "Wouldn't miss it. I love watching Ellie ride."

"You're going to get a lot more of it working at Twelve Oaks," I tell her. "Like every day."

The reminder briefly flashes annoyance over Holly's expression, but then she brightens. "I hope so, but who knows? If Kent's as much of a pain in the ass as everyone says, I doubt I'll see more than him."

"Beau Kent?" Caleb asks, passing me a smooth, strand of yarn before I can ask. Our fingertips brush and it sends tingles up and down my spine. "Wait. Is *that* the new personal assistant job you took?"

"Yes." Holly nods, but there's suspicion in her eyes. "Why?"

"Because he's here and he's drunk. I just saw him at the concession stand. Are you sure you want that job—"

But Holly's already stomping off toward the concession stand, her loose, silky tank swinging around her hips. Caleb passes one hand over his mouth. "I almost feel sorry for the poor bastard."

I grin, tightening my latest braid until it lies flat against Beckon's neck. She swishes her tail in warning. "He isn't going to know what hit him," I say. "Holly's a force to be reckoned with. You should've seen her last boss. Total nightmare."

"From what I've heard Beau Kent is worse."

"I'm not worried," I say, jumping down so I can tug Caleb in for a kiss. His arms hook around my waist and pull me to him. "She can handle him," I add, my insides coiling tight. It's only been twenty-four hours since our reconciliation, but this still feels like the beginning of something amazing.

"Dan Emerson looked in on Beckon," I say softly.

Somehow, Caleb's attention narrows even more. He's completely focused on me. "Did he? Good. I want him to see you two."

Heat climbs my face. I don't ride for Jacks or Better anymore, Beckon isn't his horse anymore, and he still wants me to shine. "If it goes well, you could be known as the farm who bred an Olympic horse."

"And the guy who's lucky enough to be the woman who rode her."

I kiss him. I can't help it. I fork my hands through his hair, and drag his mouth to mine. The heat of him always shocks me. My breath escapes in a gasp, and he holds me tight. Tighter. My lips open to him, and Caleb takes my mouth hard.

His tongue tangles with mine, finding that rhythm that melts my knees and makes my thighs tremble. My fingers dig into him, urging him on, and his hands cram my hips to his. He grinds into me and I feel his hardness against my stomach. He makes me crazy.

I make him *crazy*, I realize, and the power of it makes me drunker than any peach martini ever has.

Caleb pushes me into the stall wall, pinning me with his weight. I love it. We can't get enough of each other. This isn't just the beginning of something amazing. This *is* amazing.

His hands find my face, cradling my jaw as he turns the kiss tender. Gentle. Chills and heat and turn me dizzy, and he holds me up like he knows. His grip stays firm around me, but the kiss backs off and backs off, teasing me and teasing me until I'm following his lips.

Until Caleb breaks us apart, and we're both panting.

"Are you nervous?" he whispers, lips a mere inch from mine. This close, my body melts into his. We fit like we were made for each other, and he squeezes me like he feels it too. "However you finish today, however it goes, I'm so proud of you."

"I'm not nervous." I tangle my hands in his hair again and press my body to his. Even here, even now, he lights me up. He makes me feel like I could do anything, be anything. Behind us, Beckon snorts. "No matter how the competition plays out, Caleb, I've already won."

Looking for More?

Sign up[1] for a FREE prequel novella and get notified about Emma Ashe book releases, cover reveals, and bonus material!

...

Get the next book: **emmaashe.com/books[2]**

...

Read on for an excerpt from *Deeper Than Secrets*, Book #3 in the Deeper Than Love Series

---

1. http://www.emmaashe.com/signup-book

2. http://www.emmaashe.com/books/deeper

TEASER CHAPTER 1 | Holly

I think part of me knew Beau was up to no good even before our newest groom came running to get me. I was sitting on the bleachers, watching for our sales horse to be led in for auction and doing Beau's emails while I waited. In fact, I was almost done when I heard boots pounding down the aisle. I looked up and spotted Maisy heading straight for me, eyes nearly bugging out of her head.

"Holly," she gasps when she reaches me. "He's at it again."

I frown. 'It' is drinking, and technically, Beau hasn't stopped long enough to be at it *again*. He's more like...at it *still*.

And as his personal assistant, it's my job to stop him. Or try. Honestly, over the past two months, I haven't been that successful, but I give Maisy my best "I got this" smile and slip Beau's smart phone into my bag. "Where is he?"

She swallows. "The bar."

Of course he is, I think, trying to keep from grimacing. Appearances are important and I can feel about a dozen sets of eyes following me as I stride through the bleacher seating and take the stairs to the top walkway.

Of all the flipping places for him to have a meltdown, I think, *did it have to be here?*

Here being Atlanta's inaugural Southeast Sporthorse Auction. It's being put on by my best friend's boyfriend, Caleb Reese. He's the manager/owner/brainchild behind Jacks or Better Farm. It's also being endorsed by Adele Mar, the billionaire heiress who happens to be my boss *and* Beau's boss.

Not that Beau ever acts like he remembers it.

I spot Beau trailing through the crowd, a drink in each hand. Somehow I doubt this was what Caleb had in mind when he organized the auction's themed out food and drink menus. Then again, I wouldn't necessarily put it past him. Caleb's girlfriend is *also* employed by Adele Mar and if Caleb thought he could move Beau out of the way so Ellie could take the top rider spot, he'd do it.

Honestly, I don't think there's much Caleb wouldn't do for Ellie and if I didn't love her so much, I would be jealous as hell.

"How can you walk in those things?" Maisy whispers as we work our way through the crowd.

"These?" I peer down at my shoes. They're vintage red platform sandals and I love them. Love. Them. I'm a firm believer they go with everything, but Maisy doesn't look like she agrees. "Oh, walking in heels just takes practice. I wore them a lot for my last job. Heels, mini-skirts, I wore this see through top once that everyone loved—it was considered normal."

Maisy pales and I realize how that must sound. "I worked for a fashion designer in New York," I explain.

"Oh. I thought you'd always worked for Mrs. Mar."

"Nah, just for the last few months. I'm...rebuilding."

Which is a tactful way of saying I'm figuring out my life since the design company I worked for went under.

"Rebuilding?" Maisy looks at me in confusion again, but before I can explain the crowd thins and I spot Beau by the railing behind the bleachers. He's staring down into the auction paddock, consumed with the horses and oblivious to the stir he's creating all around him—wives sliding him sideways glances, husbands getting annoyed at their sideways glances, and excited fans struggling to get the courage to come talk to him.

I stifle a sigh. I get it. Even if he weren't a two-time showjumping gold medalist, Beau Kent is easy on the eyes. Over six feet with a lean build and panty-dropping smile, he looks like trouble.

Mostly because he is.

"Can you go get my car?" I ask Maisy, one hand deep in my purse as I search for my keys. "It's parked in the A lot. First row."

Maisy pales. "I can't drive stick."

I stifle another sigh. "Remind me to teach you. Why don't you go check on Mrs. Mar, see if she needs anything?"

The poor girl whirls away, more than happy to leave me to wrangle Beau alone. I don't really blame her. When Maisy signed on as a Twelve Oaks groom and exercise rider, she was expecting to learn from the once-upon-a-time Number One rider in the world. I should specify she expected to learn riding, not whether he's about to black out.

Ahead of me, Beau weaves further on, studying the horse being led in a circle below. The auction has been going on for two hours now, horses selling at a steady and pricey clip. The four-year-old being presented now is approaching fifty thousand and the bids are still climbing. I've been around the horse world my whole life and it still blows my mind that some people have that kind of money.

I sidle up to Beau, bracing one hip against the railing so I can lean close to him. He smells like whisky, and his skin has a clammy sheen. "We're leaving."

Unsurprisingly, he ignores me.

"Hey," I say, thumping his arm hard. It makes his drink shake and I pause. I've never seen him this bad before. Beau is usually a friendly drunk, the kind you meet at late night parties. This is...different. Worse. "We're leaving," I repeat. "Dump the whisky."

"Don't talk to me like that. I'm your boss."

"Nooooo," I tell him. "Mrs. Mar is my boss. *You* are my project. You're like a spreadsheet that has to be updated."

Slowly, Beau turns to me, brown eyes narrowed to slits. "Spreadsheet?"

"Would you rather be a pie chart?" I pretend to think. "A Power-Point presentation?"

He scowls, the Beau Kent equivalent of a Care Bear stare. It causes most women to fall all over themselves. Thankfully, I am not most women.

"You know that doesn't work on me," I say.

A deeper scowl, but when I don't start taking my clothes off or try to take his clothes off, he turns back to the horses, passing one shaky hand over his mouth and drawing my attention to his lean, bare forearms.

Usually, Beau always wears long sleeves. They hide the tattooed scripts that run up his forearms and (rumor has it) across his chest. Other guys go for barbed wire or naked women. Beau went for the names of his greatest horses and the dates of his greatest wins. They wind like veins across his skin and whenever I see them, I have the urge to trace each line with my fingertips.

Or maybe my tongue.

Like I said, Beau Kent is trouble.

"I'm not leaving," he tells me at last, eyes still tracking the horses below us even as he takes another swallow of whisky. "I have something I need to do."

Suspicion makes me tense. "Like *what?*"

I follow his gaze, and my stomach curdles. He isn't watching the sale at all. He's watching Dell Landers. The thickset businessman is sitting in the stands with a small group of people, enjoying lunch and the horses.

"Beau..." I trail off. I have no idea what to do with this. Dell owned one of Beau's horses, Arch, an up and coming Grand Prix showjumper who dropped dead a year ago.

While Beau was *riding* him.

He'd been pinned underneath the poor animal, suffering a head injury, cracked ribs, and a broken back. Everyone called it a horrific accident, but Beau's been muttering that it was intentional for *months*. He thinks Dell's groom, George Parish, killed the horse so Dell could collect the insurance money.

And as I watch, a wiry, dark-haired man joins Dell's party. Yep, that's Parish. This is going from bad to worse. I try to edge around Beau to get his attention. "Beau? What do you think you need to do?"

He drops his drink onto the concrete and hurls himself forward, striding straight down the steps for Dell.

Oh shit, I think, tearing after him. *He's going to start a fight!*

"Beau?" I catch up and grab his shirt with both hands. "No! Stop it!"

He shakes me off, and I stumble. "Beau!"

Too late. Two more steps and he's right in Dell's face, Beau jams a finger into the other man's meaty shoulder. "Buying something else to kill?"

"Excuse me?" Dell's face flushes bright red. "What did you say to me?"

"You heard me."

Dell's friends begin to shuffle around. No one knows what to do—including me. How do I play this off?

You can't, I think, planting myself firmly in between the two men. Heat radiates off Beau. I can feel it right through the back of my T-shirt. "Sorry, Mr. Landers. He's...not well."

"The fuck I'm not."

Dell jerks his jacket back into place, and behind him, Parish smirks. "Get him away from me now," Dell snaps. "If he can't speak respectfully, he can leave."

"Of course." I back up a step, trying to force Beau to move. He doesn't. "We were just leaving."

"I know what you had Parish do," Beau says to Dell, moving around me. I yank on his arm, but it makes zero difference. Beau leans into Dell like he wants to kill him, and the older man's eyes widen when he sees it. "Beau! *Please!*"

He jerks. "This doesn't concern you," he says, cutting me a dark glance.

I give him another yank. "If you can't think about yourself then think about Mrs. Mar," I whisper and to my utter relief *that* actually does it.

Beau steps back, his arm brushing my shoulder. He's shaking and for a second I think it's from the exertion and the booze, but then I see his clenched jaw. He's not sick.

He's furious.

I swallow, tugging him toward me. "I'm sorry, Mr. Landers," I say. "It won't happen again."

"You better see that it doesn't." Dell tugs at his jacket again, face almost purple with fear and fury. "And don't think I won't talk to Adele about this."

I wouldn't expect any less, I think, steering Beau up the stairs. He's moving funny, disjointed almost. All the booze must've finally caught up with him. Briefly, pity tugs at me and then I notice a couple of reporters whispering to each other. So not good. This will end up on one of the gossip sites for sure.

Beau stumbles, curses, and stalks on. He's oblivious. Wish I could say I was the same. Forget the snatched glances and subtle looks from earlier, *everyone's* staring now. My skin crawls as we leave. I'm really not sure how much more of this I can take.

TEASER CHAPTER 2 | Beau

I lean against Holly's ancient Bronco while she rummages around inside, sneaking glances at me through the window. She thinks I'm drunk. Hell, between the swaying and the uneven walk, I look drunk. But I'm not. It's the pain.

It's been a year since the accident. I'm supposed to be getting better, and I'm not. My hands are almost always numb. My back almost always feels like it's on fire. I can't ride. I can't sleep—or I can't unless I drink.

In fact, if I drink enough, I don't see Arch anymore. I don't feel that sickening impact when his body hit the ground and I followed.

Freak accident, everyone said. Undiagnosed heart condition, everyone said. But all that matters is he was my horse, and he died under me.

And I know his owner had something to do with it.

I roll both hands into fists, remembering how Dell's face had looked when I yanked him close. He was scared—and not just of me. His eyes kept skittering around, looking at anyone who might be listening. He had Parish kill Arch for the insurance money. He knows it. I know it.

Now I just have to prove it before he destroys another defenseless animal.

"Hi, Beau!" The voice is lilting and unmistakably southern. I turn, spotting one of my former clients walking through the parking lot, heading for the auction.

I lift one hand, nod. Once, she would've stopped to talk. She would've wanted to be seen with me. Kind of sucks to be reminded again that I'm well past worth being seen with, but whatever.

More people are coming in for the afternoon sales listings. I recognize a fair number of them too. Riders, trainers, some very wealthy owners. This is my world.

Was my world?

My cell rings and I pat my pockets for a couple seconds before I remember Holly has my phone. I hold out a hand for it, and she rolls her eyes.

"As *if*," she hisses at me, answering it herself. "This is Holly...no, he can't come to the phone. Can I take a message?"

Holly bends down to grab a stack of fabric from her passenger seat, and I can't take my eyes off her ass. God, she annoys me. She's uptight, rides *my* ass like she stole it, and I have never wanted to fuck a woman more in my life.

Which, honestly, annoys me even more.

Holly says something about 'no problem' and 'we'll get back to you,' and stands up, motioning for me to get into the Bronco. With those heels on, we're almost eye level. If I ever do get a chance to fuck her, I'm going to leave the heels on and revel in it every time they dig into my back.

"What?" Holly brushes a fringe of blonde hair out of her eyes. "What are you thinking about?"

"You don't want to know."

"If you're going to be sick, do it out here. I don't get hazard pay."

"What if I can't help it?" I give her my laziest grin. "What if I get sick *on* you? Accidents happen, sweet."

"I'm not your 'sweet,' and if you puke on me, I will punch you in the ear. Got it?"

She'd do it too. I look her up and down, deliberately taking my time to garner maximum annoyance. Unfortunately, it only makes me even more aware of how those curvy hips look in her skirt, how perfect her breasts look in that T-shirt.

Holly's always coming up with something interesting to wear. Gotta admit, I don't really get the whole worn T-shirt with the formal pencil skirt and sky-high heels thing, but I like the effect. She gravitates toward fabrics I want to touch.

I ease into the Bronco's passenger seat while Holly stalks around to the other side. She cranks the engine, blasting us with hot air as the retro-fitted AC begins to work. She shifts into reverse and then stops, both hands on the wheel and eyes focused on the windshield. "Beau?"

"Yeah?"

"Do you really think Dell Landers had something to do with your horse's death?"

"I know he did." I pause, another wave of pain washing over me. I moved too fast on those steps and it's catching up with me. "I just can't prove it."

Yet.

"That isn't something you can just go around saying," she whispers. "I mean, that's a serious allegation and he's your boss's childhood friend. They owned that horse together. If you're saying Dell did something like that, you're basically saying she would've known, and after everything Mrs. Mar has done...I mean..."

She trails off unable to say, *After everything Mrs. Mar has done for you.* Or maybe even *After all the money Mrs. Mar has spent on you.* Either—both—would be accurate. Not many broken down riders get kept on by their sponsors, but after twenty some years of working together, Adele and I are practically family. She's let me recover, kept me on the payroll, and hasn't even brought up riding.

Probably because, like everyone else in the horse world, she thinks as soon as I'm healed, I'm headed straight for the top again.

Holly pauses, waiting for me to say something and when I don't, she gives up, steering the Bronco out of the parking space. I stare out the window, flexing my hands over and over again in the exercises the doctors taught me. The joints catch, shooting pain up my forearms. By the time we've hit the main road, I stop. There's no point—not with the exercises, not with pretending I'll eventually get better. Arch is gone. I'm not healing. I'm not going to ride anymore.

Actually, that's not accurate: I won't be able to ride at the level I did and international showjumping? Being number one in the world? It's everything I've ever wanted, everything I've worked for.

If I lose that, what will be left of me?

TEASER CHAPTER 3 | Holly

We get back to Twelve Oaks in time to see Ellie finish exercising Beckon. The pretty, dark mare gallops around the arena like the huge jumps are nothing and Ellie's grin is practically wrapped around her head.

"They look good," I say to Beau.

He doesn't respond, and I can't tell if it's because he isn't speaking to me or if he's worried because they *do* look good. Ellie won her first Grand Prix two months ago. The mare jumped like she had wings, and people are already whispering about how the pair will win championships and Olympic gold—all the things they used to whisper about Beau.

Thanks to his accident, he's been stuck on the sideline for a year now. He hasn't been able to ride, hasn't been able to compete. It flamed his international standing. He was number one in the world. I think he's around the sixty-something mark now and with every passing competition, he falls further and further down.

I angle the Bronco into a parking spot between two of the Twelve Oaks work trucks and Beau gets out, walking off toward the paddocks. Part of me wonders if I should follow him. He's not right. I don't think he's totally wasted, but he isn't himself either.

The rest of me remembers that I have a metric ton of work now, thanks to him. That last call I took for him was from the farm vet. He didn't process her invoices and now we're behind. Plus, Beau was supposed to review the client schedules today, but I clearly that's not happening—which means I'll have to do it.

My cell buzzes, and I glance at the screen, part of me hoping it's my other best friend, Parker, *finally* calling me back, but it isn't. It's Scott. Again. We've been arguing for months now about whether I'm going to return to New York to find another job. I say I can't return until I have something firm lined up. He says I should just come anyway because everything will work out. We've been arguing about it ever since.

Scott was my *first* nightmare boss. Thrust onto the international fashion scene after being discovered in a reality television show, he burned up runways, reviews, and assistants. Scott would describe himself as exacting. Everyone else describes him as a pain in the ass. Technically, both descriptions are correct.

After design school, I went to work for him, learning everything I could about the fashion industry. I wanted to start my own dress line—I still do—but life had other plans and the company we worked for went bankrupt. Scott had savings to fall back on, but I had to come home.

I send him to voicemail and hop out of the Bronco, my heels sinking into the finely ground gravel. A smarter move would've been to wear boots, but I was running late this morning and forgot my change of clothes.

"Holly?" a voice calls. "Can we talk?"

I freeze. Mrs. Mar. She doesn't sound angry, but I'm sure Dell Landers has already called. I shoulder my bag and plaster on a smile. "Sure thing!"

She's waiting for me just inside the arched stable entrance. It might be October, but we're in the south and that means temps are still hovering in the low eighties. I'm actually a little sweaty, but Mrs. Mar looks pristine in her white collared shirt and dove gray breeches.

"Office?" she asks, tilting her head. Sunlight catches on her high cheekbones and almost black hair, and briefly, I see a glimpse of the beautiful young woman she must've been behind the stately woman she is now.

"Sure," I say, following her past rows of stained wood and brass horse stalls. The Twelve Oaks office is just off the tack room, a sunny, whitewashed space that always smells like high end leather and Chanel perfume since Mrs. Mar spends so much time in here. She reviews the farm's accounting herself, and often takes work calls here, watching her horses play in their paddocks through the huge picture window.

As I close the door, Mrs. Mar takes a seat at the antique desk, glancing over some paperwork while I get settled. I drop into the closest armchair—a fluffy, overstuffed thing by the window—and curl my legs under me.

"How's Beau doing?" Mrs. Mar asks.

I take a moment to consider my response. There's a lot I could say here: He's not doing well at all. He's drunk. He's an ass. Honestly, any of those answers would be accurate, but I hold back. "He's having another bad day," I say finally.

She nods, biting her lower lip and looking out the office window. A breeze brushes through the flowers and they wave, tapping the glass. "I heard. Emily called."

I swallow. Emily is the head of Etoile Saddlery, one of the premiere saddleries in the world. Beau's been one of their sponsored riders for years. He's photographed all the time with their saddles and bridles—or he used to be.

"She's not going to renew his contract," Mrs. Mar continues. "She doesn't approve of his behavior outside the show ring. That will make the third sponsor he's lost this year. At the rate he's going..." She trails off, refusing to say what we both know: at the rate Beau's going, Mrs. Mar is going to be the only person still by his side. "I don't know what to do," she says.

That makes two of us, I think. I don't know what to say so I decide to go for bracing honesty: "He believes Mr. Landers killed Arch. "He admits he doesn't have proof, but he still believes it happened."

Mrs. Mar swallows and glances away again. I don't blame her. Mr. Landers and Mrs. Mar grew up together. Although Mr. Landers found Arch in the beginning, Mrs. Mar was also a part owner with him and, of course, it was *her* rider, Beau, who competed the horse. I can't imagine what she thinks of the allegations. When Arch died, they both collected insurance money, which means Beau's accusations reflect on her as well.

She sighs. "I've told him again and again Dell had nothing to do with it. Parish works for Dell. He just happened to be walking by when Arch started thrashing, and he went into the stall to check on him. It's what any good horseman would do—but that's not to say I haven't heard the rumors. Everyone has. Dell's been in financial difficulties for some time. Then again, that doesn't make him an animal torturer."

I nod. I totally agree and she's completely right, but worry still clouds her expression and for a half a heartbeat, I wonder if she knows something more than she's saying.

"I'm going to have to keep them apart for a while longer, I guess," Mrs. Mar says.

"Probably for the best." The way Beau looked at Dell...I shudder. I don't want to think about what would've happened if I hadn't been there. Maisy and I thought Beau was just drinking and blowing off steam, but he wasn't. He was lying in wait for the other man.

"Well," Mrs. Mar says brightly, bringing both hands together. It makes her gold bracelets wink in the sunlight. "I think we need to focus on what we can do. How are we going to fix this?"

I blink. "Mrs. Mar...no one can fix him because he doesn't want to be fixed." I pause. "Maybe he needs rehab. Maybe he just needs a wake-up call, but you need to find another rider. I know how this ends."

"Really?" She arches a manicured brow. "I thought this was going rather well. You've lasted longer than any of his other assistants."

I try for a non-committal nod. I bet none of his other assistants ever talked to him like I do either. Beau has pretty much been an equestrian phenom since he was seventeen or eighteen, and he's ridden for Mrs. Mar since he was fourteen because she spotted his talent so early. From what I understand, Beau's taste in personal assistants ran to starry-eyed fangirls.

Which I am certainly not.

"Holly," she begins, leaning a little forward. "I know you're not seeing Beau in his best light, but I promise you he's going to come through this."

I give her another non-committal nod. Mrs. Mar's commitment to Beau borders on fanatic. She's said in several interviews he's like a son to her, but I think it runs deeper than that—they share a passion for horses and show jumping. Mrs. Mar will never ride like Beau rides, but by sponsoring him, she can experience it through him.

"Furthermore," Mrs. Mar continues, "I need him to keep it together until my company's board meeting. My new charity organizations are on the line, and I need them approved."

I wince. That's not good. One of those charities happens to be an equestrian outreach program. It's designed to bring in kids from impoverished areas and let them experience horses and the outdoors. I'd hate to see it get torpedoed because Beau can't get his crap together.

Mrs. Mar levels me a grim look. "I need you to make it happen."

I consider her for a moment, comments like "And people in hell want ice water" flitting through my head.

She smiles like she knows exactly what I'm thinking. "I know it's easy to think this is simply a hobby for me, but it's more complicated than that. I run my farms like businesses. They may be a labor of love, but they're still *businesses*—and moreover, they reflect my family's real business. I can't have Beau melting down in public. It's bad for him and it's bad for the farm's image—my family's image."

I nod. I get it. In fact, I've seen the articles on Noelle Floyd's website and in the *Chronicle of the Horse* magazine. It wasn't pretty before I came on and it hasn't been much better since. Beau's imploding and it feels like the whole world is watching and *judging*.

She studies me. "Moreover, the company's board won't approve additional charity funding if they don't think I'm on top of things. We need to look in control. We need to *be* in control." She pauses. "So what do you recommend?"

"He's not going to get better until he decides to get better. You should find another rider."

"You mean I should fire him."

I squirm. It's exactly what I mean, but saying it out loud is awful.

Mrs. Mar skims one hand over her smooth chignon. "I have another idea. If you can get him through the board meeting and the charity program announcements, I'll bonus you twenty thousand dollars."

My heart double thumps. That would be enough to start my dress line. That would be enough to start my *life*.

"What do you think?"

"I think you have a deal."

Want More?

...

Get the full version from your favorite book sellers: **emmaashe.com/ books**[1]

LEAVE A REVIEW

Thanks so much for reading! There are a lot of books out there to choose from, I appreciate you trying mine. Even if you completely hated it (really, really hoping you didn't!), I'm a big believer in the importance of reviews. If you could take a moment to **leave a review**[1] to let everyone know what you think, it would be so appreciated. Not only does it help other readers, but it also helps me become a better writer.

All the love,
 Emma

ABOUT THE AUTHOR

Hi! I'm Emma and I hate writing about myself in the third person. I write fairly steamy contemporary romance. *Deeper Than Destiny* is the first book in my Deeper Than Love series. I'm having fun with these, and I hope you enjoy them too.

...

Deeper Than Love
Deeper Than Desire, Prequel[1]
Deeper Than Destiny, Book 1[2]
Deeper Than Lies, Book 2[3]
Deeper Than Secrets, Book 3[4]
Deeper Than Temptation, Book 4[5]

An Indecent Apposal
Something Real, Prequel[6]
Show Me Your Secrets, Book 1[7]
Claiming The Secretary, Book 2[8]
Second Chance Romance, Book 3[9]
All For Her, Book 4[10]

---

1. http://www.emmaashe.com/books/deeper

2. http://www.emmaashe.com/books/deeper

3. http://www.emmaashe.com/books/deeper

4. http://www.emmaashe.com/books/deeper

5. http://www.emmaashe.com/books/deeper

6. http://www.emmaashe.com/books/apposal

7. http://www.emmaashe.com/books/apposal

8. http://www.emmaashe.com/books/apposal

9. http://www.emmaashe.com/books/apposal

10. http://www.emmaashe.com/books/apposal

<u>Better With You, Book 5</u>[11]
<u>Anyone But You, Book 6</u>[12]

...

<u>An Indecent Apposal Volume 1, Books 1-3</u>[13]
<u>An Indecent Apposal Volume 2, Books 4-6</u>[14]

...

<u>An Indecent Apposal Collection 1, Books 1-6</u>[15]

Follow me at Emma Ashe Author on Instagram and Facebook or **sign up**[16] for book release announcements, cover reveals, and bonus content.

---

11. http://www.emmaashe.com/books/apposal

12. http://www.emmaashe.com/books/apposal

13. http://www.emmaashe.com/books/apposal-set

14. http://www.emmaashe.com/books/apposal-set

15. http://www.emmaashe.com/books/apposal-set

16. http://www.emmaashe.com/signup-book